A

CRUEL OBLIVION

A
CRUEL OBLIVION

A Tess Alexander Mystery

Joan Merriam

The heart dies a slow death,
shedding each hope like leaves
until one day there are none.
No hopes. Nothing remains.

~ Arthur Golden
Memoirs of a Geisha

A Cruel Oblivion

Copyright © 2021 by Joan Merriam
All rights reserved

Printed in the United States of America

Visit the author's website at www.joanmerriam.com

Dedication

For Jody, distant in miles though not in heart,
for all your love, encouragement, and the magnificent
dogs you helped bring into my life.
Even if you don't like mysteries.

Acknowledgements

A book may be *written* by just one person, but that's not true for its *creation*. Dozens of people—some named, some unnamed—go into a book's life from conception to birth to its final emergence as a finished entity.

This book is no exception.

First and foremost, I want to thank my wonderful crew of editor-friends who scoured the manuscript for all manner of absent and superfluous commas, strangely repeated words, typos, and confusing or muddled passages. They are Ron Howard (not, not *that* Ron Howard), Elsie Durgin, Kandi World Turner, and Christi McBee (who long ago adopted me as her mom). Special thanks to my final sharp-eyed editor, Lee Zasloff. I'd have been in *such* a world of hurt without every one of you!

I also want to thank the multitude of people throughout these many years who taught and tutored and guided me in the classroom and the classroom of life about child abuse and its agonizing consequences. I've already thanked most of you in my first book that was published all those years ago, but a special thanks today to those who stood by me as we built Placer County's first child abuse prevention council. Being your director was one of the greatest honors of my life.

And on the subject of child abuse, I want to give a belated but heartfelt thanks to the wonderful counselors and therapists who helped me through my own darkness over the years, convincing me not to give up on myself or on life, and guiding me toward the light: Linda Farley, Susan Coit-Miller, and most especially, Nancy Otterness. Nancy, you were a beacon of hope in my universe for all the whirling years we were together, and I will be forever grateful for your presence in my life.

To those whose names I borrowed—Teichi "Jimmy" Oe, dear neighbors Kip, Carla, Rick, and Jan, and retired detective George Coelho (the nicest cop I've ever met)—I can only hope you're pleased with your namesakes.

And this appreciation wouldn't be enough without thanking a woman I met many decades ago when she was very young and in a very dark place, and whose childhood was also brutalized by child abuse. Without even knowing it, you changed my life.

PART ONE

Two turtle doves will show thee
Where my cold ashes lie
And sadly murmuring tell thee
How in tears I did die.

~ Nikolai Gogol

1

STANDING AT THE GRAVE, she stared down at the exquisite brushed stainless steel casket, its lid and rolled handles rimmed with a delicate lacing of burnished gold.

Nothing but the best for the daughter of Simon Matlock.

A thin veil of moisture from the morning fog gave the coffin a faint otherworldly luminosity; here and there, tiny droplets formed, some sitting patiently atop the cold metal, others inching gently down its steel sides like the tears of angels.

The elegant green velvet drape that once enfolded the coffin and obscured the open grave from the refined funeral guests had been removed, while off to one side lay a roll of impossibly green artificial grass used to cover the mounds of dirt that would soon be shoveled into the chasm, burying Rennie and her secrets forever.

A dark shadow of fog crept up the hill toward the gravesite, clawing its way across the meticulously manicured grounds and shrouding the marble headstones and elegantly engraved memorial plaques in a sheet of dirty gray.

She stood, alone and motionless except for the wisps of auburn hair swirling softly across her face. A cadre of cemetery workers stood several yards away, restlessly waiting for the woman to leave, or at least signal that they could go ahead and lower the casket.

In a moment or two she looked up and gave the men a tiny nod, then stepped back from the edge of the grave. A few clods of dirt rolled down the sides of the hole into the burial vault.

Dust to dust.

One man engaged a discreet lever, and the casket began its slow, silent descent into the earth. The speed self-adjusted once it neared the bottom, until the silver box finally settled with a nearly inaudible thump into the concrete sarcophagus.

Nothing but the best.

She stepped forward once again and the men backed away.

"I'm so sorry, Rennie." She tossed a silver-white rose into the void, where it settled atop the gleaming casket.

As the fog became drizzle, Tess shivered and turned, making her way across the sweeping, greening lawn, past the gravestones of the famous and ordinary, past the barren wisteria and the ghostlike Deodar cedar with its drooping branches weeping with the rain, and finally out of sight.

PART TWO

"The truth." Dumbledore sighed.
"It is a beautiful and terrible thing,
and should therefore be treated with great caution."

~ J.K. Rowling
Harry Potter and the Sorcerer's Stone

2

Ten Years Earlier

SHE NEVER WOULD HAVE DONE IT, had it not been for the last comment her mother threw over her shoulder as she staggered up the stairs that night, reeking of alcohol from the customary three or four martinis she'd guzzled over the past two hours. Even as she maneuvered her way from step to step aside the massive wrought-iron railing, her free hand carried one of the exquisitely hand-etched Waterford crystal martini glasses, filled nearly to the brim. Later, Rennie would remember how fat droplets of the translucent liquor marked the woman's unsteady progress up the winding mahogany staircase.

"You know you always wanted it," Cliona Matlock screeched. "You're nothing but a little whore."

Rennie felt something pop in her head, like a stretched-too-tight rubber band that finally split apart. On the marble sideboard rested an antique sterling silver letter opener, a naked, plump cherub perched on the handle's terminal. She had no memory of picking it up, no memory of racing up the stairs behind her mother, no memory of plunging the instrument into the base of her mother's skull.

When the police arrived at the stately Pacific Heights mansion in response to a young boy's hysterical 911 call, Rennie Matlock sat on the polished bottom step of that magnificent stairway, her hands and the front of her white Beatles "All You Need is Love" T-shirt smeared with blood. Splatters of red glistened on her face and in her hair as she gently rolled the bloody murder weapon over and over from one hand to the other and back again, a half-smile on her lips and her dark unblinking eyes bottomless, vacant lagoons.

News of the grisly murder spread quickly, even in those days before the nation became so irredeemably ensnared in the web of social media. The entire alphabet soup of cable news outlets led with the story, newspapers blared headlines about it, and radio and television talk show carnival barkers speculated twenty-four hours a day about the motive behind the killing of the wife of one of the most prominent businessmen in California.

Meanwhile, investigative journalist Tess Alexander was puzzled. Normally, she wasn't especially enticed by these sorts of sensational slice-and-dice news stories, but this one was different. She knew how rare it was for a child to kill a parent, and rarer still for a child to kill a mother. The limited research she'd already done showed that parricide by females was even more unusual: almost ninety percent of children who murdered a parent were male.

So, she thought to herself as she read and re-read the news reports and analyses, what the hell motivated 13-year-old Rendell Matlock to kill her mother with a letter opener in their posh uptown estate? From all accounts, Rennie was a normal, seemingly well-adjusted teenage girl (assuming teenage girls were ever terribly well-adjusted) who got good grades, was active on her school's tennis team, volunteered at the SPCA Pacific Heights Adoption Center, didn't date or have a party-girl reputation, and as far as anyone knew or would admit, shunned drugs and alcohol. What internal demons drove a kid like that to slaughter her mother?

Rather than join the journalistic herd in the City by the Bay and add to the bedlam, Tess stayed home, biding her time and gathering as much information as she could on the Matlocks. If nothing else, her long career as a journalist had taught her that if she waited long enough, the scavengers who characterized much of the mainstream press would soon move on to another cataclysm of the week, which of course they did.

Rennie's stepfather, Simon Matlock, was a major player in San Francisco's booming commercial property scene. The long-time builder-developer was reported to be quite cozy with the Bay Area's political and judicial movers and shakers, and seldom had serious problems getting his projects green-lighted. *Forbes* magazine ranked Matlock as one of the city's wealthiest and most influential business owners and a possible future contender for a Senate seat, and from what Tess could tell, he wasn't at all shy about throwing around his financial and social weight to achieve whatever ends he sought.

Over the years, rumors of bribery and illegal kickbacks swirled around Matlock, but it all remained in the realm of just that: rumor. Tess didn't take any of it at face value. She knew that, prodded by envy, people sometimes attributed the acquisition of wealth or power to less-than-stellar means, when in reality such success was often the result of doggedly hard work and perseverance.

Then again, sometimes the dude turned out to be Bernie Madoff.

Patriarch Simon was the only son of a lumber tycoon in the Pacific Northwest who made a killing in the wholesale lumber business, then parlayed his success into buying and selling commercial real estate in Seattle. Cashing in on his father's fortune, Simon rose to become one of Seattle's foremost commercial real estate developers just as the city was becoming the computing center of the universe. Eventually, he relocated his burgeoning enterprise to northern California's Bay Area, where the name S.G. Matlock became synonymous with building the largest, tallest, and most opulent commercial centers in the San Francisco region.

Soon after setting up shop in San Francisco, Simon met Cliona O'Connor, a strikingly beautiful Irish model who by then was notorious on the New York party circuit for her impulsive, alcohol-fueled escapades and captivating but volatile personality. A year later he married the wild Irishwoman and brought her west, along with her six-year-old daughter Rendell, always called Rennie, the unanticipated consequence of one of Cliona's untamed all-night sexual liaisons.

By the time their sons Phillip and his younger brother Devon were born, the family was enjoying the fruits of Simon's labors in the wealthy Pacific Heights neighborhood of San Francisco. Newspaper and gossip blogs hinted that more than once, Cliona had gone on an extended "retreat" in an alcohol rehabilitation program, but that never seemed to tarnish the Matlocks' status among the city's social elite, much less reduce the frequency of the couple's elegant and well-lubricated private soirées.

As his multi-million-dollar empire grew, Simon cemented his image as a pillar of the community through his generous donations to multiple civic causes and charities, twice honored by the Mayor's Fund for his efforts on behalf of homeless children and at-risk youth. Except for that pesky little issue of Cliona's alcoholism, the family lived what appeared to be a stable, contented, exemplary life.

Until the night Rennie slaughtered her mother.

As the immediate furor over the homicide cooled, the question of *why* kept gnawing at Tess. Nothing made sense: sure, Cliona was an alcoholic, but there was never so much as a hint that she was abusive or violent enough to provoke an attack, intoxicated or sober. As for Simon, despite the whispers that he might use friends in high places for illicit purposes and his own gain, nothing more than gossip ever surfaced. Even if it were true, how could his lust for power lead to his stepdaughter murdering her mother?

Once Tess learned that Simon had hired Mason Van Sweringen as his daughter's attorney, she knew she had a way in. Some years before, the two worked together as journalist and confidential source while Tess investigated negligence inside the child protective services system, an inquiry that ultimately resulted in a Pulitzer Prize. The attorney represented an adoptive couple whose child came from a series of abusive foster homes, and who were deeply concerned at the lack of oversight that yielded such horrific maltreatment. Tess caught wind of the complaint even before Van Sweringen filed it, then wrangled an introduction to the prominent attorney through a mutual friend.

They met over sumptuous hors de' oeuvres and a bottle of Anderson Valley Cabernet at the Intercontinental Top of the Mark cocktail lounge, where Tess presented her argument for access to the case. By the end of the evening, Van Sweringen capitulated. That decision forged an enduring bond between the two hard-charging professionals that neither ever regretted.

As she dialed the phone, she could only hope that bond would hold true.

"Mr. Van Sweringen's office."

"Hey, Gloria: this is Tess Alexander. Is he in?"

"Tess! Great to hear from you again! Whatcha' been up to since that little commendation of a Pulitzer a few years ago?" The receptionist-paralegal-majordomo possessed a piercing, nasal voice vaguely reminiscent of brawling cats, but her perceptiveness, genuine warmth, and dedication made it easy to excuse her vocal shortcomings.

Tess couldn't help but smile. "Oh, you know: just spending the time reveling in the glow of my own majesty."

She should have known better than to make Gloria laugh: it was an ear-splitting cackle that could probably be heard for miles. Tess held the phone away from her ear to salvage her hearing.

"Really, Tess," the woman said after she'd stopped braying, "I was so jazzed that you got that award. It was a brilliant article—for weeks I went around telling everyone that *I* know a Pulitzer prize-winning writer!"

"Thanks, Gloria. Couldn't have done it without Van."

"Speaking of whom, yes, he's in—he's even available. Hold on a sec."

Mason Van Sweringen's voice boomed through the phone. "Oh, my God: is this really the world-famous Pulitzer prize-winning investigative journalist Tess Alexander?"

"It is. And is this the even more legendary, brilliant legal advocate Mason Van Sweringen?"

"I confess," he said with a laugh. "Tess, what's up these days? Still prowling the grimy streets of L.A.?"

"Nope. I'm in Berkeley now, with the Foundation for Investigative Journalism."

For months Tess had struggled to find a way out of Los Angeles, fed up with the interminable traffic, monotonously unchanging seasons, and increasingly frenzied pace of daily life. She was a country girl at heart, even though she'd grown up in the middle of Sacramento, which by then had surpassed its reputation as a bush-league backwater and was well on its way to being a modern, comfortably cosmopolitan city worthy of being the capital of the third-largest state in the nation. As a young girl, she roamed the city's streets with an assortment of friends, exploring the then-rundown tenements of Alkali Flats and the abandoned railyards, honing her investigative skills and frequently getting into trouble with both landlords and police for her unauthorized exploits.

After college, she landed a position at the *Akron Beacon Journal* in Akron, Ohio, which she hated. Ohio was too rigid, too proletarian, for her liberal west coast tastes, and she frequently butted heads with her editors over the fact that, as a new hire, she was relegated to the society beat. Within a year she was working for Cleveland's *The Plain Dealer*, arguably the state's largest and most influential newspaper. A beat reporter by then, she began to garner attention for her efforts at unearthing fraud and dishonesty among some of the city's public and political elite.

Finally, the west coast called, and she started work at the *Riverside Press-Enterprise*. She hated it for different reasons than she'd hated her time in Ohio: Riverside County was chiefly desert, which was insufferably hot, flat, boring, and largely sterile of anything green unless one counted the scraggly yucca and Joshua trees.

It didn't take long for the largest newspaper in Los Angeles, the *Los Angeles Times,* to notice this headstrong upstart who had an unquestionable skill in investigative journalism. They started her as a reporter for the Inland Empire edition of the newspaper, and within a year offered her a spot as part of the main publication's investigative team. Five years later, after her last serious love affair came to a fiery end when the man dumped her for a blonde, impossibly buxom cheerleading coach—*Jeeze,* she thought when it happened: *a fucking CHEERLEADING coach??*—Tess was more than ready to get out of Los Angeles.

Then the Foundation for Investigative Journalism in Berkeley began wooing her.

The pay wasn't spectacular, but thanks to her substantial inheritance, she had the luxury of indifference to the siren's song of a six-figure income. Certainly, the Pulitzer along with her other prestigious honors like the Robert F. Kennedy Award for Excellence in Journalism, meant she could command a much heftier salary than what the Foundation offered, but there was an undeniable allure to being associated with such a respected and socially influential organization. And while it may not have been the rural lifestyle she craved, Berkeley was a lot closer to Tess's winner's circle than Los Angeles. Hell, she thought at the time, even Fresno would be better than L.A.

"So, what can I do for you, Tess?"

"I have a proposition for you."

"My dream come true, beautiful lady." The attorney heaved an ersatz blissful sigh.

"I'm serious, Van. Do you have a few minutes?"

"Sure. Propose away."

Tess didn't have to remind him of their successful partnership on the child protective services corruption case, or any of the other times they'd worked together over the years. Even considering that, asking an attorney for access to a client before and during what was likely to be a sensational murder trial was another matter entirely. If he allowed Tess to meet with Rennie, Van Sweringen would be straddling a narrow ethical line, and she wasn't sure he'd go for it. He may have trusted her, but his foremost obligation was to his client, and that could be an insurmountable obstacle.

Once she finished, the attorney was silent, clearly weighing the pros and cons in his mind. "You've probably guessed this," he said finally, "but we're going to plead diminished capacity."

"Yeah, that's what I figured, based on the reports about how they found her afterward. Do you really think she's insane?"

"You know I can't answer that, Tess. What I *can* tell you is that she's an extremely damaged kid. And that the damage is only obliquely related to her mother."

"I know you're treading on thin ice here, Van, but who *is* the damage related to?"

"I can't tell you that either. In fact, it may not even come out at trial, depending upon whether or not the judge lets it in."

"Come on, Van: you've got to give me more than that. If *you* can't tell me, let me talk with Rennie. You know me well enough to know I'll keep everything she says totally confidential, and that I won't go public with anything until the trial is over. I give you my word."

"Let me have a day or so to think on it."

"Sure. Take all the time you need." The fact that Van Sweringen hadn't turned her down cold told Tess that he would eventually agree. There might be constraints on what she could or couldn't ask, but he would agree.

And he did. The lawyer's only request was that Tess not question Rennie about the killing itself. Everything else was on the table and fair game.

3

RENNIE MATLOCK LOOKED MUCH MORE DELICATE in person than she did in the press or police photos, and was an entirely different person than the teenager who eagerly grinned out from the pages of her school yearbook and family album.

What unnerved Tess the most were Rennie's eyes: they were so dark brown as to be almost black, and were completely vacant and detached. There wasn't a person alive who could read anything in them except emptiness and desolation. Her hair, straight and lifeless as her eyes, was a dust-colored sheet sagging a few inches below her shoulders. With fingernails bitten almost to the quick, her hands lay wilted in her lap. A narrow gold band, its filigreed shank encasing a small, solitary ruby, encircled her right ring finger.

Mason Van Sweringen had cautioned Tess that Rennie was emotionally shuttered and would likely say little at first, even though the lawyer repeatedly assured the teen that she could trust the journalist. In fact, during that initial hour-long visit Rennie barely acknowledged Tess's presence, sitting silently on the charcoal grey steel bench and alternately staring at the floor and the blank concrete wall above Tess's head. Tess spent the hour quietly telling Rennie about herself: how she'd grown up in Sacramento, worked as a glorified gofer at the NBC-affiliate television station there during college, and ended up working at newspapers in Ohio and Los Angeles. She told Rennie about her move out of L.A., about her younger sister Karen who lived in Carmel-by-the-Sea, about her twin calico cats named Mulder and Scully, and her old golden retriever Luna.

Tess could only hope that all of it would help build a bridge, however tenuous, between them, and help Rennie see her as someone who had the capacity to both care and listen without judgement.

She came back the next morning to a repeat of the day before. Rennie was unspeaking and empty-eyed, her only movement twisting the ruby ring around and around on her finger. Unsure what to do next, Tess took a risk. After fifteen minutes of silence, she stood up and knelt directly in front of Rennie, practically forcing the girl to make eye contact.

"Rennie," she said firmly, "I can't begin to imagine what you're going through. I can't begin to imagine how scared and confused you must feel. I can't begin to imagine what it feels like to look at the future and see nothing. I won't say I understand, because I can't. I've never been where you are. What I *can* do, though, is listen. I can let you tell your story, no matter how painful or disturbing it may be, and I can do it without judging you in any way. If you want to try, I'm here. If you don't, then it's time for me to leave." She stayed there kneeling for half a minute in the soundless room, then stood and picked up her briefcase.

"That's it, then. Good luck, Rennie."

She'd almost reached the buzzer signaling the guard to unlock the door when she heard a sound like a kitten mewling. Rennie was crying softly, tears dribbling down her cheeks and off the edge of her chin.

"Please," she half-whispered. "Please don't leave."

Tess turned back to the girl, who had withered even further into herself on the ashen metal bench. Her back rolled into a mournful curve and her narrow shoulders quivered with suppressed emotion. The unresponsive, stony-faced teenager had assumed the form of a forlorn and frightened little girl.

At that instant, the air in the room shifted and compressed the way people recount how it feels just before a twister hits, and Tess saw Rennie, maybe nine years old, cowering in her bed with a hulking figure towering over her, his arm swinging a belt-like strap and bringing it down on her back. As suddenly as it appeared, the vision vanished, leaving Tess standing unsteadily in the center of the stuffy room.

This was nothing new for her: since her own childhood she'd experienced these sudden and unexpected flashes of sixth sense that sometimes peered back on a someone's past, or into a future that had yet to appear. She told very few people about these episodes, figuring she would be whisked away in a strait-jacket to spend the rest of her days in a padded cell—but over the years, they'd come to be a normal, if random, part of her life.

Stepping over to Rennie, Tess sat close by on the cold bench and simply waited. The girl would have to make the first move, say the first words.

Eventually, they came. "I…I'm sorry. I guess I just wasn't sure…didn't know if…" her voice drifted off.

"Didn't know if you could really trust me."

"Yeah."

"Well, you can."

"Mr. Van Sweringen said I could, but I wasn't ready to believe it, I guess. I guess I was scared that you…that you would think I was some kind of monster."

Tess took note of Rennie's repeated use of the tentative "I guess." *This girl's self-esteem is somewhere near the level of pond scum. Makes sense, if my unexpected vision is worth anything.*

"No, I don't think you're a monster, Rennie. What you did may have been monstrous, but I'm not here to talk about that. I'm here to listen to everything that led up to that day, to the truth of your life. Are you ready to talk about that?"

Rennie turned her head sideways and looked at Tess through a veil of hair. Uncertainty still blanketed her eyes, but then she seemed to reach an internal decision and slowly sat up straighter. Her gaze shifting between the empty concrete wall and the scarred and grimy linoleum floor, she began to speak.

Over the next few days, she regurgitated a story that was even more brutal than Tess's vision.

Rennie spent most nights as a child in the care of her adoring Irish-born grandmother. Daytimes were the realm of her mother Cliona, who was alternately devoted to and dismissive of the little girl. To Rennie, it seemed like every few weeks brought a different man into their lives: some kind and some not so much, but most paid little attention to her. As sweet and pretty as she was, her light simply couldn't compete with the blinding beacon that was her mother's.

Things changed when Simon Matlock appeared. Now there were lavish dresses and play clothes, a tide of new toys and games, a four-story dollhouse, and exciting trips on a private jet to faraway places. For the first time, Rennie felt like part of a real family rather than just an inconvenience to be handed off to her grandmother. Plus, she adored Simon, who treated her like a precious Fabergé egg.

She didn't remember much about it, but the photographs of the couple's wedding in Seattle showed her as a shyly smiling, dark-eyed flower girl in a pearlescent blue dress and pale blue peep-toes shoes with silk roses on top, carrying a basket of rose petals, some of them scattered on the aisle behind her. Cliona was, of course, magnificent in her custom Vera Wang backless wedding gown that featured lace, pearls, and opaque seed beads on the bodice, while Simon stood handsome and elegant in a midnight blue, satin-trimmed Armani tuxedo.

With Simon and Cliona on a month-long honeymoon in Greece, a horde of movers relocated the household into a three-story, six thousand square-foot mansion in San Francisco's exclusive Pacific Heights neighborhood. The couple returned with armloads of extravagant gifts and trinkets from the Greek Isles: a delicate antique amphora, a handmade wool flokati rug, a rare ancient Greek silver coin, an amethyst bead necklace from the 1st century B.C., a Byzantine-era bronze oil lamp, toys for Rennie, Greek olives and cheeses like Mizithra and Graviera, bottles of Greek wine and, of course, plenty of ouzo.

And for a time, all was well with the world.

Until it wasn't.

By the next year, Cliona was too absorbed with her charities and tennis lessons and shopping and vodka martinis to pay attention to her young daughter, much less the signs that something very ugly was putrefying under the pristine landscape of their lives.

It began innocently enough. A good-night kiss that lasted a little too long, a hand that touched her leg a little too high above the knee, arms that held her a little too forcefully. One night Simon's bedtime hug turned into a massage, then a few nights later he removed the top of her pajamas and nights later, her pajama bottoms. "It's our special secret," he whispered, his moustache tickling the sensitive spot just under her ear, and she felt adored and uneasy at the same time.

The child's uneasiness mounted as the sexual violations persisted, culminating with his first rape on the night of Rennie's eighth birthday party, an extravagant affair with clowns and jugglers and pony rides and a fully functioning miniature carousel atop a three-layer birthday cake.

In the weeks to come, Cliona ignored the blood on her prepubescent daughter's Cinderella-patterned sheets, even after their housekeeper mentioned it twice.

On the nights Simon came to her room, he would repeat the whispered admonition that everything was to stay "our secret," and that telling anyone would mean she would be taken away from her family forever. As the years rolled on and the eight-year-old became ten and twelve and fourteen, that lie wasn't enough for Simon: now the nighttime threat was direct, more ominous. I will kill you. I will kill your brothers. And of course, the girl believed him, because by now she'd learned that Simon Matlock was a Very Important Man with Very Important Friends, and that he could do and get anything he wanted.

Adding to the young girl's confusion, he continued plying her with gifts and phones and iPads and clothes and anything else she wanted, all the time professing the depth of his love for her. "You're my princess," he would tell her over and over, "and nothing will ever change that." Never wondering how someone who loved her so much could talk about killing her, she simply packed up each declaration in separate boxes inside her brain, believing them both.

The love came with a price beyond the bedroom. Unable to divorce his sexuality from his overwhelming desire for dominance, whenever that desire was thwarted Simon turned to violence. It didn't take much to incite his rage, Rennie explained: something as simple as an accidentally broken glass or an opinion that differed from his own could be enough to bring him to her room that night with a belt in his hand. Yet other times, he would brush off incidents like that as if they were nothing more irritating than a buzzing fly. Rennie never knew when her protector would become her persecutor, which is of course precisely what Simon wanted.

"So I learned how to be perfect," she told Tess in the later hours of their conversation. "A perfect student and a perfect daughter. A perfect little girl. Anything to keep me safe."

"And to keep your secret."

Rennie looked down, absently twisting the ruby ring and taking it off and on. The backs of both hands were parched and covered with small sores, some scabbed over and some fresh, where Rennie had scratched and picked at them over the weeks or months or years.

She glanced up, then barely nodded. "Yeah, I guess so." A curtain of scarlet crept sluggishly from her chest up to her face.

Tess let the silence drift like a murky cloud, hoping Rennie would find the strength to slice it open it and reveal whatever mysteries it held. It wouldn't happen that day, or the next, or ever. Some things we take to our graves.

She did, however, talk about how she tried to tell her mother.

"I was pretty little the first time," she said, a faraway look in those somber eyes. "Maybe right after…after it happened the first time. After he raped me. I didn't understand what happened, why he hurt me like that and then told me it meant he loved me. So I went to my mother and tried to tell her. I remember that she looked at me with this hateful look in her eyes, then she slapped me across the face. Hard. 'Don't you ever, *ever* say anything like that again,' she said in this creepy whisper, and walked out of the room.

"I tried to talk to her one other time, when I was maybe about eleven or so, and she hit me again and called me a bitch and a cunt and a liar, and told me to get out. Leave the house. So I went over to my friend Judy's place; I didn't tell her what I'd said to my mom, just that she'd been drinking and we had a huge fight. Later, Simon picked me up, saying mom told him I'd called her names and hit her, and he wanted to know why. I tried to tell him the opposite was true, but he wouldn't answer, then later that night he came in and beat me worse than ever, and afterward raped me.

"That was always how it was: he would hit me first, or do other things to me, and then he would have sex with me. It was like…like he was excited or something."

Breakfast rose in Tess's throat, and she swallowed it back down and stifled an expletive. She'd known men like Simon Matlock, men who were aroused by violence and depravity, but this was the first time she'd ever heard a daughter describe it about her father. Father, stepfather, it didn't make any difference: Simon Matlock was the only male parent Rennie ever knew, so he may as well have been her biological father. For years, Rennie choked down meals at the family table while seated across from the man who violated her; next to him sat the woman who was complicit in the crime, playing pretend because it was just too unpleasant, just too uncomfortable, to admit the truth.

4

Three Weeks Before Sentencing

TESS WOULD RATHER HAVE BEEN ANYWHERE ELSE in the world than ringing the doorbell of the imposing redbrick Georgian-style mansion in San Francisco's Pacific Heights neighborhood. As muffled footsteps approached the door, she took a deep breath and slapped on a genial, practiced smile. After what she'd learned from Rennie in the last four days, Tess detested the thought of spending time with Simon Matlock, but knew there was no choice if she wanted to get the full picture. She also knew she would have to convince him that she wasn't a threat.

Days before, the district attorney filed the 602 Petition, charging Rennie with the crime of murder. The next step was the judge's, to decide if the petition was true. Tess had wandered around legal circles enough to know what his decision would be, and that Rennie would soon find herself on trial. The juvenile system moved much more rapidly than its adult counterpart, where there could be years between an arrest and trial date. Youngsters detained in juvenile hall had just fifteen judicial days between the court's initial detention order and the jurisdictional hearing.

A uniformed maid answered the bell and invited Tess in. The two-story foyer was awash with light, even though the day was typically foggy. Boxy windows sparkled on three sides of the huge entry, and on the remaining wall curved a grand mahogany staircase with an ornate wrought-iron railing. Above, a hand-painted coffered ceiling sported elaborate medallion insets. Just beyond was the massive living room, where four arched picture windows framed sweeping views of the Golden Gate Bridge and the San Francisco Bay. Through the fog lay Angel Island and Alcatraz, and the eclectic city of Sausalito.

Tess was escorted into the library, where a fire burned in the limestone fireplace and soft jazz played quietly through invisible surround-sound speakers. The breathtaking view echoed that of the living room, this time captured through a huge bay window accented on both sides with a pair of French doors. Four huge marble pillars stood guard on the outside terrace, supporting the third-floor balcony.

In front of the leather sofa was a glass-topped mahogany table, where tendrils of steam rose from two cups of coffee. Cream, sugar, napkins, and dainty sterling silver spoons sat on an engraved silver tray between the two cups.

"Please to sit," said the maid, her eastern European origin evident in both her accent and grammar. Maybe Ukraine, guessed Tess. That country was the nexus of the thriving human trafficking trade, and the thought flitted through her mind that the maid could be one of those unfortunate victims. She stopped herself before her overactive imagination took her any further down the rabbit hole.

Just then, a side door opened and the man Tess instantly recognized as Simon Matlock strode in. He was shorter than she envisioned him, probably no more than five-foot nine, but even through his cable-knit sweater she could tell he was lean and powerfully built. An unmistakable aura of unalloyed power and domination rolled in waves toward Tess, compelling her to take an instinctive step backward before catching herself and moving toward him, her hand extended. The instant her fingers came in contact with Matlock's, invisible snakes slithered across her hand and up her arm. Checking the instinct to recoil from the chilling sensation, she gripped his outstretched hand firmly and shook it.

"How do you do, Ms. Alexander? Welcome to my home. Please, sit and have some coffee. May I offer you anything to eat? Some fresh fruit and cheese, perhaps?" He was smooth and charming, with a dazzling smile and deep, warm voice. His eyes were the same shade as the curving bay beyond the window, a stunning deep azure that matched perfectly the uppermost color block of his sweater, the elegant face of the Rolex watch on his left wrist, and the background of the patterned pillows scattered on the couch and overstuffed chairs. Impressive, thought Tess. And thoroughly calculated. A man always in control of his surroundings, who needs to be the center of attention, who wants you to *see* his supremacy. A classic narcissist.

"No, thank you, Mr. Matlock." Her smiling face was a mask of friendliness and sincerity. "But I'd love some coffee."

"Please: it's Simon."

"Of course. Simon."

"So, Tess—may I call you Tess?" He didn't wait for a response. "I presume you want to talk about my daughter."

"Yes, that's right. I've spent quite a bit of time with her, but wanted also to speak with you. May I record our conversation? Just for accuracy: I wouldn't want to misquote you."

His eyes narrowed for an instant, then relaxed. "Of course. There's nothing I have to say that I wouldn't want the world to know."

Yeah, right. She flipped the switch on her digital recorder, then sat back and took a sip of coffee. Kona, undoubtedly. "What delicious coffee," she gushed, squirming inwardly at her sham ingenuousness. "So, Simon, can you tell me about Rennie's childhood?"

Matlock embarked on a forty-minute monologue about how entranced he was by the little girl the moment he met her, how they formed an instant bond, how within days she fell in love with him as the father she never knew. Everything he said revolved around his own relationship with the girl, not the girl herself. It was as if she had no existence beyond the one she shared with him. And always, always, it was "my daughter." Not "Rennie," not "my stepdaughter," not even "our daughter" or "Cliona's daughter." Always *my* daughter. He owned the child.

It was because of *his* influence that Rennie became such an excellent student: he sent her to the most exclusive schools in the city and made sure she had the best private tutors. *He* was the one who encouraged her to play tennis, practiced with her twice a week to sharpen her game, and inspired her to join the school's tennis team. He monitored her friends to make sure they were the "right" kind of girls, and was always the one to drive the kids to parties or school events and bring them home. Any sleepovers were always at the Matlock house, never anywhere else. Rennie was, he told Tess, "my princess," and he would never allow anything or anyone harmful near her.

Inside, Tess quivered like the leaves of an aspen tree under assault by a violent winter wind. The parallels between Matlock and the husband of her murdered sister Kat were shocking, and the taste of disgust burned in her mouth.

Yet ever the consummate actress, she continued stroking his ego. "It sounds like you were a wonderful father—she was lucky to have you in her life. What about her relationship with her mother?"

Matlock snorted. "What relationship? When Rennie was little, Cliona was too busy with her modeling, then after we married, she was too busy with her shopping. I ended up raising Rennie."

For the next hour, he continued sketching himself as Rennie's perpetual knight in shining armor, barely even mentioning his recently murdered wife. The evening fog had rolled in with a vengeance by this time, obscuring the view and smothering even the nearby streetlights with its sodden blanket. She knew it was irrational, but the last place Tess wanted to be was in Simon Matlock's house after dark. As if he were any less menacing in the daylight.

"Thanks so much for your time, Simon," Tess said as she switched off the recorder and stood to leave. "I need to get going."

Before she could move, he was standing directly in front of her. "What's the hurry, Tess? Stay for dinner, and we can talk more. I have a lot to tell you that I know you'll find very interesting and useful in your story. Besides," he added with his most alluring smile, "I'm sure you'd like to meet my sons, and talk to them too." He tried to hook Tess with the promise of more revelations, and now he was reeling her in.

"I'd love to, but I really can't," she said sweetly, looking for a way out. "I'm meeting a colleague for dinner in North Beach." It wasn't true, but she had no compunction about lying to a man like Matlock. She stepped sideways around him. "Can we pick this up tomorrow morning? Say, around ten?"

He touched her arm, and the snakes returned. "Just call your colleague and tell him—it *is* a 'him,' isn't it?—your plans have changed." It was a decree, not a request. Then he smiled, the amiable charmer again. "Easy enough, right?"

Tess's heart was thumping so hard she was afraid Matlock could hear it, or see the frenzied pulsing on the veins of her neck. She was both furious and unnerved at his attempt to intimidate her, but had no intention of letting him know it. "I wish I could, but actually, the colleague is really one of my bosses, and I just can't afford to stand him up. As someone who knows all about the corporate hierarchy, I'm sure you understand. Is ten o'clock tomorrow okay?" The muscles on her face ached as she maintained an innocent smile.

They stood facing each other for a few seconds, then Matlock coughed a hard, rasping laugh that sounded like dead leaves skittering across a sidewalk. "You know, Tess, one day all that sweetness and light is going to get you into trouble. All right: tomorrow morning it is."

Once she reached her car, she got hit by a tsunami of nausea. Unconcerned about whether or not any of the affluent Pacific Heights residents saw her, she dropped to the curb, putting her head between her knees to stop the violent spinning in her head. After a few minutes the mad Tilt-a-Whirl slowed and finally stopped, leaving Tess shuddering and drenched in sweat. At that moment, she knew that Simon Matlock would be a very formidable adversary, if it ever came to that.

❧

The night's gelatinous fog was magically gone the next morning, leaving the city's saturated streets glittering like Christmas ornaments in the brilliant sunshine. In the distance, sunbeams reflected off the bay's cobalt waters as Tess approached the Matlock estate and once more walked into the light-filled library. An elegant coffee urn sat on the sterling tray, bracketed by a pair of coffee cups identical to the ones from the day before. On the table was a silver-rimmed basket of petite breakfast muffins still warm from the oven, alongside a platter of fresh strawberries. This time, Simon Matlock was already in the room, silhouetted against the bay window with his hands on his hips and legs apart, looking out over the cityscape like a commanding general.

"Good morning," he said, his back still toward the room. "How was your dinner meeting with your boss? And where did you go?" It felt like a challenge, one Tess was prepared for.

"The meeting went very well, and dinner was wonderful; we ate at the Park Tavern on Stockton Street." She was almost embarrassed how easily the lie slipped off her tongue. Almost.

Matlock turned around and locked eyes with her. Seconds ticked by with neither one conceding: Tess in her fictitious guilelessness, Matlock in his dominance. Then in an instant, he transformed into the urbane host, smiling and gesturing to the couch, his voice warm brandy. "Sit, please, Tess, and help yourself to a muffin. They're Tory's specialties, and quite delicious. Totally organic. And there are fresh strawberries as well. Organic also."

Tess wasn't the least bit hungry, but reasoned that allowing Matlock this small conquest would help ease whatever sting he felt from her refusal to join him for dinner the night before. She bit into one of the warm blueberry muffins, and was instantly transported into culinary heaven. "It's wonderful, Simon. Tory must be a marvelous cook."

"Yes, she is: a rare find. She's been with us for almost ten years."

"So," said Tess, continuing the small talk, "how long have you lived here? It's a magnificent home."

"It is, isn't it? I moved here right after I married Cliona."

Not "after Cliona and I were married"…"after I married Cliona." As if she had no choice in the matter. I wonder if she ever understood how absolutely he dominated her.

Tess set up her recorder and arranged herself in the middle of the couch. The day before, Matlock was seated in one of the occasional chairs across from her, but this morning he moved toward the sofa, forcing her to shift to one side and leaving barely three feet between them. Claiming his territory.

At noon, two dark-haired boys scuttled down the stairs and into the library, shyly introducing themselves to Tess. The youngest was four-year-old Devon; Phillip, standing a full head above his brother, was five. Tess had only seen professional pictures of Cliona as a young model and newspaper society shots of her with Simon, but she could tell that the boys bore only a vague resemblance to their mother. On the other hand, each son's likeness to his father was remarkable: both had the same deep azure eyes with full, dark lashes; both shared his aquiline nose and square jaw; and both had the same wide smile, although theirs carried none of their father's frequent artifice.

"Tory said lunch is almost ready, and that we should ask if Ms. Alexander will be joining us." Phillip spoke in the practiced, clear manner of a boy who'd already been well-schooled in social skills. No *Hey, dude* here.

Matlock didn't even look at Tess. "Of course she will. One of you run into the kitchen and tell Tory." Only then did he turn to Tess. "I know we didn't discuss this beforehand, but really, Tess, you must stay, if only to sample more of Tory's superb cooking. It's the least I can do, for all the time you're spending here and with my daughter. She says she admires you greatly, by the way, and finds you very easy to talk to."

"That's really nice to hear," Tess responded, then struggled to find the right expression. "She's a…a…remarkable…young woman. Much deeper, more discerning, than I expected." She wasn't about to reveal how much she really knew about the perverse secrets Rennie shared: the only way she could keep Matlock engaged and talking was if he thought she believed his version of events.

"Indeed she is. So now, you *will* join me and the boys for lunch."

Saying no would likely bring their future interview sessions to a screeching halt, so Tess generated the most genuine smile she could muster and accepted his invitation.

Tory was indeed an extraordinary chef: for the main dish she served scallop rosettes with avocado and tandoori spiced summer squash, accompanied by warm dill-and-garlic crescent rolls and South Indian coffee spiced with chicory. Dessert was an airy, fragrant lemon panna cotta.

Tess tried her best to engage Devon and Phillip during the meal, but noticed that after each question she asked, no matter how innocuous, each boy would glance furtively at his father before answering, as if needing his assent. Her skin prickled in discomfort every time it happened, and soon allowed the conversational ball to volley back into Matlock's court where he effortlessly refocused the talk onto himself.

Eventually the boys tired of the adult conversation and asked to be excused, and twenty minutes later, Tess and Matlock returned to the library. Sun still glinted off the motionless waters of the bay as the thick fog bank slumbered well beyond Alcatraz Island. The city's Chamber of Commerce must have been orgasmic.

It was close to three o'clock when Tess raised the question of Cliona's drinking, and the effect it might have had on Rennie. "Forgive me for bringing this up, Simon—and please know I'm not condemning Cliona in any way—but alcoholism can have a pretty profound impact on other family members, especially kids. Did Rennie ever talk with you about it? About how she felt?"

Tess was thunderstruck when Matlock replied. "I can't imagine where you got the idea, but Cliona wasn't an alcoholic. Sure, she loved her martinis a bit too much sometimes, but it never caused any problems. Not with my boys, not with me, and not with Rennie. She was a terrific wife and mother."

Tess knew she was treading on very thin ice, so softened her voice to a near-whisper. "I don't know quite how to say this, but one of the staff at an alcohol treatment facility confirmed she was there. Twice, at least. I'm sure this is embarrassing for you, and you have to know I'm not blaming anyone. Not you, not Cliona." She learned toward him on the couch and touched the cushion between them in a gesture of kindliness and understanding. "Simon, you invited me here, and gave me permission to talk to Rennie, because you said that you wanted people to know the truth, that it was important to you. That's all I'm asking you for: the truth."

For an instant, Matlock seemed to deflate like a popped balloon, but seconds later he recovered, any trace of uncertainty or weakness vaporized. "You remember what Jack Nicholson said in *A Few Good Men*, don't you? 'You can't handle the truth.'" He broke into a wide grin, then winked as if the whole thing was a colossal joke. "Okay, you win. Here's the truth: Cliona *was* a drinker, but she was pretty much harmless. Never took anything out on the kids. When the drinking got out of hand, I sent her to rehab, simple as that. No big deal, no big secret."

"Do you think it had anything to do with why Rennie did what she did?"

"Not in the least. I think Rennie just snapped. Some wires in her brain shorted out, and she went crazy. Can't blame her, any more than you can blame a rabid dog for biting. It just happened. But that's all I can say right now: my attorney advised me not to discuss anything related to the murder, and you agreed to those constraints when we set up these interviews."

He was right, at least about their agreement. Ordinarily scrupulous in her ethics, Tess admitted that every once in a while she nudged her toe over the line. Especially when she was dealing with rancid individuals like Simon Matlock. Nevertheless, there comes a time when acquiescence is the better part of valor.

"Of course," she said apologetically. Her mind roiled at his analogy between Rennie and a rabid dog. "I certainly didn't mean to overstep. Please forgive me."

Back in charge and sidestepping Tess's plea for absolution, Matlock returned to boasting about his picture-perfect relationship with Rennie, and how much she adored and trusted him. Tess's nausea threatened to make an unscheduled reappearance.

As the afternoon wore on, San Francisco's ubiquitous fog skulked its way back into the city. First to disappear into the nebula was the fingertip of Belvedere Island, just five miles distant across the bay from the city's shoreline. Within thirty minutes it swallowed Angel Island, Alcatraz, and finally all but the soaring, 750-foot-high towers of the Golden Gate Bridge.

At 4:30, Tess pled an impending migraine, just to escape Matlock's self-serving smugness. She'd been with him long enough to know that he wasn't going to reveal anything of importance, and the longer she stayed, the greater the chance that her sugary façade would begin to dissolve. It wasn't time to show her hand just yet.

At the library door, she turned and extended her hand, this time prepared for the reptilian onslaught. Unexpectedly, Matlock stepped closer and pulled her into an embrace. Tess stiffened, instinctively shifting into a flight-or-fight response. The bottoms of her feet tingled, the wispy hairs at the back of her neck levitated, and miniscule beads of stress perspiration dotted her forehead. The man's powerful hold trapped Tess's arms at her sides.

Her first reflex was to deliver a swift knee to the groin, something to inflict maximum pain while allowing her to escape. But an instant later, she realized how foolish she was being: Simon Matlock was simply a lecher. Like many prominent men, he was innately predisposed to assume that a woman would be lured by his power, and would tolerate, if not welcome, his advances. If she hoped to maintain a decent relationship with him, Tess had to disabuse Matlock of that notion without insulting him.

"Hey, Simon," she adopted her most charming, guileless smile while using every ounce of strength she had to pull back from him so he could see her face. "You're a great guy, but I'm seriously involved with someone. How's about we just keep this professional?"

For a few seconds, he just stared, his eyes shuffling back and forth between hers, trying to detect any hint of deceit. Then he relaxed his hold and laughed. "Oh well, you can't blame a man for trying."

All Tess wanted at that moment was a long, hot shower.

5

TESS TALKED WITH RENNIE a few more times before the jurisdiction hearing, California's version of a juvenile court trial where the judge decides if a young person is responsible for the crime. It was a foregone conclusion that Rennie was guilty, but Mason Van Sweringen made the case that she was insane at the time of the killing due to her prolonged abuse and her mother's refusal to acknowledge it. Unfortunately, the judge ruled all that as inadmissible for lack of evidence. At that point, both Rennie and Van Sweringen knew Rennie was destined for the California Youth Authority facility in Ventura, the only one in the state that housed females. The question was, for how long.

The answer came at the end of the sanity hearing. Sane, the judge intoned, and sentenced her to the Youth Authority until she was 25, the maximum age for holding anyone in a juvenile facility. No one was surprised.

Weeks later, Tess sat across from Rennie in the CYA's big visitor's area, tying up loose ends as best she could. The teenager was no longer prohibited from talking about the killing, but she refused to take Tess anywhere near that day.

She would talk about almost anything else, but not that.

Tess went back to Berkeley once Rennie was whisked off to the Youth Authority. After several weeks of intense research, and bolstered by those last exchanges with Rennie as well as conversations with some of Matlock's former employees and other Bay Area movers and shakers, she was satisfied that the man was thoroughly dirty. The problem was, just as with Rennie's abuse allegations, no one could or would offer any proof or evidence.

Tess decided to slip off her veneer of benevolence and shake the man's psychic tree to see what dropped out. It would be one of her final meetings with Simon Matlock.

On that last morning, she walked into the mansion's library to find the former high school prom king standing once more against the wide bank of bay windows, but this time he faced into the room. Behind him, the San Francisco fog had lifted just enough to reveal the faint outline of the two offshore islands, while closer in, the huge main cables and vertical suspender ropes of the Golden Gate Bridge glistened vermillion in the sun.

Icy claws tiptoed up Tess's spine when she realized that the glass-topped coffee table was barren of its customary cups and saucers and baked delicacies from chef Tory's oven, and that not a single note of Matlock's favorite smooth jazz flowed from the room's hidden speakers. Even the atmosphere in the room was leaden, as if its air was now something more viscous and suffocating.

Staring at her across the room, Matlock's eyes were a stony, frozen sapphire, and his lips creased into an acidic smile. "Well, Ms. Alexander," he said, his voice taking on a sarcastic edge, "I hear you've been roaming around the city and asking some very peculiar questions about me."

"Peculiar, no. Pointed, yes." Her heartbeat ratcheted into a higher gear.

"To what end?"

"To the end of what I told you when we first met: finding the truth."

"*The* truth," he snarled, "or *your* truth? I thought all this was about my daughter, but now I see it's about me, and your petty attempt to damage me. I haven't the vaguest idea why, unless it's that you're simply unhinged, on some sort of lunatic mission that has no rational rhyme or reason."

"I can assure you, Mr. Matlock, that my mission is anything but lunatic." As she spoke, her posture stiffened, her unguarded smile vanished, and her voice lost its girlishly naïve, compliant tone. "As I said, I'm simply looking for the truth—more specifically, the truth about what would drive a seemingly ordinary, rational young woman to plunge a letter-opener into the base of her mother's skull. People don't do things like that without a reason, and I have a pretty fair idea of what those reasons are. A lot of them relate back to you. You've insisted that you treated Rennie like a princess, made sure she had nothing but the best, had everything she wanted or needed, and loved her like she was your own. Let me ask you, though: does your idea of loving someone like she was your own include rape?"

Before he could respond, Tess rolled on. "Then there's the little matter of your influence, and how you wield it. For favors, for advantages, especially in your real estate development business. Like the zoning change on that big chunk of land in south Oakland where you ended up building a huge office park, when for ten years no other developer was able to get the zoning commission to budge.

"I also understand that the Fair Political Practices Commission investigated you, several times, in fact, for making illegal campaign contributions to various local and state candidates who later authored or supported legislation that benefitted your various projects. But you're a little like Teflon: for some reason, the charges never stick."

There were other things she knew. How Matlock got the contract for a multi-million-dollar government building when he wasn't anywhere near the lowest bidder. How several of his big commercial projects got approved almost magically, in less than half the time as other developers' projects, and with much looser restrictions. That wasn't even considering his donations to charities whose board members included certain highly-placed public officials who suddenly embarked on lavish vacations and generally spent a lot more extravagantly than usual.

But all that she kept to herself.

Matlock's mouth dropped open in astonishment as she spoke, then snapped shut while he did his best to steady his uneven breathing. What he couldn't control was his face, which swiftly reddened in obvious fury. Simon Matlock hated to be played—something else Tess's research revealed—and now he was suddenly face-to-face with the reality that he'd been badly misled by this erstwhile sweet-talking reporter who'd metamorphosed into a female version of Mike Bradley.

"You print any of that—you so much as whisper any of it in your fucking sleep—and I'll make your life a living hell. You won't have a life left. You talked to the wrong people, lady: people who are more powerful than you could imagine. They'll make sure—*I'll* make sure—you never work another day in your life: there won't be a magazine, a newspaper, a goddamn association for the protection of garden gnomes, that will hire you. You have no proof of any of it."

"Maybe not, but I just wanted to give you the opportunity to contradict the rumors. Assuming they *are* just rumors. Clearly, you can't contradict them with anything but threats."

Despite her bravado, she knew he was right. She couldn't prove a damn thing. And she knew too that Matlock's group of powerful associates would close ranks around one of their own in a heartbeat, making him virtually untouchable. But at least she put him on notice that someone suspected his corruption.

That had to count for something.

Knowing the story was dead, Tess returned to the Foundation's offices. There was no way she could print the kind of volatile allegations against Matlock without evidence.

Surprisingly, Rennie took the news well. Over time the two had established an honest, if still wary on Rennie's part, connection. She admitted to being disappointed when Tess told her she had to drop the story, but said she wasn't surprised.

"After all, it's not like he did recordings of when he was with me. And no one ever knew he hit me, because he always made sure the marks and bruises were in places that didn't show. I never told anyone except for my mom those two times, so there's no one to corroborate anything. Even if she were alive, she wouldn't do it. She was loyal to Simon, more than to me. That's just the way it was." Her sable eyes held no sadness, no regret—just resignation.

During the first few years of Rennie's incarceration Tess made the trip from Berkeley to the prison as often as she could, and in between visits stayed in touch with repeated letters and phone calls.

The Ventura Youth Correctional Facility, which at one time went by the ludicrous moniker of the Ventura School, is actually in Camarillo, a small town plopped down along U.S. Route 101 between Santa Barbara and Los Angeles. The institution was once cited as a "paragon of dysfunction" and known for its inhumane living conditions and violence. Not surprisingly, the vast majority of girls imprisoned there have a history of physical and sexual abuse, often at the hands of their fathers or other male family members, yet for decades, its therapy staff consisted of only males. No one in authority seemed to grasp that young women who were molested or raped by men might be averse to disclosing the details of that abuse to a male.

Rennie said that whatever "counseling" she received in those once-a-week sessions was fundamentally meaningless; as the years wore on, she resorted to reading tattered, decades-old self-help paperbacks from the prison library and whatever books Tess sent or brought to her. Slowly, she began to peel back the layers and acknowledge the twin origins of her lifelong despair and fury: Cliona and Simon.

But then, knowing and healing are two very different things

PART THREE

When shall I be dead and rid
Of all the wrong my father did?
How long, how long 'till spade and hearse
Put to sleep my mother's curse?

~ T.H. White
The Once and Future King

6

Present Day

TESS CLOSED HER EYES, and it all came careening back.

The garish crimson path slicing across Rennie's open throat, its borders just beginning to darken to the color of an overripe fig. A burgundy lagoon seeping into the tattered bedspread. Arterial spray congealing on the dungy walls. On the bed, an extravagantly engraved Sheffield silver straight razor, clotted with red. And the festering, metallic scent of blood, its vile pungency like a thousand sharpened spikes driven into her nasal cavity.

It would take weeks, perhaps a lifetime, for the nightmare vision to fade from her mind.

None of it made any sense: the last time Tess spoke at any length with Rennie, she was surprisingly buoyant. Looking forward to starting over, moving into an apartment of her own in a new city, even starting college. She shared with Tess her hopes of someday becoming a veterinarian, even though she knew the road toward that goal would be long and grueling. "I'm up for it," she'd said, the smile palpable in her voice.

So, what the hell drowned that embryonic hope in a pool of blood in a ratty motel in the middle of nowhere?

Freed from the Youth Authority at twenty-three, two years before the statutory limit because of her exemplary behavior, Rennie had spent a decade behind bars, where her only escape from the drugs and violence and despair was to crawl inside her mind to discover a path toward redemption. So she read and studied and learned everything she could about what made her and what destroyed her, and how she could go back to the world at least a little more whole and live a life that meant something.

Along the way, she earned a high school diploma and began taking undergraduate college courses. She somehow avoided the frequent inmate brawls, and even though she got almost nothing out of it, kept meeting with the prison's pseudo-counselors, hoping to gather from them even a faint glimmer of insight. Five years into her incarceration, she entered the CYA dog grooming program, then moved on to canine training classes. These dogs, she told Tess, helped her understand what genuine, unconditional love felt like, and solidified her desire to work with animals when she was released.

One constant during the two decades of Rennie's imprisonment was Simon Matlock, a blackened thread binding her to her former life. He called, he wrote, he visited, reaffirming that he was there and would be there for her, always. By now, he had risen to even greater heights. Elected to the California state senate two years after his wife's murder, he was well into his second term of office and on his third appointment as chair of the powerful Senate Appropriations Committee. His roster of rich and influential friends had grown incrementally over the years, and while murmurs about clandestine dealings and bribery schemes continued to churn around him, the man remained virtually untouchable.

Tess offered to drive Rennie home after her release, but Matlock rebuffed her, demanding the privilege of being there so Rennie could return home with him. You'll need time, he told his stepdaughter, to rest and heal and re-learn about the world. You need somewhere where you can be safe.

For Rennie, of course, living with Simon Matlock was anything but safe. Every day, every night, brought new terrors—if not in reality, then in the dark recesses of her mind. Would this be the day he would snap? Would this be the night she'd hear again the soft *snick* of her door opening, feel again the fervent press of his hot body against hers? As weeks rolled into months, she waited and dreaded and fell deeper and deeper into a moldering pit of despair.

Once or twice she called Tess, her thin, strangled voice relaying the fear consuming her. I can't go on like this, she whispered across the electronic miles. I give up. And Tess did her best to comfort the young woman, to offer a shred of hope that somewhere, somehow, she could build a better life.

That hope materialized into actuality when Tess learned about Bess Worthington and her organization, New Promise. Deeply concerned about Rennie's state of mind, one day she reached out to an old college friend who ran a private mental health treatment facility in Connecticut. He made some calls and came back with the name of Betsy Worthington and New Promise, a small but highly regarded California nonprofit that provided financial and emotional support for formerly incarcerated women, helping them find direction and purpose. The woman proved to be a gold mine of knowledge and compassion, and immediately reached out to Rennie.

Just before Christmas, Rennie phoned Tess with a note of subdued optimism in her voice, announcing she was leaving her father's clutches in San Francisco: Betsy found her housing in Sacramento, Rennie explained, and helped her enroll in community college there. Rennie called a half-dozen more times between then and the new year, first to tell Tess about her apartment, then her classes, then a part-time job she'd snagged in the college admissions office. The boulder of dread growing in Tess's chest since Rennie's release began to dissolve.

Then came the second week of January, and this time Rennie's voice was flat and hard, saying she found evidence of her stepfather's larceny and more, much more. Enough that would annihilate him, destroy his reputation and his career and maybe even put him behind bars. I need to give you the information, she said, just in case.

"In case of what?" Tess's pulse vaulted.

"In case…just in case I need someone to back me up. Someone to go to the authorities for me."

"Why wouldn't you be able to go to them yourself?"

"Tess, please trust me here. I just want you to know what I know. What I've found."

Rennie went on to say she drove into the mountains to get away for a few days, and was staying in a small motel outside the former logging town of Hammond Mills, a few miles north of Truckee in the heart of the Sierra Nevada. A friend from her childhood had a summer home near Hammond Mills, and Rennie remembered watching videos of the girl's large, boisterous Italian family gathered around food-laden summer picnic tables, arms and hands linked in affection, joking and laughing and mugging for the camera, and Rennie feeling a stab of envy at their obvious joy in life and one another.

That's why, Rennie said, she chose Hammond Mills as a place to go to clear her mind, to figure out the logistics of how to make her escape and how, or if, to tell Matlock. It seemed a safe place, away from her stepfather and his house and its wandering ghosts.

"Can you come up here so we can meet? I need to talk with you in person."

By now, Tess had left the Bay Area and moved into the mountains, buying a home in the small community of Deer Valley, about seventy miles northeast of Sacramento. The light-filled house with its stunning view of the nearby peaks was her joy and sanctuary, one she shared with a gentle, broad-shouldered golden retriever named Cooper. Like his predecessors Dancer and Luna, Cooper was a rescue dog from Homeward Bound Golden Retriever Rescue, whose adoption volunteer Jan called Tess right after she moved to Deer Valley and proclaimed they had the "perfect" dog for her.

And he *was* perfect—of course, Dancer and Luna had been perfect too—with deep mahogany eyes and a thick coat the color of light amber honey. He was actually a golden mix—with what, no one knew for sure—but had the devoted, benevolent heart of a true golden. Tess called him her Velcro dog, not just because he stuck to her, but because he would stick to almost anyone. Despite being an incurable lover of anything human, Cooper's heart belonged solely to Tess.

Even though she lived 200 miles away, she still worked and wrote for the Foundation's *Panorama* magazine: the digital revolution and even more, the COVID pandemic, had changed the way everyone worked. Like millions of others, Tess's job no longer demanded that her backside be glued to a chair inside an office. When she wasn't traveling, she could do ninety percent of her work from home, with the added benefit of having Cooper sleeping contentedly on her feet. It was rare that she needed to make the trip to the Foundation's offices in Berkeley.

Deer Valley put her much closer to Rennie's temporary lodgings in Hammond Mills, and she figured the hour-long drive wouldn't be too bad if the weather held. The drive over Donner Pass in the middle of winter was always a crapshoot.

"Yeah, okay," Tess replied. "I should be able to get over the pass as long as the weather cooperates. And even then, I have four-wheel drive, so it shouldn't be a problem."

Rennie's sigh of relief was audible. "You don't know what it means that you're willing to come up here, Tess. I'm thinking it might be better to meet somewhere other than here, though, since this place is a little…uhh…sketchy. But it's all I could afford, since I'm soon to be a member of the peasant class," she joked. She knew Simon would likely cut off financial support once he discovered she was moving, penance for what he would see as desertion.

Tess suggested they meet in Moody's Bistro on Truckee's Bridge Street the next afternoon, but that meeting never came to pass.

It was permanently deferred by Rennie's brutal death.

The first thing Tess noticed about Rennie all those years ago was her eyes. Hollow, obsidian, murky pools of nothingness. They were the eyes of someone whose soul simply wasn't there anymore.

Rennie's eyes in death didn't look so very different than they did in life: those of someone whose essence was murdered long before she finally gagged on the nightmare of her own life, a life that ended with a straight razor's slash to the throat.

The police photographer's flash blinked again, freezing the scene in a bloody instant of time. Moments later, a pimple-faced ambulance attendant reached down with a quavering hand and closed her eyelids, then stood up and took an involuntary step backwards. It was his first night on the job, his first call of the night. Some initiation.

An older man in white motioned the young recruit to help him lift the lifeless body onto the lowered gurney, then together they covered her with a soot-gray plastic shroud and hoisted the stretcher onto its wheels. As they began to roll their cargo toward the door, one wheel jammed slightly against a hump in the matted carpet and the young woman's hand dropped outside the covering, dangling there as the gurney bumped its way across the threshold.

Thoughts careened through Tess's mind as she watched Rennie Matlock's lifeless hand hideously waving and dancing to the rhythm of the gurney's wobbling wheels. *Rennie finally quit biting her nails. Never noticed that before. As a matter of fact, I never noticed before how pretty her hands were. Small and delicate, like a child's.*

"Miss Alexander?" A burly police lieutenant touched her lightly on the shoulder. "Could I have a few minutes of your time for a statement?"

The words snapped Tess out of her reverie, even as the doors of the coroner's van clanged shut on another life. A leaden weight of sorrow and defeat sat in the middle of her chest, only amplifying her emotional exhaustion. She'd spent the last hour in this scruffy, rancid-smelling motel room after discovering Rennie's body, and what she really wanted was some time alone to think. And to be home in her own bed, Cooper curled up at her side.

Cooper had come with her on the ride that night, as he did on many of her travels, except when he wasn't allowed inside and it was too hot—or like tonight, too freezing—to leave him in the car. Once the police arrived, the motel manager agreed to let the dog wait in his office where it was warmer.

She looked up at the khaki-clad officer—*Lt. William Schiffler, Sheriff's Homicide*, announced the plastic badge on his shirt pocket—and almost told him she'd get back to him the next day, then realized it would only postpone the inevitable.

"Is there somewhere else we can go?" she asked, motioning toward the deathbed, soaked in crimson. "I'd rather not talk here."

"Oh, of course. Sure, ma'am," Schiffler said with embarrassment. "I get so used to crime scenes that I don't even think about how it might affect other people. 'Course, this one was pretty bad…." His voice trailed off as he stared at the bed and the blood-spattered wall beside it. "There's an all-night cafe only couple miles away, if that would be better."

"As long as the coffee's fresh this time of night."

"That's anybody's guess," he said ruefully, as they stepped out into the biting midwinter air. The frozen cloud of his breath hung in front of him. "Sally can put on a new pot when we get there."

"Fine. I need to get Cooper, then I'll follow you." Tess took the dog back to her car, parked in front of the motel office. The neon sign flickered a garish yellow green. " O VA ANCY." There's one now, she thought.

It was even colder than before, and an icy wind caught her coat and flung it over her shoulder as she struggled to open the car door. The gust whirled across the windshield of the maroon Lexus, picking up a handful of snow dusted there and carrying it off it a miniature funnel-cloud. It looked like an ugly night was going to get even uglier.

Ten minutes later she pulled into the tiny cafe's parking lot beside the lieutenant. He scurried around to her side of the car and wrenched open the door against the wind, blocking it from slamming closed on her.

Tossing a blanket over the dog, she said, "I'll be back, Coop. You be a good boy." Thanks to his nearly impenetrable undercoat, he would probably have been fine without the blanket, but Tess was a worrier when it came to her dogs. He could always shake it off if he got too warm.

The big officer gripped her arm and they scuttled together across the icy parking lot toward the glass door, then stood inside for a moment, breathless after the exertion of their icy sprint and the freezing night air.

"Sally!" the lieutenant barked. "Hey, Sal! Ya' got customers."

A stick-figure of a woman emerged from a darkened area behind the counter, delinquent strands of bleached-blonde hair straggling down the sides of her weathered face, fugitives from the ragged chignon at the back of her head. She wiped the sleep from her eyes as she walked out, then grinned as she saw the officer.

"Hey, you old fart! Where you been?" Her sandpaper voice rasped from too many decades of cigarettes, and an invisible, odorous cloud of tobacco enveloped the woman as she approached the pair of midnight patrons.

"Hey, Sal, been a long time. Ya' got any coffee?"

"Lemme make a new pot," she said, turning back toward the counter area. "Sit wherever you want."

They settled into a booth with cracked, greenish-beige plastic upholstery that Tess immediately christened baby-barf yellow. The bulky cop sitting across from her appeared to shrink by several inches as the padded bench beneath him sagged and complained.

Schiffler rubbed his broad hands together in an effort to warm them, then launched into a verbal history of the little café. From there, he veered off into a monologue about art of good coffee-making, his family, his neighbors, and how the country's main problems were a decline in morals and values, coupled with illegal immigration.

Sidestepping a debate over the state of the nation, Tess smiled thinly and said, "Lieutenant, you wanted to ask me some questions?"

"Oh. Right." Just then, Sally brought two steaming mugs of coffee that smelled like heaven. "Anything else?" she asked? "Piece of pie?"

Schiffler looked at Tess, but she shook her head. "Uhh, you have any of your prize-winning apple-rhubarb?" A note of hope was in his voice.

"Sure do, loo," she said with a smile, revealing deeply yellowed, tobacco-stained teeth. "Bring it right over. Warm it up first."

Shifting uncomfortably on the seat, Schiffler blissfully dove into the pie overflowing with chunks of apple and red-tinged rhubarb, and with his free hand skimmed through his notes from the evening. Tess noticed tiny beads of sweat on his forehead and upper lip. *Nerves, or the fact that the temperature must be nearing eighty degrees in this restaurant?* A cast iron pot-bellied stove in a nearby corner popped and sizzled, the heat radiating off its steel stovepipe in waves that she could almost see. Peeling off her heavy coat, she wished she'd worn a T-shirt underneath her sweater so she could take that off, too. She thought about opening the window that flanked the booth, then reconsidered, remembering the time-and-temperature sign on the Bank of the West that blinked "10º F" as she left Truckee.

"OK: let's go over again just how you came to be at the scene this evening."

Between sips of coffee, Tess gave her statement, explaining how Rennie Matlock called to say she discovered something very important about her stepfather, something that could finally put him away. She'd tried to get Rennie to give her at least a thumbnail sketch, but the young woman was reluctant to share anything confidential on the phone.

Tess reflected to herself that this semi-paranoia was neither new nor surprising: actually, her only surprise was that the disintegration wasn't worse. Beneath the veneer of her privileged and favored life, Rennie Matlock was seriously broken, thanks in large part to her stepfather's violence and incestuous predilections and not incidentally, her mother's complicity. The instant his hand had touched hers, Tess sensed the malevolence in Simon Matlock, a venom he frequently took out on his stepdaughter.

So, Tess explained to the perspiring lieutenant, two days ago Rennie called, saying she needed to talk to Tess about her stepfather. She was tired of protecting him, she said, and what she called his evil. She wanted to stop him, wanted the truth to come out. "He has secrets," she said on the phone that day. "Ugly, disgusting secrets, and I've just discovered some of them. Things that if the public knew, if his political cronies in the Senate knew, would ruin him. Send him to jail for years. And that doesn't even count what he did to me." Her voice dropped to a hiss. "You realize, don't you, that once I got out, that bastard would come after me again?"

It was inevitable: Simon Matlock's prized possession had come home, and he was going to claim her once more. Just like he did during all those years before Rennie tried in vain to tell the truth about it all. The intimidation, the sex, everything. And now that she was back home, it would start all over again.

Tess agreed to drive across the mountain pass the next day, and they arranged to meet at two o'clock that afternoon at Moody's Bistro in Truckee. But when Tess arrived, she saw a text from Rennie that she couldn't meet until that night. She would call when she could, the text said.

There was nothing Tess could do but wait. Figuring it would be a long night and reluctant to brave the mounting snowstorm and Donner Pass in the dark, she grabbed a room at the nearby Best Western, where she and Cooper settled in.

Eight o'clock, nine, nine-thirty, ten o'clock ticked by, with no call from Rennie. Finally, at 11:15 Tess's phone brayed, jerking her awake from where she'd fallen asleep on the bedspread.

"Rennie?" There was silence on the other end.

"Rennie, is that you?"

Finally, after another long pause, Rennie spoke, sounding very frail and far away. "I'm sorry."

"Sorry? About what? Where are you?"

"Just go home." Rennie's voice seemed to be getting smaller and smaller, as if she were shrinking into nothingness.

"What do you mean, 'just go home'?" Her fingers tightened around the telephone. "Rennie, answer me. Talk to me."

"I'm done, Tess." The line clicked dead.

With Cooper at her heels, Tess dashed out the door into the freezing sleet, grabbing her coat on the way but not even bothering to put it on. The crippling feeling of dread was almost paralyzing, making her feet as if they were encased in concrete.

She had no idea where she was going, except that it was called the Two Pines Guest Lodge about ten miles outside of Truckee, near a forgotten town named Hammond Mills. She stopped at a seen-better-days Beacon station to get directions, where an attendant crab-walked to her car from the ramshackle convenience store after she honked her horn repeatedly. He ogled her through the car window, grinned and told her to get on Highway 89, then take Old 89 to the right. "You go maybe a quarter a mile on the old highway, then Hammond Mills Road comes in. Go for about a mile, past the campground, then right away there's a road on your left. Two Pines is there on the right, honey," he said with a leer. "Have a good time!"

Tess gunned the engine and intentionally spun her wheels through the grimy slush that coated the station lot, splattering the unsuspecting gas-jockey. How's that for a good time, you shithead, she thought, wagging her fingers cheerily in her rear-view mirror.

Twenty minutes later she pulled into the only vacant spot in front of the manager's office and clambered out of the car.

"Rooms To Let: Day Week or Month." The neon letters reflected off the snow in crimson streaks.

What apartment number did she tell me? 6? No, 9. Apartment 9. Can't be too far down.

The tiny complex had a thoroughly slimy feel about it that had nothing to do with the obvious poverty of the place, a squalid tenderloin where furtive liaisons were the norm rather than the exception, where cigarette butts and empty beer cans dotted the half-shoveled walkway, and where life and death was bought and sold with total indifference. Bedspreads and towels functioned as curtains in some of the windows, at least one of which was illuminated by a pale red light.

Truth in advertising, anyway.

Behind one of the doors a dog barked as Tess's footsteps crunched by in the icy snow. "Nock Before Entering" was scrawled on a bedraggled piece of cardboard nailed to the door.

Apartment 9. A dingy yellowish glow seeped through the gap under the front door and from behind the flimsy curtains. Torn, yellowed masking tape patched a cracked windowpane.

Tess knocked, quietly at first, and called out Rennie's name. Nothing. She knocked louder, rattling the locked doorknob. A light came on in the next-door apartment and a groggy voice hollered, "Shut the fuck up!"

The black hole in Tess's stomach grew deeper as her calls for Rennie went unanswered. Desperately, she pushed at the door with her shoulder while twisting the knob violently, and the door abruptly burst open with a loud crack. The rusted handle flew from its tentative hold on the flimsy wood, bounced off the doorstep and rolled under a parked car, but Tess never saw it. What she did see made her gasp for air and then retch.

Rennie Matlock, dressed in a T-shirt and jeans, lay in the middle of a flaccid double bed atop a stained, snuff-colored chenille bedspread rapidly turning a sickening scarlet. Her head tilted sideways at an insane angle, exposing a hideous gaping wound in the middle of her milky-white neck. Her eyes were open and staring, as if transfixed by the splatters of gore that dappled the filthy wall next to the bed. Near one hand rested a glistening, bloody razor.

Tess was a statue, transfixed and unmoving, until a huge, rough hand smelling of oil and diesel fuel clasped her arm.

"Jesus H. Christ," the man said quietly under his breath. "Oh, shit. God damn son of a fuckin' bitch. Crap."

He roughly pulled Tess outside, shutting the door behind them as best he could without a doorknob, and commanded, "Stay here." She started to shiver uncontrollably in the bitter cold as he plunged through the berms of gritty snow surrounding the parking lot and toward the motel office. Several seconds later he reappeared with a torn and ragged olive-green Army blanket. As he wrapped it around her shoulders, she caught a whiff of something in the blanket that smelled vaguely familiar. *Hay? Pipe tobacco? No, not quite. Oh, yeah: weed.*

"Come with me." He piloted her back to the office and pushed her down into a 1950s-era aluminum kitchen chair with a grimy blue vinyl seat. "The cops'll be here any minute, but 'til then you stay in here. I have a real strong feelin' they're gonna want to talk to you."

"I...I need to...need to get my dog. In the car. Too cold."

"Shit, lady: a fuckin' dog? Okay, I'll go get him. Unless he's mean—he don't bite, does he?"

Tess shook her head.

"Okay. Wait here."

Tess couldn't shake the bloody images of Rennie from her mind. *Such a horrible way to die. Or, maybe not. Maybe it was quick.*

Then the sheriff's officers and the ambulance and the coroner were there, and they all wanted to know what happened and said to please come back inside to the murder scene and tell them what she saw. This time it wasn't so bad seeing Rennie, maybe because she knew what to expect. Plus there were so many men milling around inside this one tiny apartment that wasn't really much more than a room, that the whole scene took on a kind of surreal aura.

Except for the fact that it was very, very real.

"That's it, Lieutenant," Tess concluded. Her coffee was ice cold, and after sneaking a glance at the wall clock, was startled to see it was nearly four thirty in the morning.

"Do you have any idea at all why the victim might have taken her own life?" Schiffler stifled a yawn before taking a last gulp of his coffee and dabbing his index finger on the plate to capture any remnant flakes of the pie crust.

"No, except that her whole life was a living hell. It's odd, though, because she seemed to have so much hope for the future lately." Tess shook her head. "Frankly, Lieutenant, I'm astonished that she could summon any hope at all. That man robbed her of most of it a long, long time ago."

"That man?"

"Her stepfather. Simon Matlock."

"Oh, yeah. Heard something about him during the girl's trial." He swallowed another yawn. "Well, Miss Alexander, we know how to reach you if there are any other questions. Hope you're not planning on heading back to Deer Valley right away. I hear they're closin' down the interstate this side of the summit."

"No, I'll go back later tomorrow—that is, today—presuming I can get over the mountain." She glanced outside through the window, searching the winter sky for signs of stars. Only blackness greeted her.

"Thank you for your time, ma'am." The lieutenant stood up, brushing at the wrinkles in his drab pants and adjusting his gun holster. "Sorry you had to be the one to find the body."

"Me, too."

He tossed a twenty-dollar bill on the table, shouted a quick goodbye to Sally, and they stepped out into the winter morning.

It was no longer snowing, but the wind remained as fierce as it was two hours before. Though her motel was less than ten miles away, at the snail's-pace Tess was forced to creep it took nearly twenty minutes before she pulled in under the welcoming Best Western sign. The outside air was as frigid as the interior of a meat locker.

While Cooper was occupied with investigating all the new smells in the room, she kicked off her boots, stripped off her sweater and jeans, and placed a call to the front desk. "Yes, this is Ms. Alexander in Room 1202. I'd like a wake-up call around noon. If there are extra charges, just put them on my bill."

Even more than bed, Tess needed a hot shower, to feel clean again after all the blood. She half expected to look in the mirror and see herself covered in it, even though logically she knew that simply couldn't be, as she touched nothing in that death room, not even Rennie.

She caught her own gaze reflected in the mirror. The phrase an old lover used to say whistled through her mind. *You look like you've been rode hard and put away wet.*

Stepping into the steaming shower, she let the warmth envelop her as the tension and at least some of the horror of the night flowed with the water down the gurgling drain.

Tess Alexander was in good shape for a woman of forty-something, notwithstanding those five extra pounds she claimed to be carting around on her five-foot seven-inch frame. Her parts were all her own, even if one or two were tucked and lifted. Her shoulder-length hair still shone a warm ruddy auburn, with only a half-dozen strands of errant silver that no one but Tess could ever see.

An avid hiker, she loved getting out on the trails and back roads for a three- or four-mile jog, despite the frequent lectures from her orthopedist about the evils of running on knees like hers. In deference to Dr. Bones—yes, that actually was his name—she tried to limit her runs to a couple of days a week, while the rest of the time she walked.

The bathroom air was cold and clammy when she stepped out of the shower, so she dried herself hurriedly and pulled on her flannel nightshirt. Wiping the steam off the large vanity mirror with a spare towel, she again caught her reflection in the glass. She looked haggard and worn, ten years older than she did six hours ago. She sighed with a mixture of exhaustion and grief, absently blotting her hair with the bath towel and wishing she was anywhere other than where she was.

Then the mirror mysteriously fogged up again. At least, that's the first thought that whizzed through Tess's mind, until she felt the little pulses of what felt like electricity marching down her back like a colony of ants. *Oh, this again.* The cloudy mirror appeared to bulge into another, deeper dimension, through the wall and beyond, into total blackness. Struck suddenly blind, she staggered against the edge of the vanity and heard a distant, muffled crack. Then a misty, indistinct vision emerged through the not-mirror. It was Rennie, sitting on the bed in that squalid motel room, her head sagging against the threadbare headboard at her side. Now a hand, holding something silver blinking in the room's half-light, then like an adder's tongue, flicking and slithering toward Rennie's alabaster neck.

Instantaneously, the image vanished, replaced with Tess's own face in the clear, cold mirror. At her feet lay the shattered remnants of a small travel mirror. Regaining her balance, she carefully picked up the pieces of glass and dumped them in the wastebasket, then wiped that part of the floor with the wet towel to make sure there were no shards left.

Cooper was already asleep in the complimentary dog bed, his legs twitching in the midst of a dog dream. Spreading another towel across the pillow to keep her wet hair from soaking it, Tess lay down and re-imagined her vision, then realized she had witnessed the moments before Rennie's suicide. That night's mediocre coffee mixed with bile scorched her throat, but she managed to swallow it down.

She closed her eyes and tried to quiet her racing thoughts, but it wasn't her newest vision that kept rising to the surface: it was the memory of Rennie's lifeless body. As fatigue and lack of sleep finally took hold, a dusty moth of unease flitted through her mind, tickling at her consciousness as if she were trying to identify a barely-out-of-tune instrument in a symphony orchestra. Something was off. Something she was too mentally depleted to identify. *Maybe tomorrow it'll come to me.*

Then she plunged into a fitful sleep, where she dreamed until morning of faceless children screaming through a crimson rain.

7

THE MORE SHE THOUGHT ABOUT IT, the less understandable it was.

Barely twenty-four hours before, Rennie was eager to meet with Tess and reveal what she discovered about her stepfather. She made it clear that the information was so damning, so explosive, that she couldn't talk about it on the phone or by email, instead insisting they needed to meet in person.

At the same time, she was embarking on a fresh chapter in her life, thanks to Betsy Worthington. Set to move into her new apartment in north Sacramento in less than a week and start college, she was hopeful for the first time in months, and actually looking forward to the future.

To end it all with a razor to the throat simply flew in the face of everything Tess knew about Rennie. Had she missed something? Some sign that she was so desperate and depressed that she couldn't think of any way out other than suicide?

If it was *suicide.*

The thought slammed into Tess with the force of a blacksmith's hammer on a steel anvil. But of course it was suicide, she reasoned. Everyone agreed. The EMTs, the investigators, the sheriff, the coroner. Suicide, pure and simple.

But then it came again, that indefinable itching in her consciousness as the synapses fired and re-fired in an attempt to unearth a crucial memory. It was there, she knew, just beneath the surface. She just needed to find the right psychic shovel to mine it.

Closing her eyes, she replayed the grisly scene of Rennie's death. No, nothing there. On to the arrival of the motel manager, then the sheriff's deputies, then Lieutenant Schiffler, and finally the two men from the coroner's office. Nothing. Rennie's lifeless body, being wheeled away on the metal gurney. Her hand flopping outside the ugly plastic shroud.

Her hand. Something about her hand.

And then Tess saw it. More accurately, *didn't* see it. Rennie's cherished ruby ring, the one she'd worn since grammar school, the one given to her by her beloved grandmother so many years before.

Where the hell was the ring? And why did she suddenly feel such a powerful intuition that it was connected somehow to Rennie's death?

Then another thought surfaced: why wasn't there a note? From her long experience as a journalist, Tess knew that fewer than half of all suicide victims left notes—but in this case, reason held that Rennie would have left something for Tess. She'd been extraordinarily anxious to reveal the evidence implicating her stepfather in…in what? Whatever it was, Rennie believed it was enough to bring the universe crashing down around his shoulders. It was absurd to think Rennie would suddenly abandon such a strong compulsion to bring Matlock to justice, and leave nothing behind that could accomplish that goal.

So, we have the missing ring and the nonexistent note. And someone who was in the midst of reclaiming her life, of moving beyond the horrors of the past and making a future for herself. It doesn't take a Ph.D. to see that none of that points to suicide.

CR

Tess made her way back home once CalTrans opened the highway, and called her editors at *Panorama* to let them know she was on the trail of something big. Okay, possibly big. Possibly also something that could fall as flat as the Kansas prairie.

The main condition she laid out before she agreed to work for the Foundation was that she could take on investigative projects without expressly clearing them first. The editor-in-chief knew her work well enough and trusted her enough to permit that latitude, although he retained the authority to ultimately turn thumbs-down. It was her own reputation on the line as much as the Foundation's, which they hoped would keep her from diving off the deep end into an empty abyss.

There were times she teetered perilously close to that edge. One of her previous investigations almost cost Tess her life. Twice. But ultimately, the series on sex trafficking that resulted from that venture in Ukraine and London earned her yet another Pulitzer Prize. Even better, it put one of the main traffickers in prison, and another dead on the smutty floor of a train station.

Her second order of business that day was to call Mason Van Sweringen and tell him about Rennie. He'd probably already heard the news reports, since anything related to Simon Matlock was bound to create headlines.

"It's a hell of a deal," he said over the phone, his voice cracking with emotion. "I hadn't talked with Rennie much in these last years, but she always sent me a card at Christmas and a note about how she was doing. This year, it was a full-scale letter, telling me all about how you'd hooked her up with New Promise and how they'd found her a place to live in Sac, and that she was going to start college in a few weeks. She sounded so up, so confident and optimistic. And then this. It just doesn't compute, somehow."

"No, it doesn't, Van. And it goes deeper than that: a few days ago, Rennie called to say she stumbled across something incriminating that would finally put Simon Matlock where he belongs, in a cell. She was afraid to say anything over the phone or even by text or email, so I agreed to meet her so we could talk it over and decide what to do. She went up into the mountains to get away, staying for a couple of days near a little place called Hammond Mills."

"Yeah, I heard that on the news. Where the hell is Hammond Mills?"

"It's a few miles northeast of Truckee, off an old abandoned highway. Barely more than a bump in the road with a few houses. Anyway, we agreed to meet at Moody's Bistro in Truckee that afternoon, but she called to postpone it, and said she'd call me. She finally did a little after eleven, sounding completely out of it, and saying she was sorry. I asked her what for, but she didn't answer—just told me to go home, and that she was 'done.' I drove like a bat out of hell to the place she was staying, and pretty much broke down the door to her room and…and found her."

"Jesus. I'm so sorry, Tess. That had to be awful."

"Yeah, it was pretty nightmarish." She paused and took a ragged breath, remembering the scene. "It's what I realized afterward, though, that has my mind buzzing like a swarm of locusts. The ring she always wore, the ruby one her grandmother gave her when she was just a kid, was gone. Hell, Van, she wore that thing the whole time she was in prison, never once took it off. Why would she take it off just before she killed herself? And if she did, where is it? Far as I know, the cops didn't recover it.

"And there's one more thing: she didn't leave a suicide note. Nothing. Not even anything for me, even though she said she had solid evidence that would undermine Matlock, and wanted me to have it. Why wouldn't she have left a note or something for me, if she planned to kill herself? It was incredibly important to her that Matlock be brought down—it just makes no sense that she'd give up on that, even if she gave up on her own life." Tess decided not to tell the lawyer about her motel-room vision.

Van Sweringen was silent. Tess could almost hear the gears spinning in his mind. "You're right," he finally said. "Something doesn't add up. So, what are you going to do?"

"What makes you think I'm going to 'do' anything?"

Snorting derisively, the attorney replied, "Come on, Tess. You think I don't know you after all these years? You could no more let this go than set up a colony of Tibetan monks on Jupiter."

Tess couldn't help but smile at the image. "Thanks for bringing some humor to someone who hasn't found much to smile about in the last few days."

"Happy to be of assistance. So what *are* you planning?"

"I'm not one hundred percent sure yet. And frankly, even if I was, I wouldn't tell you, only because I don't want to expose you or anyone else to whatever fallout it creates. Simon Matlock is a powerful and possibly dangerous foe, but he's *my* foe, not yours."

"I should know better than to ask this—but are you being careful?"

"Of course I am," Tess scoffed. "Aren't I always?"

"In your dreams."

8

Now that she was ninety percent convinced that Rennie's death wasn't suicide, Tess revived her in-depth research on the Matlock family, trying to learn everything she could about Cliona, Simon, and the children. It was crucial that she dig up every existing ounce of information to exhume the truth. And the killer.

Her excavation turned up some curious information about Rennie's brother Phillip, the dark-haired pillar of perfection she met at Simon Matlock's lunch table just before Rennie was convicted. Some years ago, Tess cultivated a relationship with a particularly adept gray-hat hacker who, while he was averse to undertaking anything malicious, wasn't beneath infiltrating government and other official computer networks just to poke around. Her initial aim in contacting him was to find anything in the juvenile records about Rennie, but the hacker turned up something else.

"Hey, did you know that Phillip Matlock has a juvie record?"

"Uhh, no. What kind of record, JD?"

"A not-very-nice one. Guess he had a propensity for shanghaiing the weaker kids in his school and, like, doing weird things like chaining them to the sports field bleachers, or chopping off their hair. He even got busted for slicing a kid with a pocket knife—not enough to do any permanent damage, but enough so the kid probably ended up with a scar." The hacker's voice was as wooden as a two-by-four. He might as well have been reciting the alphabet as talking about a possible psychopath in bloom.

"Shit. Anything violent? Other than the slashing?"

"Lemme look some more. I accidentally bumped into this while I was trying to find stuff about Rendell. Rennie. Y'know, these outfits really need to beef up their security. Any script kiddie with bad intentions could crack their systems, no problem."

"Probably true, JD, but today that's not my issue. Maybe someday when I'm feeling magnanimous, I'll have a chat with one of the head honchos or do a story on it. Get back to me if you find anything else, okay? About Phillip *or* Rennie. Might look at the other boy, Devon, too."

"Got it."

A few days later JD called back. "Got something. When he was twelve, dear ole' Phil ended up in juvie—'course, rich daddy got him out in less than a day—for beating another kid fucking near to death. Guess the kid said something objectionable about Rennie."

"What happened? To Phillip, I mean?"

"Probation, six months. And mandatory counseling. Nothing on how long, or, like, whether it did any good. But after that, his record is clear—so maybe he turned over a new leaf."

"Maybe. You dig up anything else? On Rennie or Devon?"

"Nah. That's it."

"Okay, thanks, JD. I owe you."

She clicked off, then almost immediately dialed a psychologist she used to date. They remained friendly after the mutual breakup, and she occasionally bounced ideas off him when she was stumped in an investigation that involved mental health or personality dynamics. Once they got past the pleasantries, Tess asked him about juvenile psychopathy.

"First, Tess, keep in mind that thanks to Hollywood, the public tosses around terms like 'psychopath' and 'sociopath' like they were Mardi Gras beads—but in fact, there are no such terms, clinically speaking. They're more like traits under the heading of antisocial personality disorder.

"That being said, we're especially careful about labeling any juvenile as a psychopath, because kids' brains are really, really plastic, and don't mature until they're well into their twenties. There's a measurement tool called the Youth Version of the Psychopathy Checklist that some experts swear can accurately forecast whether a kid with psychopathic tendencies is going to become a psychopathic adult, but very few studies have been able to prove its long-term predictive validity. Some kids labeled 'psychopathic' stay that way into adulthood, but others seem to even out as they mature, and effectively grow out of their anti-social behavior."

"Okay: so, in terms of what I described about this twelve-year-old kid, do you think it's possible that he could have grown up to become a murderer? Specifically, to murder his sister?"

"Anything's possible, Tess."

"Likely? Would you bet on it, or pass?"

"From my own experience, I might place a small bet on it—but I'd be prepared to lose."

"Shit, you're a big help, Sam. So, you're saying it could go either way: he could have become a perfectly normal, well-adjusted adult or another Jeffrey Dahmer."

"Leave it up to you to come up with that kind of analogy. But yeah, I suppose so."

Looking at Phillip cast a new light on the case. Of course, there remained that nagging question about why he would have killed his sister, and in such a vicious, coldblooded way. The use of a knife usually signified that the act was highly personal, not to mention that Rennie's killer may have been facing her when he sliced her throat, adding even more of a personal dimension. What could have compelled Phillip to such savagery against his sister, especially since he'd once beaten a kid within an inch of his life for denigrating her? And what did he have to gain from Rennie's death?

A few weeks later on a gorgeous spring Saturday afternoon when the weeping cherry tree in Tess's garden was in full splendid bloom, her phone rang. It was a voice she didn't recognize.

"Tess? Tess Alexander?"

"Yes, who is this?"

"It's Phillip Matlock."

The skin on Tess's arms prickled. *Chickens dancing across my grave.* "What can I do for you, Phillip?"

"I know this is going to sound weird and totally out of the blue, but I…I just found something, and…well, I know you were friends with Rennie, and she really trusted you, so I figured it was something you should know. I remember back when Rennie first went to jail you were going to do an article on her, on the case, but Father told me it never panned out for some reason, and I never knew why, and Rennie never told me and neither did Father…." His voice was gaining more and more urgency, his words tumbling out like collapsing house of Legos.

"Hold on, Phillip," she said gently. "Take a breath, okay? Now, start at the beginning." She was well aware she could be chatting with a killer.

"Yeah, yeah, I'm sorry. It's just that I've been thinking about this for quite a while, and just didn't know who to talk to until I thought of you. Uhh, did you know that I moved out of the house in San Francisco about a year ago?"

"No, I didn't."

"Well, I have my own place now, down in San Jose. Trying to get my life together. To get away from my old man. Started college, doing pretty well. Well, at least I was until Rennie…until she died. And now…now the whole thing is even crazier. Even worse."

"How so, Phillip?"

She heard him take a deep breath and then let it out in a loud, shuddering *whoosh*. "I…I think Rennie was murdered."

As the young man talked, Tess had wandered into her back yard and watched as Cooper vainly to catch a butterfly, but at this unexpected revelation she thumped down onto a wrought-iron bench. Overhead was the loud, trilling song of a sparrow, and in a different tree, the sharp *chit-chit-chit-chit* of a red-winged blackbird. Cooper gave a short bark of frustration as the yellow-and-black butterfly sailed away, while somewhere nearby, a chainsaw coughed to life. Tess was deaf to it all.

"I'm sorry, Phillip: what…what did you say?"

"I said I think my sister was murdered." His voice was flat and unemotional.

"What makes you say that?" Tess frantically made her way back inside to grab a pen and paper. She needed to get this down.

"Well, I know that Rennie used…was killed with a cutting straight razor, right? Not too many of those around these days. Except for collectors. Like my father. He has twenty or thirty of 'em he's collected for as long as I can remember. Most are in this big glass case that he used to keep locked when we were little, but now he doesn't bother locking it because there's no kids around any more.

"Anyway, about a month ago Sofia and I were talking, and she said something about somebody stealing one of Father's collectible straight razors. I came home a couple weeks ago to get some of my stuff I'd left there, and when I walked by the case, I remembered what Sofia said, so I looked. I have a really good memory—one shrink told me it was close to eidetic—and I saw right away she was right: one of the razors was missing. It wasn't where it should have been, where it always was, in the case. "

Tess interrupted his rambling monologue. "Phillip, I need to make sure I can remember everything you're saying, so I'm going to record this conversation, okay?"

"No!" The man practically screamed the word. "No, you can't! It's too dangerous! I don't even want you to write it down!"

That isn't going to happen, thought Tess, but agreed not to use the recorder. "Okay, go on. So, one of the razors was missing."

Catching his breath after his outburst, Phillip continued. "Yeah, and I knew exactly which one it was. It was one I'd always admired, ever since I was a kid: it was antique, engraved silver handle, really cool with swirls and scrolls and fleur-de-lis. Father once said it was worth around five grand.

"Then I saw the news reports about Rennie, and the cops interviewed me and said she used a straight razor, but at first I didn't really pay any attention. All I cared about was that Rennie was gone. It was totally bogus, that she killed herself when she was just getting her shit together. I mean, she seemed happy for the first time in a long time, and was really looking forward to moving to Sacramento and starting college again. She was getting her life back, and then...." His voice trailed off.

"Did you look for the razor after you realized it was missing?" asked Tess.

"Yeah, I must've searched for two hours. Maybe more. Every drawer, every cabinet, but nothing. It's not there. But why…why the fuck would someone steal the razor, and then kill Rennie with it? And *who* would do it? He'd have to be a monster."

Tess bit her tongue to keep herself from saying what she was thinking. "With your memory, I'm guessing you would know it if you saw a picture of it, right?"

"Absolutely."

"All right, here's what I want you to do: *nothing*. Do nothing, say nothing, to anyone. I'm going to look into it, see what I can find, and I'll get back to you."

"You promise? You won't just drop this and go on with your life?"

"No, I won't drop it. I've spent the last couple of months trying to figure it out myself, and now you've given me something very strong to go on. But you've got to give me your word that you'll stay out…that you'll stay silent. Deal?" Tess was deeply concerned that the young man might snoop around on his own, and the result could be something she didn't even want to contemplate.

Phillip agreed, and said he'd keep a low profile until he heard back from Tess.

Two weeks later, he did.

9

TESS STEPPED OUT OF THE CAR and into a mound of filthy slush. The last of the winter snow was melting on the warm asphalt outside the county sheriff's substation, thanks to the early spring temperatures that even at this elevation neared fifty degrees in the daytime. She'd called ahead before making the trip up the mountain, and the desk clerk in the Records office grudgingly agreed to resurrect the files and evidence boxes from Rennie's case and have them waiting for her.

Sidestepping a Volkswagen-sized puddle, she trudged across the lot to the front door, announced herself on the speaker, and an invisible hand buzzed her inside. On the right side of the L-shaped counter were three cardboard file boxes marked "Matlock, R," and the date of her death. Alongside sat a fifteen-inch computer monitor and gray-black keyboard with badly worn keys, and a cheap, three-button optical mouse. At least the county had joined the digital age.

"You'll need to stay here at the counter," the desk sergeant announced robotically, pushing away a stray lock of bristly gray hair that had fallen across her forehead. "Plastic gloves must be worn at all times. You are not allowed to open evidence bags unless they are unsealed. Do not remove anything from this room and return all evidentiary items to their proper box. On the computer, bookmark any pages from the reports or photographs you wish to copy. The cost is $1.50 per page, cash or check." It sounded like she'd said these words a thousand times, until they no longer had any meaning at all. May as well have been reading a menu.

Tess put on a pair of blue latex gloves, pulled over a tall stool and cautiously arranged herself on the wobbly, unpadded seat. *Guess they don't want you staying long.*

Lifting the lid off the box marked "1," she saw the bags containing the blood-soaked sheets and bedspread, and Rennie's bloody T-shirt and jeans. Pushing the box aside, she opened carton number two, which contained paper bags holding a clean pair of jeans, socks, bra and underwear, a baby-blue thick cable-knit sweater, and two books. In the third box, she found what she was looking for: the weapon that ended Rennie's life. Still dotted with specks of blackened blood, the instrument was a nevertheless beautiful piece of sartorial art. Even in the room's dull fluorescent light and inside a plastic evidence bag, the polished Sheffield silver steel blade gleamed and winked. Both the shank and handle were stunningly engraved with scrolls, leaves, and stems in swirling patterns, while an elegant fleur-de-lis adorned the handle's reverse side.

It stood to reason that if they retrieved Rennie's ruby ring, it would be here too, but the only other items in the box were a hairbrush and comb, along with a mirrored makeup case containing foundation, mascara, lipstick, and eyeshadow.

Tess turned to the static computer monitor and clicked on "Incident Report." Here was the reporting officer's narrative of the scene, in law enforcement's characteristically parched, detached language.

CASE NUMBER: 00247-C06-2019.
REPORTING OFFICER: Lt. William Schiffler.
PERSON 1: Victim. Adult female, 5'6" 125 lbs. Name, Rendell Matlock.

PERSON 2: Witness. Tessalyn Alexander.

INJURY: Approximately four-inch open incised wound to the throat, fatal.

REPORTING OFFICER'S NARRATIVE: At 12:45 a.m., Dispatch received a 911 call regarding the discovery of a body at the Two Pines Guest Lodge in Hammond Mills. The caller identified himself as Butch Fogerty, manager of the establishment. Sheriff's Officer Brian Burley was dispatched and arrived at the scene at 1:12 a.m. After confirming the presence of the body, R/O secured the scene and contacted Dispatch, requesting backup and EMTs. Reporting Investigator Lt. William Schiffler proceeded directly to the scene.

R/O Burley reported that he entered the Two Pines Guest Lodge office and was directed by an adult male who identified himself as Butch Fogerty, to apartment 9. An adult female who identified herself as Tess Alexander (Person 2), accompanied Fogerty and the R/O. On the bed in the apartment was the body of an adult female, whom Alexander identified as Rendell "Rennie" Matlock (Person 1). R/O requested Fogerty return to the office and direct backup and medical personnel to R/O's location. R/O then secured the scene and cleared the area, finding no other persons present in the vicinity.

R/I Schiffler arrived at the scene at 1:40 a.m. and called Deputy Coroner S. Applegate and a CSU team to respond.

EMTs R. Jackson and P. McDaniels arrived at approximately 2:05 a.m. and confirmed the victim was deceased. R/I Schiffler conducted a preliminary inspection of the scene. On the double bed, lying prone atop a brownish bedspread, R/I observed a lifeless human body, a female estimated to be in her mid-20s, wearing a white T-shirt with the slogan "California Dreaming" printed on the front, and blue jeans. The legs were slightly apart with both legs moderately straight. The left arm was slightly bent over the chest. The right arm was bent 45° at the elbow with the hand extended slightly parallel to the neck.

On the bed approximately 3 inches from the victim's right hand was a silver-colored straight razor with its blade open and covered with what appeared to be blood. Several large-to-medium-sized splatters of what appeared to be blood were present on the wall behind the victim's head.

The bedspread and front of the victim's T-shirt were saturated with what also appeared to be blood. R/I observed large open wound to the neck approximately 4-5 inches in length.

No personal items were immediately visible on the body or in the vicinity.

Deputy Coroner Susannah Applegate arrived at the scene at approximately 2:10 a.m. and pronounced the victim deceased at 2:12 a.m. by tactile observation that the victim did not have a palpable carotid pulse or any indications of heartbeat or respiration. Deputy Applegate visually examined the body and observed what appeared to a major laceration to the neck. Based on her examination, Deputy Applegate made a preliminary determination of suicide. Deputy Applegate noted that rigor mortis was not yet evident. Early indications of lividity were observable on the posterior of the body, leading her to speculate that the victim had been dead approximately 2 to 4 hours.

CSU arrived at the scene at approximately 2:20 a.m. and was instructed to process the scene.

Body of the deceased was placed into the custody of Deputy Coroner Susannah Applegate and removed from the scene at 2:30 a.m. by EMTs R. Jackson and P. McDaniels and transported to the Coroner's office.

No matter how often she read police and crime reports, Tess always found it jarring to find such dispassionate language in the chronicles of a human tragedy. She bookmarked the report for printing, then closed that tab. Next, she clicked on "Crime Scene Photographs" and mentally prepared herself to be catapulted back to that room in the Two Pines Lodge.

Scrolling from one picture to the next, Tess was on the alert for two items: the straight razor, and Rennie's ruby ring. Here was a close-up of the weapon, still smeared with blood, then two different views showing the razor's elaborate hand-engraving. She tagged the second and third photos, and continued searching. When she got to the photos of Rennie's body, the shock of finding her came roaring back. She looked so fragile, lying on that wretched blood-soaked bed, her dead eyes fixed upward on something invisible to the rest of the world. Tess enlarged the view, focusing on Rennie's right hand. The orientation was wrong, hiding any details of her fingers. She clicked from one photo to the next and the next, scrutinizing each one for a clearer shot of the young woman's hand.

And there it was, perfectly, unconditionally clear. Rennie's barren right hand. Zooming in revealed the tiny indentation in the ring finger produced by decades of constant wear. So Tess's memory was genuine: there was no ring. She tagged the photo, and tried to figure out what the hell it meant.

Ensconced once again in her Best Western lair with Cooper, Tess texted Phillip the death weapon photo. A few minutes later, he called and confirmed that it was absolutely the missing straight razor from Matlock's collection. No doubt, one-of-a-kind. He even found a photo of it, along with the rest of the collection, in his father's insurance files, and compared the two.

As they were talking, Phillip dropped the bombshell that he planned to have Rennie's body exhumed and an autopsy conducted, hoping something was found to prove murder.

"Devon and I are Rennie's closest living blood relatives, and we're in agreement about this, even though Devon doesn't want Simon to know he's involved. I understand: he works at his company, and things could get dicey if Simon figured out that Devon was part of it. Myself, I don't much give a shit: what matters is that I'm convinced some fucking son-of-a-bitch killed my sister. What I don't know is why or who." Phillip had only recently begun referring to his father as Simon. Tess figured he was trying to distance himself from the man, suspected his father was guilty of something, or because he himself was.

"I presume you have an attorney handling it for you?"

"Yeah, it's my best friend's father: he used to clerk for one of the state Supreme Court judges, then went on to become a partner in some hot-shit San Francisco law firm, and also teaches law at Stanford. Great guy, always treated me like a member of their family. I told him about my feelings—then after I found out about the razor, he said he'd do what he could to help. Personally, I think he's just doing it because he figures it'll bring me some kind of closure and not necessarily because he believes it was murder, but I'm just grateful he's helping. I need to find out the truth of what happened to Rennie." His voice broke with spontaneous emotion, sounding genuinely like a brother who wanted nothing but justice for his murdered sister.

Either that, or like a psychopath.

Tess was torn. On the one hand, her own psychic reactions to Simon Matlock pointed to someone who, while he may not have been actually *evil*, was nevertheless malevolent. Phillip, on the other hand, came off as authentically concerned and determined to get to the truth surrounding his sister's death—but then, she thought, there was that tiny issue of his past antisocial behavior. A boy who could kick a classmate almost to death wasn't exactly a candidate for Good Citizen of the Year.

Setting aside her perplexity, she began organizing a plan for the next day. First stop would be the coroner to get the report on Rennie's autopsy. Then the sheriff's office to convince her pal Lieutenant Schiffler to reopen the case. After that, back up to the Two Pines Lodge to see what, if anything, the manager knew, and talk to any of the tenants about anything they'd heard or seen. Too bad the weather was so damn brutal that night, or maybe someone might have caught something that looked out of place. As it was, the blizzard that blew in had everyone hunkered down, so the chances that some poor sot ventured outside to take a stroll were somewhere between slim and none.

That night she slept better than expected and woke at 5:30 with Cooper's head on the pillow next to her.

"You're not supposed to be on the bed," she whispered conspiratorially. Cooper opened his eyes and winked.

It was another gorgeous spring morning in the Sierra. After brushing her teeth, she pulled on tights and a sweatshirt, laced up her Adidas, snagged Cooper's leash and they set out for a sunrise run. The air was chilly, crisp with the scent of Ponderosa and sugar pine and somewhere, fresh coffee brewing, while overhead a majestic Northern Harrier cruised the skies in search of a morning meal. A fluffy-tailed, chubby gray squirrel darted across the trail in front of her, then stopped, turned, and stared as if trying to figure out what this strange human and her dog were doing out at such an early hour. Cooper was too busy exploring bushes for the best place to pee to notice. Lucky for the rodent.

Emerging from the shower an hour later, Tess absently wiped the fogged mirror with an extra towel, then stared gloomily at her reflection.

Shit, girl: here we go again. Another day alone in another anonymous hotel room in an anonymous town, on the scent of another Big Story for…for what? Another Pulitzer? Maybe an Oscar this time if they make it into a movie? Yeah, I hear ole' Oscar is tons of fun to go hiking with. Absently blotting her hair with the bath towel, she felt the serrated knife's-edge of sorrow, and pictured Roger's face in her mind.

She met Dr. Roger Holland when, in the course of investigating an international sex trafficking ring, she found herself at the Stanford Medical Center after a terrifying and almost lethal attempt on her life. Over time, their doctor-patient relationship blossomed into friendship, then into romance. A year later, they were married.

By then, he was out of the hospital and in a private practice in Auburn, a growing foothill town about thirty miles from Deer Valley. They were just settling into their life together when one evening, well past the time for Roger to have gotten home, she answered the doorbell to find the county sheriff standing there, his head bowed and shoulders hunched.

She had only a whispered recollection of what he said, how Roger was hit head-on by a truck-and-trailer rig that veered into his lane. It was instantaneous, the sheriff intoned, grief lacing his voice. The last words she heard before dropping to the floor were "I'm so sorry, Tess."

It was all just so senseless. And Tess didn't even have any-one to blame: the truck's deadly course was the result of its driver suffering a sudden heart attack, not because he'd been stupid-drunk or loaded or fallen asleep. All she had was just the crushing agony of loss, day after week after month.

So she did what she always did: threw herself into work. She told herself that was what Roger would have wanted, for her to continue turning over rocks in search of human vermin, to keep fighting for justice. But none of it filled the deep empti-ness that took up residence in her heart. None of it brought Roger back. But at least it kept her from collapsing in on herself like a child's deflated balloon. Having Luna, their beloved white retriever, helped, of course—but a year later Tess lost her, too, and the emptiness returned.

And then there was Kat, her beloved sister. She felt Kat's gentle presence often, no more so than on that day she stood above Rennie Matlock's coffin. An earworm of uneasiness began to nibble, and Tess recognized its bite. The ghost of her sister whispered what Tess already knew: *Rennie shouldn't be here, in this cold, wet ground. Something's off, doesn't make sense, like a jigsaw puzzle with the wrong pieces mixed in.*

Tess pushed the memory away for now.

After allowing herself a moment of mourning for the losses, she frowned, huffed a pessimistic sigh, and finished drying her hair and putting on makeup. An hour later, after breakfast of a massive ham-and-cheese omelet—half of which she saved for Cooper—she was on the road to the county coroner's office, reinforced with a travel mug of dark, hot coffee. It turned out that Deputy Coroner Susannah Applegate was the one to greet Tess at the department's front desk that morning. Once she introduced herself, a look of recognition crossed Applegate's face.

"Yes, of course. You're the woman who discovered Rennie Matlock's body over in Hammond Mills. I saw you at the scene."

"I saw you as well, but at the time an introduction seemed somehow terribly inappropriate."

"Yes, I agree," said Applegate with a small smile. "What can I do for you, Ms. Alexander?"

"I hoped to take a look at Rennie's autopsy report."

The deputy looked puzzled. "Oh, there was no autopsy. It was an open-and-shut case of suicide, and her father wanted to transport her body immediately to the Bay Area."

Tess stifled an expletive, then glued on a beneficent smile. "Well, I guess I'm a little surprised: I thought pretty much any case of suspicious death demanded an autopsy."

"That's true, but in this case, the death wasn't suspicious. All the evidence pointed to suicide."

"What kind of evidence?"

"The razor next to her hand for one," Applegate replied with a slight edge to her voice. "And the lack of anything at all that would point to an intruder, or even a second person in the room. No wet footprints on the carpet from someone having come in from the snow, no broken locks on the door or window, no fingerprints except for Ms. Matlock's."

Tess kept pushing. "But isn't it unusual for someone to commit suicide by slitting their own throat?"

"It's rare, certainly, but it does happen. And most often with women."

"So, what about DNA, or a toxicology report to see if there were any drugs in her system?"

"Again, Ms. Alexander, there was no need. The law gives a coroner the latitude to determine whether an autopsy is necessitated, and in this case it wasn't. Ms. Matlock, unfortunately, died by her own hand. That was the coroner's ruling, and that's what our report says."

"I'd like a copy of that report," said Tess, swallowing her irritation.

"Certainly." The deputy reached into a desktop cabinet, then handed Tess a form. "Just fill this out, and I'll make a copy of the report for you. It'll be ten dollars."

"No problem."

Five minutes later Tess sat in her car with the windows rolled down and Lady Gaga warbling on the audio system, skimming the three-page Coroner Investigation Report and hoping something would jump out at her. Nothing did. The paperwork detailed Rennie's personal characteristics—height, weight, ethnicity, eye and hair color—and the incident information, including time and place of death, when she was last seen alive, who discovered the body, and the extent of livor and rigor mortis. Under Cause of Death, the coroner wrote, "Suicide, as a result of self-inflicted transection of carotid artery." The rest of the report consisted of a mass of checkboxes detailing evidence, wound location, weapon, case history, and who the body was released to, followed by a narrative section that fundamentally echoed what was in the sheriff's report. No mention of a ring or suicide note.

With the breakfast omelet still rumbling in her stomach, Tess skipped lunch to see if she could meet with Lieutenant Schiffler. She'd talk to him about the missing ring and the absent suicide note, and maybe prod him into re-opening the case.

She found a perfect parking spot, bathed in the shade of a thick-leafed maple. She left Cooper asleep in the car, was buzzed into the dingy sheriff's headquarters, and approached the duty officer. Yes, Lieutenant Schiffler was in. Yes, he was available. A minute or so later Schiffler appeared in the lobby and stiffly shook her hand.

"What can I do for you, Ms. Alexander?"

"Perhaps it's more what *I* can do for *you*, Lieutenant. Is there somewhere we can talk?"

"Uhh, sure. Come with me." She followed him up the stairs to his closet-sized office and sat down across from him in the cramped and stuffy boxlike room. The furnishings consisted of an ancient steel desk painted gunmetal grey, and two excruciatingly uncomfortable metal chairs with padding that had long ago ceased to exist. A four-drawer filing cabinet painted to match the desk completed the look. The walls were a lighter shade of gray, and the pockmarked linoleum was an ugly hue of yellow that reminded Tess of baby barf. No wonder cops were chronically depressed. Even the Dalai Lama would be depressed in a room like this.

"Coffee?" His own mug was half full of the muddy liquid.

"No thanks. Lieutenant. I'd like to talk with you about the Matlock case. The coroner's office said they ruled it as a suicide, but didn't do an autopsy. Is that customary here when there's a possible suicide?" She took care to keep her tone neutral and friendly.

"It's the coroner's call. If the investigator on scene doesn't find anything suspicious, and everything points to suicide, then that's pretty much how it's ruled. Nine times out of ten, there's no need for an autopsy."

"I have a question about your coroner's office: I know many smaller counties have a sheriff-coroner system, simply because they don't have access to or the budget for a forensic pathologist."

"Yeah, that's sure true here. We have a really low violent crime rate, so there's just not that much call for a pathologist. I think that Ms. Matlock's was the first—uhh, unusual—death we've seen in about five years. Around here it's usually some-thing like a car accident, maybe a drug OD, or of course natural causes like old age or sickness. We just don't see many suicides."

"What if Ms. Matlock's death *wasn't* a suicide?"

Schiffler sat up straighter in his chair and furrowed his brow. "But it was. The coroner ruled it."

"But what if he was wrong?"

"Ms. Alexander, I can't imagine where you're going here, but if…"

"Lieutenant," she interrupted, "I have some information you may not be aware of. That the coroner may not have been aware of. Rennie always wore this small ruby ring, a gift from her grandmother when she was younger. Rennie never took it off. I mean *never*. She wore it the entire time she was in prison, and still wore it the last time I saw her alive. She treasured that ring."

She pulled out the crime scene photos that showed Rennie's bare hand. "As you can see, there's no ring on her hand. The CSIs didn't find it in the room or in her car. It's gone. Why would Rennie take off that ring—and what would she do with it—if she was going to kill herself?"

"People who are going to kill themselves often do strange things. She could have left it home."

"But she didn't. It's simply vanished. There are other things, too: first, Rennie linked up with a nonprofit called New Promise and was on her way to beginning a whole new life in Sacramento, moving into an apartment the very next week and starting college three weeks later. She aimed toward becoming a veterinarian, even though she knew it would be a really tough haul. She was hopeful and determined, looking toward the future. That doesn't describe someone who's ready to kill herself."

"It isn't…"

"Pardon me, Lieutenant, but please let me finish. There was also no suicide note. Yes, I know: often there isn't. But aside from that, she called me two days before with some critical information about a crime that was committed by a member of her family, and she needed to give it to me. But that wasn't at the scene either—it's disappeared too.

"Finally, there's the weapon. Did you know it's part of Rennie's father's collection? Her brother told me that an engraved antique silver straight razor was missing. I looked at the evidence and case files yesterday, and not only saw the razor but got a copy of the crime scene photo showing it on the bed. I sent her brother the photo last night, and he confirmed it belongs to Simon Matlock." Tess paused for emphasis, and locked eyes with the lieutenant. "I'm beginning to wonder if someone in the Matlock household killed Rennie. Maybe even Simon Matlock himself."

"That's preposterous," he snorted. "Senator Matlock is a well-respected member of the legislature, and apparently he's just as well regarded in San Francisco and the entire Bay Area. Why would he want to murder his daughter? He was by her side all through the trial, and all the years she was incarcerated. I understand he even welcomed her back into his home when she was released."

You've come a long way from that January night when all you could remember about Matlock was that you'd "heard something" about him during Rennie's trial. Wonder how it is you know so much more about the man now? "I'm not saying I'm convinced it was her father. All I'm saying is that someone in that house had access to the weapon that killed Rennie Matlock. Do you know anything about Phillip, the oldest son?"

"Nope. No need to investigate him, or any other member of the family, in a suicide."

"So, you're not aware that Phillip had a juvenile record?"

The lieutenant bristled. "Lots of kids have juvenile records."

"But lots of kids don't get popped for chaining other kids to school bleachers out in the hot sun, or shaving their heads, or cutting another boy badly enough that he's going to wear a scar for the rest of his life. Not to mention when he was twelve, he beat and kicked another kid half to death."

"I…I hadn't heard that. What happened to him?"

"Spent a day in juvenile hall 'til Matlock bailed him out, then got assigned probation and anger management counseling. One has to wonder whether or not he grew out of those little personality quirks, or grew *into* something worse."

Schiffler fidgeted in his chair and mumbled something under his breath.

"Phillip's not the only Matlock with problems. Are you aware that Simon Matlock began molesting Rennie when she was just six?" Tess hadn't planned on revealing this tidbit just yet, but needed something more to bolster her argument.

The lieutenant's bushy eyebrows shot up in disbelief. "How do you know that?" he demanded.

"Rennie. Once she figured she could trust me, she divulged everything. That is, almost everything: as I've mentioned, she uncovered something else after she got out, but died before she could tell me what it was."

"So," growled the officer, "what you have is the word of a now-decreased, very disturbed young woman who murdered her mother, against a sitting two-term state senator who's known for his dedication to dozens of social causes and frequent large donations to charity. I'm sorry, Ms. Alexander, but it just doesn't fly."

"Fly or not, Lieutenant, that's what I'm beginning to think. But leaving that aside for now, what about everything else I've mentioned? Don't all those other facts provide at least some basis for reopening the case?"

"I'm afraid these 'facts,' as you call them, are little more than coincidences and conjectures. Nowhere near enough to revive a closed case that everyone involved agrees was a straightforward suicide."

"Just because everyone believes it, doesn't make it true."

"And it doesn't make it untrue." The two had clearly reached an impasse. "Is there anything else I can do for you, Ms. Alexander?" He pushed his chair away from the desk and stood.

"No, Lieutenant. I'd just hoped you would reconsider, in light of the information I laid out for you."

"Thank you for stopping by." He made his way to the door and swung it open.

Tess forced a smile as she walked toward the portly officer. "I hope you realize that I'm going to continue investigating this." She stepped through the door, then turned back to face the lieutenant. "And that I'll be back *when*, not if, I have conclusive proof that Rennie Matlock was murdered."

10

IT WAS STILL EARLY ENOUGH in the day for Tess to make one more stop, this time at the Two Pines Guest Lodge. She surprised herself by making only one wrong turn on the way there.

A shrill buzzer sounded when she opened the door to the office, something she didn't remember hearing that night. Manager Butch Fogerty, whom she *did* remember, emerged from a side door, a beer in one hand and a thick submarine sandwich in the other.

"Yeah, can I help you?" He didn't sound especially eager to have her accept the offer.

"Mr. Fogerty, I'm Tess Alexander. We met back in January when Rennie Matlock died here. I'm the one who found her."

His eyes widened in recognition. "Oh, yeah, I remember you. You were pretty messed up from seeing it, that's for sure. Hell, *I* was messed up from seeing it." He took a huge bite of the sandwich, and a glop of something that looked like Russian dressing dripped onto the front counter. He looked down, then wiped it up with the sleeve of his shirt. "So, what can I do you for? You lookin' to rent a room?" His face bore the same unctuous leer as the gas station attendant, just before she hit the accelerator and splattered him with muddy asphalt slush. She wished she had a handful of it now.

"I'm investigating Ms. Matlock's death, Mr. Fogerty, and need to ask you a few questions."

"Investigating, eh? You a P.I.?"

"No, I'm a journalist. And before you ask, no, I can't pay you." She'd dealt with guys like Fogerty before, and knew they took every opportunity to squeeze out some cash in exchange for information.

"That's too bad. Oh, well, guess it can't hurt for me to listen."

Tess retrieved the small notebook from her purse. "On the night of Ms. Matlock's death, did you notice anything strange?"

"Strange, how? Like aliens or something?"

"Strange, like cars you didn't recognize in front of the rooms, or people you didn't know hanging around?"

"Shit, lady, in this place there's always strange cars and stranger people. I don't take no note of them. Didn't that night, either."

Tess tried a different tack. "Okay: did anyone come into the office? Anyone you didn't know?"

Fogerty's chocolate eyes narrowed, and he took another swig of his Budweiser. A thin smile crossed his lips. "What if they did? What's it worth to you?"

Tess doubled down. "Listen, I have no intention of paying you anything. But if you have no conscience about the death of this innocent woman, you can bet your last Budweiser that I'll let the sheriff know that you withheld critical information with regard to a crime. That means all kinds of cops crawling all over this place, harassing your tenants and sticking their noses into your business—and somehow, I don't think that would make you terribly happy. On the other hand, you can just tell me what you know, and I'll get out of your hair without saying anything to the boys in blue. Which is it?"

The manager's demeanor had gone through a series of minor contortions as Tess spoke, from fury to alarm, each expression producing a different shade on his face. Right now it resembled a bleached tomato.

"Okay, okay: I was just foolin' with you. There were a couple people I saw that night, one of 'em a guy who came into the office. Figured he was lost, 'cause nobody with any brains would be out on a shitty night like that on purpose. But turns out he was lookin' for her, the dead girl. He give me five hundred bucks to tell him what room she was in. Said he was a relative, and she was on drugs, and he needed to stop her before she did something stupid."

Tess was stunned. "What time did this guy come in?"

"Shit, how am I supposed to know? It was dark and snowing like a sonofabitch. I'd been watching one of them dumb comedy shows that comes on at…oh, yeah: at 8:00. So guess it was somewheres between 8 and 8:30."

"Tell me what he looked like."

"White guy, not too tall—maybe five-six or -seven—with the craziest blue eyes I've ever seen. I don't mean crazy-crazy, but they were a really weird shade of blue, like super-blue. He was wearing a thick ski jacket, so I couldn't tell how he was built, but he didn't look like he was carryin' around a lot of blubber. Had a really strong handshake."

With his mention of the blue eyes, Tess's pulse skipped.

"About how old was he?" *Simon, or Phillip? Or maybe some mystery third party who just happens to have sapphire-blue eyes?*

"Middle-aged. Around forty-five or fifty."

Not Phillip. Tess pulled out a photo of Simon Matlock. "Is this him?"

"Hmmm," the man said, looking first at the photo and then back to the strikingly beautiful woman standing in front of him. "Could be, could be not. My memory's not so good these days."

Yeah, right. Your memory would probably go from zero to sixty if I handed you a fistful of bills.

His face bore the barest trace of a sneer as he looked Tess up and down. "I might be persuaded to think about it harder, ya' know what I mean?" Now the sneer was full-on.

Tess stifled a retch. "Listen: I don't have time for your bullshit, *Mister* Fogerty. Either you recognize him or you don't. Doesn't bother me one way or the other. Of course, it *might* bother the sheriff."

"Okay, okay…can't blame a guy for trying." Tess shivered inwardly, remembering that Matlock said the exact same words. He looked down at the photo again, and said, "Yeah, that's definitely the guy. What'd he do?"

"Did you see the car he was driving?" Tess ignored the man's question.

"Kinda. When he pulled away from the office, I could see it was some hot-shit car, maybe a BMW or Audi, one of them that cost a fortune. Black or dark blue."

"Did you see him leave?"

"Nah. Went back to my TV show, five hundred clams richer."

"You said you saw a 'couple' of people that night. Who was the other one?"

Fogerty's eyes shifted to the left. "Mmmm, maybe a young guy. I don't know, maybe not."

It was obvious the man was lying. But why? "Describe him."

"Didn't get a good look. 'Cause 'a the storm." Still looking left, away from any direct eye contact. "Coulda even been a woman."

Tess wondered if Fogerty was just trying to throw her off by bringing up the notion of it being a woman, but the question kept coming back to *Why?* What was he hiding?

"You mean, you can't tell the difference between a man and a woman? Somehow I doubt that."

"Oh, I can tell the difference all right," he shot back. "Come to think of it, it really coulda been a woman. A real tight-assed chica."

Tess ignored the remark and kept pushing. "Look, it either *was* a woman, or *wasn't*."

Fogerty brought his gaze back to Tess. "Couldn't tell. Too bundled up."

"How could you tell she was tight-assed if she was bundled up?" Tess was tiring of the man's games.

Fogerty struggled for an answer, then showed his teeth in a wicked smile. "I can always tell. From the way they walk. Don't matter what they're wearin'. Butch always knows if they're puttin' it out there."

Tess locked eyes with him, refusing to take the bait. "So, exactly *when* did you see this maybe-woman? Before or after you saw the man whose picture I showed you?"

"After. Probably." Playing games again, and still hiding something.

Tess gave up. "I need to talk to any of your residents who were here that night."

He paused and half-closed his eyes, ticking something off on his fingers. "There's only two guys who were here back in

January that are still around—well, one guy and a couple. Don't know if they'd talk with you, but I'll give you their apartments."

Tess wrote down what he told her, then looked up. "One more thing: did you tell the police any of this? Did they question you?"

"Nope. They never asked, I never offered. Not then, not since. You might have guessed I'm not too big a fan of cops, so I say little as possible anytime I have to deal with the fuckers. Besides, what difference would it make? The broad committed suicide. End of story."

Tess gritted her teeth and handed over her business card. "Okay. Get in touch if you think of anything else."

He saluted her with his beer bottle and bit off another chunk of sandwich. This time, a ragged piece of cheese-coated meat slid out and landed on the front of his shirt, clinging there like a banana slug.

She didn't gather anything more from her Two Pines expedition. Neither the single man nor the couple were any help. They hadn't seen or heard anything until the police arrived, and then holed up in their apartments until the coast was clear. Apparently they weren't such big fans of the cops, either.

The back of Tess's neck began tingling as she walked across the rutted pavement to her car. Reaching for the door, the lights went out in her head, followed by a blurry image of a vague figure sitting on the bed beside Rennie in the scabby motel room. Something silver glinted on the bedspread. Rennie held a Pepsi-like bottle in one hand and a telephone in the other, her eyes heavy-lidded and almost closed. Her mouth sagged as a tiny trail of spittle drooled from its corner. She said a few words into the phone, but it played like a silent movie without the organ music in the background. Tess struggled to see if the woman's moving lips conveyed anything intelligible, but it was just a blur.

And suddenly she was back standing next to her car, the spring breeze, perfumed with the honeyed scent of white fir, ruffling her hair. For an instant the trees around her seemed to spin and whirl, then she grabbed for the door handle to steady herself and dropped into the driver's seat accompanied by Cooper's enthusiastic welcome.

The vision brought with it a dawning awareness that Rennie was drugged before she was killed. That explained why her voice on the phone that night sounded so thick and distant. Coupled with Fogerty's revelation about Simon Matlock being at the motel that night, Tess's uncertainty about Rennie's death vanished.

Simon Matlock murdered his own daughter.

Now all she had to do was figure out why, and prove it.

11

THE EMAIL LANDED IN TESS'S INBOX at the Foundation, where it automatically rocketed through cyberspace to a special folder in her personal Gmail account at home. This was only one of several electronic access points she maintained, including the encrypted ProtonMail service on the darknet which she used to communicate securely with confidential sources.

The email address and sender's name weren't familiar, but that wasn't terribly unusual: readers, admirers, and haters alike often contacted her to offer their accolades or insults in response to one of her articles in *Panorama,* even months after it appeared. But it was the subject line of this particular email that caught Tess's attention: "Simon Matlock." Just that, nothing more.

She clicked it open and began reading.

Dear Ms. Alexander:

We have never met, but I know you were friends with Rennie Matlock both before and after her conviction, and largely responsible for Rennie's efforts to start a new life. I know you were also the one who discovered Rennie's body.

I have worked for Simon Matlock for three years and have been his executive assistant for eighteen months in both his San Francisco and Sacramento senate offices. I spent much time at the house and got to know Rennie after she was released, even though I do not know if she completely trusted me because I was connected to Simon. But I could see the sorrow in her, and how much it lifted when you connected her to New Promise. (She told me that much, but swore me to secrecy, as she felt Simon would do everything he could to dissuade her from leaving.)

I spoke with Phillip, and he assures me you are trustworthy, and that like he and I, you are not convinced that Rennie committed suicide. I do not wish to explain it in an email, but I have some information that you might find helpful to your investigation.
Can we meet?
Sincerely,
Sofia Frantonio

Tess wondered as she hit "Reply" if this could be a crucial lead or if, like so many others over the years, it was just another dead end. Only one way to find out.

Dear Ms. Frantonio,
I would be happy to meet with you and discuss your information. I can be in Sacramento whenever it's convenient for you; I suggest we meet somewhere off the legislative beaten track so there's less chance being spotted together. Just let me know day, time, & location.
Tess Alexander

It only took thirty minutes for Sofia to respond. They settled on meeting the following afternoon at a small coffee shop near the state university. Chances were extremely slim, Sofia agreed, that a well-known state senator would be frequenting that area of the city.

Sofia Frantonio was exquisite. Tall, curvaceous, with legs that seemed to go on forever and deep mahogany hair pulled back in an elegant twist. Her olive skin, square jaw, and full, sensuous lips paid tribute to her Italian heritage. The moment she opened her mouth, it was apparent that she had emigrated from that country to the U.S., as the melodic, rolling lilt of her voice still held traces of her birthplace.

The two women chatted amiably as they settled at a small table at the rear of the café. There was only one other customer there, but they both recognized the need for caution in not allowing their conversation to be overheard.

"To begin, I must admit that I was not wholly correct when I spoke of being Simon Matlock's executive secretary. I am that, but I am also more. We have been lovers for the past year, even though I feel some shame in the admission."

Tess wasn't the least bit surprised that, considering Sofia's beauty, Matlock had managed to broaden the role of executive secretary to include certain extracurricular activities. "Shame? Why?"

"Because he is a monster."

Unprepared for such a candid response, Tess's eyes widened and she inhaled sharply. "Perhaps you need to begin at the beginning."

"Yes, of course. I met Simon three and a half years ago at the annual San Francisco Museum of Modern Art gala dinner. I was there as a guest of my then-employer, one of Simon's chief business rivals. I knew, of course, that in addition to being a very influential developer in the Bay Area, he was also a powerful state senator.

"During the evening, I made every attempt to draw his interest, which frankly was not difficult. Eventually, he approached me and asked if I was looking for a change in my employment. I intentionally demurred, saying I was very happy where I was, but knowing he would not take no for an answer. A week later I received a telephone call from him, asking me to join him for lunch at Boulevard. I knew I had ensnared him.

"He was utterly charming, respectful, and courteous throughout our time together, and did not even mention the job until we were almost finished. Somehow, he knew what my salary was, and offered me double if I would come and work for him. I said I was flattered, and that I would consider it. Of course, I took the job." As she spoke, she reflexively smoothed and re-smoothed the napkin next to her coffee cup.

She took a deep breath and paused, her lips hardening into a straight line as the sparkle disappeared from her eyes.

"Now," she said, "I must tell you another truth. Six years ago, my younger sister Francesca was raped." Her voice dropped to almost a whisper. "By Simon Matlock."

Tess felt the hair bristle on the back of her neck, but said nothing, knowing Sofia needed to disclose the story at her own pace.

"They were on two dates before, but she had no concern as he was always a gentleman. That night, they went to a formal event in the city, and she had a little too much champagne. According to people who were there and saw her, she was not drunk, perhaps just a bit tipsy. He drove them back to the mansion and Francesca went inside with him, not thinking a thing about it. He poured them both a Galliano, but about ten minutes later she said she began to feel very woozy and disoriented, and tried to stand but couldn't. She told Simon she was not feeling well, so he said he would take her to a bedroom where she could lie down."

Sofia swallowed, cleared her throat, and her eyes grew damp. "Instead, he took her to *his* bedroom, and the last thing she remembered was him kissing her roughly, pushing her down on the bed, and tearing off her blouse. When she woke, it was morning and she was alone in Matlock's bed, naked, and there was a note on the nightstand that said, 'Hope you had as wonderful a time last night as I did.' She went into the bathroom, threw up, then called me.

"I left work and took her to the emergency room; they said there was evidence of…of trauma…and the blood test showed she was given Rohypnol, the date-rape drug. But there was no semen, so no way to prove it was Simon except for Francesca's word. The female officer from the Sexual Assault Unit took her statement, but Francesca got the feeling that she didn't believe her when she said it was Matlock, or that he raped her. They talked with him later, but he insisted the sex was consensual. And that was pretty much the end of it. Until Francesca killed herself two months later."

"Oh, God, Sofia." Tess reached out and touched the woman's hand. "I'm so, so sorry."

Once Sofia began to recount her sister's story, memories of her own sister intruded on Tess's consciousness, then surfaced like scum levitating to the top of a stagnant pond as she remembered Kat's lifeless body on a coroner's gurney, her skin gray and cold.

Kathleen Alexander—she always went by Kat—unknowingly sealed her fate the day she met Ray Granieri. The suddenness of the marriage troubled her father, but for Tess, it was simple: Ray simply made her skin crawl.

With all the accoutrements of a successful life in a succession of ever-more expansive homes in the affluent seaside neighborhood of Corona Del Mar in Newport Beach, Kat and Ray *seemed* happy enough. Looking back, though, everyone was blind to some of the warning signs and red flags: Ray's relentless control of Kat, her increasing isolation, how the couple so often missed family holidays and vacations. *Wish we could join you at*

Lake Tahoe, but several of my European executives will be here that week. Sorry, can't make it for Christmas because I'm meeting with suppliers in Germany. I know you'd like to be here celebrating Kat's birthday, but she has the stomach flu.

The truth, as Tess learned later, was that a summer bathing suit would reveal the roadmap of ugly bruises—some new, some in the greenish-yellow stages of healing—on Kat's body. The trip to Germany happened to follow on the heels of Kat's broken arm and clavicle. The missed birthday was really because Kat was in the hospital with three broken ribs, a punctured lung, and ruptured eardrum.

If anyone asked, there were always perfectly reasonable explanations.

The bruises? She was very thin-skinned and bruised easily.

The broken arm? She slipped on the stairs.

The fractured ribs and ruptured eardrum? A wakeboard accident.

It all made sense, as long as you didn't take too much time to think about it.

Then came the call to her father from the Orange County Sheriff's office, relayed in habitually dispassionate cop-talk style: *We're sorry to inform you that your daughter Kathleen Granieri collapsed three hours ago in the Newport Coast Shopping Center; the EMTs attempted to resuscitate her, but she died in the ambulance on the way to the hospital. Her husband Raymond is currently under arrest for her murder.*

Tess eventually learned that Ray's vicious kick to his wife's belly ruptured her spleen. Later that day, she left home to buy that same man a birthday gift, and bled to death on the upscale shopping center's elegant travertine floor.

After her sister was buried and Ray sent to San Quentin for life, Tess discovered Kat's journal, hidden inside a baggie with a frozen steak, chronicling her abusive matrimonial journey that progressed from petty manipulation to emotional assault to sadistic rape and ultimately, to violent battery.

Until the day his madness killed her.

The knowledge of her sister's violent, solitary passage was Tess's bellwether, the helmsman that kept her on course as she navigated the treacherous waters roiling between evil and good. Shining a journalistic light into the dark caverns of injustice was the only way to atone for Kat's death, and her own blindness.

Shaking off the invading memories, Tess got up and refilled their coffees at the counter. When she returned, she'd gathered herself enough to listen to the rest of Sofia's story.

From the instant of her sister's suicide, Sofia said, she was determined to bring Matlock to justice. So she asked her boss to take her to the SFMOMA dinner, wrangled an introduction, set her trap, and waited for Matlock to take the bait. He hired her three months later.

At this point, Sofia dropped her head and began twisting her fingers together. "My shame is because I later became involved with Simon, in the hopes I could find something. From working with him as long as I did, I was sure he had dishonest dealings with many people, and that he bribed city officials to get his projects through, but I did not have enough for proof. I knew I would need to get…closer…to him to find evidence, so I allowed him to seduce me." A single tear rolled down her cheek, leaving a raindrop spot on her emerald green silk blouse.

She took a deep, uneven breath, then raised her head and looked at Tess. "So that is why I wanted to meet with you. I believe in my heart that Simon killed Rennie. Why, I do not know. As I told you, I have talked with Phillip, who told me about the missing straight razor, and that it was the very weapon used in Rennie's death, but that this is not enough for the authorities to restart the case. I fear it will also not be enough to convince them to exhume her body."

Tess frowned and said, "You're right, it might not be enough. The sheriff and coroner up there are pretty single-minded that it was a suicide, and that there was no reason to do an autopsy. Unfortunately, even when blood relatives request it, the authorities need to believe there's a legitimate reason for an exhumation."

"Can you do something? Something to convince them?"

"I don't know, Sofia. All I can say is that I'm turning over every rock I can, hoping something rotten will crawl out that implicates Matlock. In the meantime, I need *you* to do something."

"Anything. I will do anything to see justice for Francesca and now, for Rennie."

"I need you to look for Rennie's ring. Do you remember seeing it on her hand?"

"Oh, yes: it was a sweet little thing, with gold latticework and a single ruby. I asked her about it once, and she told me it came from her grandmother who she loved very much."

Tess nodded. "She'd had that ring since she was in grammar school, always wore it, twenty-four-seven, even during the ten years she was in prison. There's just no way she would take it off voluntarily, yet it wasn't on her hand when she died. It's just one more thing that doesn't fit. But if you can find it in Simon's house…well, that might be enough to open the eyes of the authorities."

"Why?"

"Sometimes, killers will take what's called a 'trophy' from their victims. In this case, maybe Simon took the ring because he wanted a physical memorial of Rennie. Something to tie her to him for eternity."

Sofia shuddered. "I see. But I will search everywhere I can for it. It is difficult, because when I am in San Francisco it is usually because Simon is also at the house. But there are times when he stays in Sacramento for legislative conferences or committee meetings, and he sends me back to San Francisco to work at his district office. I can use that time to search for the ring."

"There's one more thing you can do, Sofia: see if you can find solid proof of Matlock's dirty dealings. I don't know what that might be, or even *where* it might be, but it could be an important link in the chain that takes him down. Even if you're never able to conclusively prove that he raped Francesca, at least he would be in prison, and that would be some measure of justice."

Sofia's jaw set in grim determination as she listened to Tess's words. "Yes, it would. I will do my best, and also look on his computer, although he is always careful to close it and also lock his filing cabinets when he leaves. But I will work to find proof of both things: his treachery, and his guilt for Rennie's murder."

"Just remember one thing: BE. CAREFUL." She emphasized each word, keeping her eyes focused directly on Sofia's. "It's critical that he not suspect you. We both know that Simon Matlock can be dangerous, and is a powerful adversary. There's no telling what he might do if he feels threatened."

The warning lingered in the air, a toxic cloud they would both do well to elude.

12

SOFIA FRANTONIO WAS RECOUNTING a story as she and Tess sat in the little Sacramento coffee shop where they had their previous clandestine meeting.

A week before, Simon Matlock was in one of his furies, driven by the discovery that Tess was sticking her nose into things again and asking questions. He was also drinking heavily, and that meant he was even more disposed to burst into rages over anything he considered an obstacle or even an irritation. He was far from a happy drunk.

"That fucking cunt of a reporter is driving me crazy!"

Sofia sat silently on the couch that evening, shocked by Matlock's sudden outburst. Thus far, all her attempts to acquire any information or evidence about the man's involvement in underhanded schemes or illegal dealings turned up nothing. She was just as unsuccessful in her quest for Rennie's ruby ring.

"What reporter?" she asked innocently.

"Tess Alexander, that's 'what reporter'," he growled, slurring *Tess* so it came out as *Tesh*. "That bitch has been sniffing around, talking to cops and coroners, asking a whole lot of nosy questions. Plus, she's trying to get them to reopen the case, because she has this bizarre idea that Rennie didn't commit suicide. I'm sick of the whole fucking thing, and mostly, of this fucking woman. It's been four months, for chrissake—why can't this bitch leave it alone?" He was working himself up into an even greater state of infuriation as he paced back and forth across the engraved Aubusson rug like a caged animal, a sloshing tumbler of Irish whiskey in his hand.

After draining the glass, he headed over to the bar and refilled it. Sofia wavered between apprehension and eagerness, knowing his intoxication could lead to either violence or foolhardiness, or both. She hoped for the latter.

"Simon, just ignore her: she will get bored soon and move on to another story. Besides, what proof could she possibly find? Everyone knows Rennie killed herself."

"It's not just the shit with Rennie. She's back to snooping into my business dealings in the city, too. You know how I feel about all that, because of…you know, because of all the people who are out to get me. Who want to destroy my business." The alcohol was fueling his paranoia.

Sofia recalled asking who would want to destroy his business, which set Matlock off on another irrational tirade about rivals and competitors who wanted nothing more than to ruin him, because he was so successful.

Sofia sensed she had a tiny opening and stepped through it. She told Tess her voice was quivering so badly that she was afraid Matlock would pick up on her nervousness, but he was oblivious to anything other his own annoyance.

"I asked what kind of computer safeguards he used to protect his information, and he said he had top-of-the-line computer security, and no paper files. That focused me on the computer, so I asked him to show me the program he had in place. Since my background is in computer software engineering, he has always relied on me to oversee digital security at his offices, so I hoped he would think it logical for me to inquire about what security steps he used at home, too."

After Matlock drained his glass, Sofia obligingly refilled it and took his arm, directing him upstairs to his office. He stumbled once or twice on the stairs, but his massive ego always in command, tried to make it appear as if it were purposeful.

Making his way across the room, the man sat down heavily in the black leather executive chair, switching on the massive HP Workstation and its thirty-two-inch monitor. From across the room, Sofia heard a repeated series of keystrokes, each one peppered with increasingly angry expletives, until Matlock exploded again.

"Sonofabitch! What's wrong with this fucking thing?"

Sofia approached him from behind and touched him on the shoulder. "What's wrong, Simon?" then realized in trying to enter his main password, he was getting one error popup after another. This last one warned him that he only had two more attempts remaining before the machine automatically shut down.

"This fucking thing won't take my password, goddammit!" The silver-gray computer mouse jumped as he smashed the desk with his fist in frustration. He tried again as Sofia watched, something he never allowed. Matlock was especially obsessed with keeping his passwords secret, but was drunk enough this time that the only thing in evidence was his frenzied, infuriated reptilian brain.

E-M-B-R-A-C-S-D-E-R-P-#-Q

This time the popup materialized in a bright red box, and the word "WARNING" was highlighted with a string of bold exclamation points. "YOU HAVE ONE MORE ATTEMPT TO ENTER YOUR CORRECT PASSWORD BEFORE THIS COMPUTER SHUTS DOWN FOR TWENTY-FOUR HOURS."

Sofia figured it was now or never. "Simon, you are typing the wrong password."

"It's *not* the wrong damn password, you stupid bitch! It's this asshole machine!"

She plunged on, softening her tone. "Darling, you are hitting incorrect keys accidentally. Let me do it for you. Let me help. You know you can trust me."

Matlock turned his head sideways, fixing her with a penetrating one-eyed glare. She remembered that for several seconds, the only sound in the room was the computer's faint electronic hum and the rhythmic *tick-tick-tick* of the antique pendulum clock on the far wall. Feigning guiltlessness, she held Matlock's gaze; then he indignantly pushed himself away from the desk and gestured to the huge screen. "Fuck, just do it."

"What's the pass-phrase?"

"Embarcadero hashtag one. My first billion-dollar development deal."

Typing carefully, Sofia entered the code, then pressed the small password eye symbol to reveal the characters.

EMBARCADERO#1

"Is this right?" She needed to make absolutely certain.

"Yeah, that's it. Hit the damn key."

She hit the Enter key, and a flock of icons magically appeared on the bland desktop screen.

"I'm really impressed by your ingenuity," Tess said, taking another sip of her coffee. They'd been sitting in the café for well over an hour while Sofia explained how she finally managed to gain access to Simon Matlock's home computer.

"But so far, it has not been enough," she said, her unsmiling face a witness to her disappointment. "Having his passcode is only part of it: I have looked through most of his files, and there is nothing there except what you would expect on anyone's home computer. Now I need to get into his Folder Lock, and for that I need time and luck."

"Folder Lock is an encryption program, right?"

"Yes and no," explained Sofia. "It uses government-level 256-bit AES encryption to scramble and protect data, but it also uses other things to protect files, like a master password that restricts access to the application itself, and even more advanced security called stealth mode. Then if you need even *more* security, you can set it to shut down the application or even the whole system after a certain number of incorrect password attempts. I do not know whether Simon has set any of these security features on his Folder Lock files. He is somewhat knowledgeable, but I am not sure if he has the know-how to activate something that advanced, or if he would even consider it necessary. He may think that AES encryption is enough. What I need is a block of time alone in the house to dig into it, something I have not had since the night I learned the computer passcode."

Tess shared Sofia's frustration. "Looks like this is one of those things that will take however long it takes. But what's most important is that you keep yourself safe. It's bad enough that you live under the same roof, but if Matlock is Rennie's killer like we suspect, you're even more vulnerable. That concerns me a lot."

"Tess, this was *my* decision to help you, and no matter what happens, I will not regret that. Of course, I hope we will get to the truth in the process, but even if we do not, for me it will have been worth it."

"I'm glad to hear that."

Just then Sofia's phone chimed to announce a text. Apologizing for the interruption, she gave it a quick read, then stuffed the phone into her purse. "I am being summoned," she joked humorlessly. "Simon needs a document from his office for a committee meeting he is scheduled for."

"No problem. Go ahead and take off. I'm going to stay here and finish my coffee, then head back up the hill."

They said their goodbyes, then Tess wandered up to the counter and ordered a cinnamon-raisin bagel. While she was waiting for it to be warmed up, she turned back toward the bustling café and her pulse suddenly launched into a rapid-fire jitter. For an instant, she froze in place.

The man could have been Gabriel's brother. Not a twin, but enough like him that Tess was momentarily fooled into thinking it was him. The height, the thick shock of molasses-colored hair, the sensual, almost carnal way he strolled through the coffee shop like a feral cat on the hunt for prey, oddly enticing and sinister at the same time. She'd never seen another man move like that.

But of course it wasn't Gabe. Gabe was in far-flung Australia, the last she knew. Married, settled. Maybe even a kid by now.

She watched the not-Gabe drift out the door as a swarm of brittle memories hurtled back. It had started with a chance meeting on a ferry boat cruising from Los Angeles to Santa Catalina Island. It ended a year later with him suggesting they take a break from one another, claiming he needed "space." By the end of the third month with nothing but silence, Tess no longer clung to the hope that he would return. It was an excruciating blow, especially since they talked about a future together just weeks before he made that "we need space" announcement.

As she sat nursing the last of her coffee, ignoring the plump bagel on the table in front of her, she thought back on those weeks and months after Gabriel's exodus, and how she'd slipped further and further into a bottomless, barren pit of depression. It was a testament to both her own resolve and the skill of her therapist that she finally clawed her way back into the light.

There were times in the intervening decade that Tess wondered what her life might have been like had things turned out differently between her and Gabe. She had fallen deeply in love with him, and trusted the feeling was mutual. Then suddenly, it wasn't. At least for him.

She sighed, picking a raisin from the bagel. *God, he was a terrific lover. Tender, inventive, incredibly sensual. Like the way he moved. I could have lain in bed all day and just watched him walk back and forth across the bedroom.*

She wondered, then acknowledged, that this relationship in which she'd been so profoundly invested was at least partly to blame for her chronic state of singlehood. Until Roger came into her life.

As she gathered her briefcase and what was left of the bagel, she couldn't help questioning whether she'd have stayed single as long as she did, had it not been for the love affair with Gabe. *Or maybe I'd have allowed myself to be wooed and won by some destitute artist with a beautiful soul or a fabulously rich dot-com exec who could spirit me away to Bimini to live out a life of luxury. Or maybe I'd have never met Roger, never discovered what genuine love was like.*

She walked out the door and toward her parked car, ancient sorrow catching in her throat like a jagged shard of granite.

13

IN A CASE SWARMING WITH MYSTERIES and ambiguities, one was especially plaguing: how did Simon Matlock know where Rennie was staying that night? Did she tell him she was driving to Hammond Mills? That was doubtful, since part of the reason she escaped that day was to finish planning her move to Sacramento and away from her stepfather.

Considering what she now knew about both Phillip and Sofia, Tess was certain that neither of them would tell Matlock where Rennie was going. Who else was there? Tory, the cook? The housekeeping staff? So unlikely as to be ludicrous. She needed fresh eyes, a fresh perspective.

That made her think of an old friend who just retired from the Los Angeles Police Department. Javier Coelho spent twenty years as an LAPD detective, and Tess was convinced there was almost nothing the man didn't know about finding answers to insoluble questions.

"Tess Alexander, as I live and breathe!" Coelho's bronzed, unlined face beamed at her through the video chat screen. "Girl, whatcha been up to? I hear you left La-La land, exchanged it for the People's Republic of Berkeley, and then headed for the hills." Coelho's playful, easygoing personality was legendary, not just in the LAPD but among everyone he came into contact with. Whether it was in his role as a rookie cop, a seasoned detective, or merely a civilian, his even temperament and basic decency had defused an untold number of sticky situations in the potentially combustible urban environment that was the City of Angels.

"I've missed you too, Javier," Tess laughed. "You look like retirement is agreeing with you." It was true: his brow was less furrowed than when she last saw him, and his deep brown eyes bore a renewed twinkle that seemed to be largely missing in the last year of his career. But then, hunting down a multi-state serial rapist and murderer would do that to you.

After exchanging trivia about their lives since they were last in touch, Tess shared the details surrounding Rennie's murder and her suspicions about Matlock, then popped the sixty-four-thousand-dollar question: how the hell could Matlock have known where Rennie was, when from all she could tell, no one told him? She was sure the man wasn't a clairvoyant, so how did he find out?

Coelho was listening attentively, his eyes never leaving the screen. Now he began stroking his thick moustache with his left hand, something he did when he was deep into the process of deciphering some complexity.

"Is it possible he had her followed?" he asked after several seconds.

"I thought of that, but doubt he would trust anyone enough to do it, especially once it came out that Rennie was killed. It would just be too much of a political and personal risk."

Coelho nodded and went back to massaging his moustache. Ten seconds went by, then twenty, then thirty. Finally, a barely perceptible smile curled the corners of his mouth. "GPS."

"What? GPS?"

"Yep. He outfitted her car with a GPS locator."

Tess let out a sharp, snakelike hiss and rolled her eyes. "Shit. Of course. Why didn't I think of that?"

"Because you're a mere prize-winning journalist, my dear, and I'm an illustrious, eminently-qualified, worldly-wise doyen of the constabulary." His wide grin revealed etchings of laugh-lines on either side of his eyes.

"Okay, mister smart guy: how do we prove it? It's for damn sure he didn't leave it on her car after he brought it back to the city, and by now I'm sure the thing is buried ten feet deep in the county landfill. And for some reason, I don't think he saved the receipt so he could claim a tax deduction."

"Well, he probably bought it online: safer than going to your neighborhood Walmart or Best Buy and risk being filmed by their security cameras. So all you need to do—and I have my tongue firmly planted in my cheek when I use the word 'all'—is get into his phone or computer, resurrect his browsing history, which he's probably erased, and find where and when he picked up the little goodie. So easy even a child could do it."

"No need for snarky sarcasm," Tess groused good-naturedly. "Luckily, I have access to an extremely accomplished computer software engineer, who just so happens to be living with Mr. Matlock at the moment and who would like nothing better than to see him permanently ensconced in a five-by-seven concrete cell. If there's an Internet record to be found, I have a hunch she can find out."

"There you have it," Coelho said. "Case closed."

"From your lips to God's ears," Tess chuckled, then gave a broad wink. "Thanks for the help, you gorgeous Spanish hunk. And give my best to your lovely Anita."

❧

"Unless he has completely replaced the hard drive," Sofia pronounced in the melodious accent of her Italian birthplace, "I can absolutely track his Internet browsing history, even if he thinks he deleted it. Again, it will take a bit of time and a guarantee that he will not interrupt me in the middle of my spy game, but I can do it."

Tess breathed a sigh of gratitude that the faith she'd placed in the woman's technological abilities hadn't been misplaced. "Any idea of when…?"

"It might be as early as this evening. Simon has a subcommittee meeting, and then several of them are going out to dinner afterward."

"Let me know the minute you find anything."

Tess's phone buzzed on the far side of midnight, jerking her out of a bittersweet dream of sailing lazily on a sapphire lake with Roger, his arm around her waist and lips brushing her cheek.

"Yes? What?" She hadn't even bothered to look at the caller display.

"It's Sofia, Tess: sorry to wake you, but I knew you would want to know. I found where Simon purchased the tracking device."

Tess sat up in bed and switched on the light, fully awake. "Explain."

"Do you want the technical details, or just the results?"

"Break it down for me."

"First, most people think that when they delete a file, the operating system destroys it. That is not true: what the OS does is just remove the file's reference from the directories, then *moves* the actual information to free space on the hard drive. Eventually, new files will overwrite the supposedly-deleted data, but that can take weeks or even months, which means someone can use a special file recovery tool to resurrect the file.

"That is what I did here. I not only recovered the URL of each site he visited, but the exact pages he viewed, including the one that has GPS trackers for sale. Then, because I understand how scrupulous Simon is about tracing his expenditures, I knew he would have saved the order information, and recovered its actual image. The tracker he bought was very high-end, apparently used by a lot of private investigators: it operates on a 5G network, is portable, can last up to a week on one charge, and has a waterproof case that mounts with a very strong magnet underneath a car, and transmits the automobile's location every ten seconds. It was all he needed to know exactly where Rennie was."

As Sofia detailed what the tracker could do, Tess slid out of bed and reached for the writing pad she always kept in the drawer of her nightstand. Now, she had the proof they needed to put Matlock at the scene and prove how he got there—but her initial feeling of victory vanished, replaced with a powerful revulsion that brought a sour, acidic taste to her mouth. Rennie was marked for death even before she left San Francisco, just as much a victim as she was twenty years before.

"That's great news, Sofia," she said, her voice flat and muted. "You've done a terrific job."

"What is wrong?"

Her throat began to tighten, and she had to swallow several times to get the words out. "I just realized that Rennie never had a chance. He was going to destroy her, keep her from talking, at all costs. And we may never know what it was she wanted to say."

Silence hung like a dead weight between them.

"We will find out, Tess," Sofia said softly. "Besides, I found something else on the compu…" She stopped mid-sentence, paused, then spoke hurriedly, her voice barely above a whisper. "I must go. He is home." The connection broke.

Tess was curious about what else Sofia may have discovered on Matlock's computer, but assumed she would tell her the next time they talked.

14

THERE WERE TIMES WHEN TESS'S PAST haunted her, and then there were times like this when it was worth a fortune. She was riffling through a pile of unread papers and mail and magazines on her desk, when the bold black-and-white **IRE** logo caught her attention. It was the brochure she received a few months before, announcing the annual Investigative Reporters & Editors Conference. At the time she was so absorbed with the turmoil surrounding Rennie's death that she just set it aside.

Truth be told, that was one of Tess's flaws: as methodical as she was in her work, when she was in the middle of a story, she became a serious procrastinator about everything else in her life. Bills often lay unpaid on her desk and in her bank's Bill Minder account, dental and doctor appointments got swept aside, long-ago-scheduled social events were missed, phone calls went unreturned—not because she was rude or even forgetful, but because they were all things that she pledged to take care of "later." When things calmed down. When she could focus. More often than not, she kicked the proverbial can down the road so far that it disappeared, often leaving friends, family, and colleagues feeling irritated and ignored.

She picked up the glossy brochure and looked at the cover for the first time. A familiar face gazed out: Teichi "Jimmy" Hisakawa, one of the world's most eminent forensic pathologists, who as Chief Medical Examiner for New York City was often called to consult on high-profile deaths throughout the nation. Currently the president of the American National Association of Medical Examiners, he was even awarded the Order of the Sacred Treasure by the Emperor of Japan for his "exceptional contribution to Japan in the area of forensic science." Hisakawa was the keynote speaker at this year's IRE conference at the historic Omni Hotel in downtown San Francisco.

Looking at the dates, Tess was shocked to see that it was the following weekend: Hisakawa's address was set for that Saturday's conference luncheon. She quickly opened her laptop, logged onto the IRE member website, and made a reservation. Even if she didn't attend the entire three-day event, she knew it would be good to rub elbows and connect with long-lost colleagues and investigative reporters from other regions. Plus, she could pigeonhole her old pal Jimmy and see if he could do anything to convince the county coroner to exhume Rennie's body and perform an autopsy. It never hurt to have friends in high places.

Even though they hadn't spoken in at least a decade, Hisakawa recognized Tess's voice the minute he picked up the phone. "Well, hello Tess," he said, the surprise evident in his voice. "It's been a long time!"

"Too long, Jimmy. How've you been? How's Akiko?"

"I'm good, she's good, the kids are good—did you know that Ted just graduated from Stanford? Going to become a doctor."

"That's terrific: a chip off the old block."

"Nah. He wants to go into pediatric oncology. But both the kids seem to be taking a page out of my own morbid book of dealing with the dead and dying: Maizie as a homicide detective, Ted an oncologist, and me a pathologist. Poor Akiko can't escape it!" Part of his charm was that he never hesitated to poke fun at himself and his chosen profession, often regaling friends with macabre but uproariously funny pathologist jokes and stories.

Tess told Hisakawa that she would be at the IRE conference and wanted to get his advice about a story she was working on. Could they possibly get together for an hour or so after his keynote? Only, he replied, if you agree to have dinner with me and Akiko that evening. A deal was struck.

The Omni San Francisco was a relic from another era. Built in 1927 as the Financial Center Building, it reopened as the Omni San Francisco in 2002. Now on the National Trust for Historic Preservation's list of Historic Hotels of America, the seventeen-story Florentine Renaissance building was meticulously renovated to reflect its 1920s ambiance, including guest rooms with soaring ceilings and elaborate crown molding, luxurious residential style mahogany furniture, and private bathrooms with Italian marble floors and walls.

Tess called her dog- and house-sitter Priscilla to see if she was available, then booked a room for Saturday night so she had more time to mix and mingle during the conference panels and workshops. It also meant she didn't have to worry about a late-night drive home when she might have had a glass or two too many of Napa Valley Bordeaux over dinner with the Hisakawas.

She had heard Jimmy Hisakawa speak before, so she knew what to expect: a thoroughly engaging amalgamation of humor, forensic education, and fascinating personal anecdotes about life as "pathologist to the VIPs." The only problem with that, he cracked, was that by the time he got to meet these celebrities and luminaries, they were dead.

Once he finished with the post-presentation chatting and congratulatory handshakes, he spotted Tess from across the room and headed in her direction.

His face crinkled into a wide grin as he grabbed her in a warm, welcoming hug. "Like I said on the phone, Tess, it's been too long!" She caught a light scent of cool, citrusy aftershave.

"Well, if you didn't live on the other side of the country, Jimmy, we wouldn't have to go on meeting like this once a decade."

"I know, I know. I keep thinking about retiring and moving west, but Akiko says they'd probably find me stretched out on some other coroner's table in just a few months because she'd have gotten so sick of me hanging around with nothing to do that she had to kill me."

"Like you would *ever* have nothing to do," Tess laughed. "You'd probably be out on some cross-country speaking tour and spending the rest of your time as a big shot consultant for CNN. She'd see you even less than she does now."

"I suspect you're right. So: you want to bend my ear about a case you're involved in?"

"Yeah. How about we find somewhere a little more private?" They wandered into the vast hotel lobby under a trio of huge crystal chandeliers, choosing one of the intimate seating areas in a far corner.

Tess got right to the point. "Jimmy, I need you to use your influence to convince a county coroner and sheriff to exhume a body and do an autopsy."

"Uh, sure," he joked, snapping his fingers. "I'll get on it right away." Then he turned serious. "Maybe you better give me the details."

Over the next thirty minutes, Tess explained about Rennie Matlock's death, the coroner's ruling of suicide, and what she and Sofia Frantonio discovered about Matlock's possible role in what they were both convinced was murder. "Honestly, Jimmy, I know getting an exhumation order isn't easy: our evidence is pretty much just circumstantial at this point, and the fact that we're implicating someone as rich and powerful as Simon Matlock makes it even tougher. The deck is stacked against us, even with Rennie's two brothers, her only living blood relatives, in agreement. But I was hoping that with your prominence and expertise as a forensic pathologist, you might be able to work your magic and persuade them that an autopsy is absolutely essential. That it's a matter of justice."

Other than occasionally arching one eyebrow, Hisakawa barely moved as he listened intently to Tess's story. He sat silent for some time after she finished, his fingers laced together in a steeple like a slender modern-day Buddha contemplating some great existential truth. Finally, he leaned across the small marble-topped table and locked eyes with Tess. "Get me the sheriff and coroner reports, and I'll take it from there."

Over a sumptuous dinner of wild-caught California spiny lobster, calamari, and cabrilla, the three friends caught up on their lives over the past years. Even though they always exchanged Christmas emails, those abbreviated blurbs weren't anything like sitting around a table with good wine, good food, and good friends. Tess's cheeks ached from laughter, something in perilously short supply lately.

Back at the hotel, she handed Hisakawa a large envelope with copies of the two official reports on Rennie's death, along with a short synopsis of Phillip's suspicions, Sofia's discoveries, and her own findings. She knew from experience that the more information he had, the better he could make his case.

"I'll be in touch once I've talked with these folks," Hisakawa said confidently, then smiled and winked. "Never say die." Akiko and Tess groaned in unison.

A few days later, Tess got a text from Sofia.

Must speak with u. In SF this week, can we meet?

As apprehensive as Tess was about communicating with sources over an insecure phone, in this case she had to trust Sofia's insistence that Matlock suspected nothing and would have no reason to snoop through her call or text logs. Tess only hoped she was right.

Where?

A few minutes later, Sofia texted back.

Golden Gate Park, teahouse, tomorrow 11AM

It was a characteristically foggy day in San Francisco. Summer was well on its way by now, a season when the city provided a deliciously cool respite from much of the rest of California's scorching temperatures.

In a stroke of luck, she snagged a parking spot on John F. Kennedy Drive inside the park itself. From there, it was just a short walk to the Japanese Tea Garden, created for the 1894 California Midwinter International Exposition and rambling through four acres of the thousand-acre Golden Gate Park.

Undeterred by the damp chill and with Cooper trotting happily at her side, Tess strolled along the paths that wound through the lush, meticulously landscaped garden and its forest of Japanese maple, gnarled and twisted Monterey pine, cherry trees, and wisteria and azalea in full, riotous bloom. Nearby, a waterfall splashed and burbled, while huge koi swam leisurely through a string of lily-covered ponds. Overlooking it all was the exquisite five-story centenarian pagoda with its bronze Peace Lantern, a gift from Japanese schoolchildren to commemorate the U.S.-Japan peace treaty.

She hadn't been in the park for years, and only visited the Tea Garden once as a small child when her family was on a summer vacation in San Francisco. It was like another world, this near-silent, serene oasis deep within the heart of the second most heavily populated city in the nation, and gradually, Tess's breathing slowed and her mind halted its incessant racing. The sense of peace was palpable.

Just before entering the diminutive Tea House, she encountered a benevolent, eleven-foot-high bronze Buddha. Mesmerized by its mystical aura, she was standing before the imposing statue when a hand lightly touched her arm. She turned quickly to see Sofia standing beside her, dressed in a conservative, businesslike deep blue dress and belted sapphire jacket. She bent down and lightly touched Cooper's head.

The threesome walked inside and settled at a corner table. The only other patron was an elderly Japanese woman. Nevertheless, Tess and Sofia kept their voices low.

"I cannot stay long, as Simon is returning to the district office shortly after noon. But I wanted you to know I accessed his Folder Lock. I will not bore you with all the technical details, but I found two separate folders, one of them labeled "P." So far I have not been able to open that one, as it has an additional level of protection that I haven't yet hacked. But the fact that it is protected *inside* another protected folder tells me it is something very, very important. I shall keep trying to get into it.

"The first thing I found was a file folder that held program files for a Tor browser. Do you know about Tor?"

"Absolutely. Use it frequently to communicate with sources."

For investigative reporters like Tess who frequently dealt with sources who were easily spooked because they wanted to stay anonymous or who would be in grave danger by talking to a journalist, digital security was crucial. It was just as important in safeguarding her own online privacy and security. Web browsers like Google and email programs like Gmail were fine under normal circumstances, but reporters like Tess often found themselves in decidedly less-than-normal circumstances, which is where programs like Tor came in.

The year before, she found herself giving a talk on investigative journalism to a group of journalism students at Laney College in Oakland. She made a wild-ass-guess that probably most of them were functionally illiterate when it came to the intricacies of the Web, so Tess started off by describing Tor and the darknet.

"How many of you use a browser like Google to find things on the 'net?" A sea of hands went up. "Okay: and I'm guessing that most of you think you can find just about anything that way, right?" Nods all around. "Well, you're only about ten percent right. Because that's about how much of the Web is visible to Google. The other 90 percent—or *more*—is hidden." Several faces were open-mouthed in shock.

She went on to explain about the difference between the surface web, the deep web, and the dark web.

"The dark web is *part* of the deep web, but it's 'beneath' it, like a subterranean basement that has some really dangerous, hidden corners where all kinds of nasty things live. This part of the web also has an impenetrable door with a bolt that can only be opened using a specific key. The door is a network called an onion network, and the key is a special browser called Tor.

"On the regular Internet, your laptop or phone communicate *directly* with the server that hosts the website you want to visit. But in an onion network, to get where you want to go you use the Tor browser, basically because you don't want anyone to know where you're going. Think of it like hacking into the GPS on your car. Poof! Mom and Dad think you've driven to the library to study, when actually you've gone to Reno for the weekend." Laughter.

Continuing, she said that Tor scrambles the user's data and directs them to a number of other places before they reach their destination. It's like peeling an onion, she said, which is why it's called an onion network. These 'onion layers' allow the user to stay anonymous, and at the same time allows them to reach darknet websites without anyone knowing. While this perfect anonymity is great for criminals, it's also great for people like whistleblowers and investigative journalists who need to protect the identities of their sources.

Tess pulled herself back to the present, and Sofia's question about Tor.

"Sorry…so, you were mentioning Tor?"

"Yes. I was able to open the Folder Lock folder containing the program files for Tor. I just thought it odd that he'd feel the need to hide it. But in addition to the "P" folder, I also found an Excel file in the Tor folder that I do not understand, and that is not part of the program. The file contained this long list of IP addresses and nicknames, and columns of numerical entries associated with each address. The numbers appeared somewhat random, although many were identical: the most common entry was 10000. Do you think they could be dollar amounts? But for what?"

Tess shook her head, perplexed.

Sofia glanced at her watch, then stood up. "I need to go, but please let me know what you come up with. In the meantime, I will keep trying to unlock that other file on his computer."

15

YOU'VE GOT YOUR EXHUMATION and autopsy." Jimmy Hisakawa's voice bore a note of satisfaction, if not downright jubilation.

Tess was ecstatic at the good news. "Jimmy, you're my hero! How the hell did you manage to convince those hidebound bureaucrats in Aspen County to change their minds? Or do I even want to know?"

The exhumation was complicated by the fact that Rennie was buried in a different jurisdiction than where she died. That meant her brothers—or in this case, Hisakawa, acting on their behalf—needed to convince the coroners in *both* counties to concur on the exhumation warrant. At the same time, the Aspen County sheriff had to be brought into the loop, since the basis of the exhumation request was that Rennie's death was a homicide, not a suicide, and the coroner wouldn't agree to the exhumation without the sheriff's consensus. Tess also knew that the private pathologist wouldn't ever agree to a postmortem without involving law enforcement.

"No, you probably don't want to know how I pulled this whole thing off," Hisakawa laughed. "Let's just say you're going to owe me big-time."

"I have no problem with that! Maybe an extended tour of our beautiful foothill wine region the next time you and Akiko come out to the left coast?"

"Ahh, that sounds perfect. I'm going to hold you to that."

"So, what's the timing on the exhumation and re-examination of Rennie's body?"

"The authorities will exhume Rennie on Tuesday, and Benjamin Dambudzo will undertake the autopsy that afternoon."

"Wait: Benjamin Dambudzo? The same Benjamin Dambudzo who recovered evidence of murder and torture on the victims of the Rohingya genocide in Myanmar?"

"One and the same."

"Jesus, Jimmy: how did you get someone like Dambudzo to agree to handle the autopsy? I'm guessing you know him, and that *he* owed you big-time as well?"

Hisakawa's chuckle echoed across the miles. "As a matter of fact, he *did* owe me. But he was also fascinated by the case, even before I brought it to him. He knew Cliona Matlock before she emigrated to the U.S., and said he felt something was hinky about her murder from the beginning, that there was a lot more underlying it than just a thirteen-year-old kid going suddenly berserk. Then when Rennie was found dead and the authorities insisted it was a suicide, that piqued his interest even further. So it wasn't hard to convince him to step in and handle the autopsy. Plus, of course, he lives in Sacramento, so the trip into the city isn't an issue for him, and Phillip and Devon have ample enough resources to afford his fee. It all just fell into place."

"Jimmy, I don't know how to thank you. This is huge."

"Well, the autopsy hasn't been done yet, Tess. As you know, anything can happen. It could come up empty. Although," he added deliberately, "I doubt it."

"I think that wine country tour is going turn into a two-week vacation to pay you back for all this," Tess said. "You're a rock star."

"Now I just need the bank account to match," the pathologist replied with another laugh. "Happy to help. Just keep me informed as things move along, okay? Oh, and one more thing: watch your back, Tess. If our suspicions play out, Simon Matlock is a much more dangerous character than anyone knows, and this could put you in his crosshairs. If you're not there already."

Tess had no desire to observe either the exhumation or the autopsy. The recurring image of Rennie's lifeless body on the killing field of that bloody motel bed was appalling enough.

Jimmy Hisakawa persuaded Dr. Dambudzo to email Tess a copy of the autopsy report once it was completed, so for a week she anxiously watched her inbox for any sign of it. Friday morning it finally arrived, with a brief note from the pathologist that he'd sent his report to both the Aspen and San Francisco county coroners, cc'ing Rennie's brothers. He added that he was unconditionally confident of his conclusions.

She took her laptop outside and started for the small gazebo in the side yard, calling for Cooper to come along. He pranced out ahead of her toward the little building, his feathered tail like a golden pennant, looking back over his shoulder and grinning.

Washed by the soft morning light, Tess opened the report. She skipped over the lengthy notes of Dambudzo's external examination of Rennie's body and clothing, to the section marked "Injuries." Taking a deep breath in anticipation of the gruesome descriptions, Tess began to read.

Incised injury of neck, transecting the right internal jugular vein. It commences on the right side of the neck, at the level of the midlarynx, over the right sternocleidomastoid muscle; it is gaping, measuring 4.5 inches in length with smooth edges. It tapers superiorly to 1 inch in length cut skin. Dissection discloses that the wound path is from right to left through the skin, the subcutaneous tissue, and the sternocleidomastoid muscle with hemorrhage along the wound path and transection of the right internal jugular vein, with dark red-purple hemorrhage in the adjacent subcutaneous tissue and fascia. No bruising of wound edges are present, and there is no tissue bridging. The direction of the pathway is upward and slightly front to back.

Internally, there is almost no blood present in the heart and great vessels and tissues due to exsanguination from the wound. X-rays of the head and neck. The chest and upper abdomen show no obvious fractures or foreign bodies. The internal structures of the neck, including the carotid arteries, show no injuries except for the large neck injury passing into the muscle as detailed above. None of the major organs show any injuries.

Toxicology was conducted on the blood, urine, gastric contents, and liver to determine the presence of any drugs.

LABORATORY DATA

Cerebrospinal fluid culture and sensitivity:

Gram   stain: Unremarkable
Culture: No growth after 72 hours

Drug Screen Results:

Urine   screen   {Immunoassay}:   NEGATIVE
Cardiac blood {GC/MS}: 0.2 mg/l benzodiazepine (Lorazepam)

Vitreous Humour {GC/FID}: 0.033 µg/mL benzodiazepine (Lorazepam)

Liver, right lobe {GC/MS}: 314.8 mg/kg benzodiazepine (Lorazepam) wet weight tissue

No evidence of other contributory drugs found.

MANNER OF DEATH

Homicide

Three things jumped out at Tess from the report. First was the word "homicide." Second was the toxicology report showing an elevated level of lorazepam in Rennie's system when she died. That explained why she sounded so loopy on that last phone call. But, Tess wondered, would someone that drugged have the strength and dexterity to slice through her own skin, fascia, and muscle?

More telling, however, was the pathologist's determination of the neck wound's directionality: from *right* to *left*. To cut her own throat that way would require right-handed Rennie to contort her arm, wrist, and hand into a bizarre and almost impossible position. However, for a right-handed killer standing face-to-face with Rennie—or, she realized with a start, a left-handed one standing behind her—the razor slice from right to left was perfectly natural. Tess closed her eyes and pictured Simon Matlock eating lunch, gesturing, picking up a cup of coffee, smoothing the front of his shirt—all with his left hand.

Glancing at the computer display, she did a quick time calculation and called Jimmy Hisakawa at his office in New York. "Hope I'm not disturbing you, Jimmy."

"Not at all. What's up?"

"First, I wanted to thank you again for pushing through the exhumation, and getting Dr. Dambudzo to do the autopsy. I just got his report, and wanted to check one thing with you. Would someone loaded on lorazepam be able to cut their own throat?"

"Ahh, you caught that, too."

"I should have known Dambudzo would cc you on the report," Tess replied. "So, yeah, I caught that. Am I wrong that it would be unrealistic?"

"No, you're not wrong at all. Since there was no evidence that Rennie was a benzo addict or chronic user, chances are her tolerance would be fairly low, and she'd be as wobbly as Gumby fairly soon after being dosed."

An image of the green cartoon figure popped into her head and she smiled for an instant, then returned to the significantly more grisly subject at hand. "What I can't figure out is why someone—Matlock—would tranquilize her before he slashed her throat. What's the point? So she couldn't fight back?"

"That's my guess. Just one more way to exert his control over her. Plus, drugging her was the only way he could force her to call off the dogs. That is, you."

"I'm guessing you know Matlock is a southpaw."

"I suspected, but you just confirmed it for me. So, that's one more checkmark in the Matlock-as-killer column. Proving it, however, is something else. But the directionality of the transection, coupled with the high levels of lorazepam, should be enough for the sheriff to open a homicide investigation. Of course, whether he'll even so much as glance in Matlock's direction may depend on whether or not he experiences a sudden infusion of capital."

"Didn't know you were such a cynic, Jimmy," Tess snorted. "But," she added, "knowing Matlock, I wouldn't put it past him."

"Where do you go from here?"

"Sofia has something else for me, but beyond that, my lips are sealed. What you don't know won't hurt you. Bottom line, I can't begin to say how much I appreciate your help on this. It's made a huge difference already, and with any luck, the bastard will be going down for what he did. Soon, I hope."

"Just keep your head up, Tess. I'd really prefer not being called on to execute my pathologist's skills on your body."

"No more than *I'd* prefer that not happen."

16

THERE'S GONNA BE A PRESS CONFERENCE with the sheriff of Aspen County." It was her editor from *Panorama*, his voice raspy from the early morning hour coupled with too many cigarettes and too much Scotch over too many years. Tess was in her back yard, enjoying the quiet and the remnants of an espresso she picked up at a neighborhood coffee shop, when her phone chirped to announce a call from the magazine.

"Hey, Ed. Good morning to you as well."

"Fuck good morning," he growled. Early hours were not his favorites. "Just got an alert from a pal at the *Chronicle* who remembered you were friends with the Matlock kid—sorry, with Rennie—and figured I'd be interested. It's at ten this morning. Suggest you be there."

"No shit, Ed." Tess was annoyed that he felt the need to prompt her, since he had to know she probably was grabbing her car keys that instant. "Where's it going to be held?"

"Sheriff's office. It's on…on…"

"I know where it is. I'll be there. And thanks for the call: it's always so lovely to hear your cheery voice first thing in the morning." During her time with the magazine, she and Ed Willoughby often engaged in these kind of mockingly acerbic exchanges, a mark of their friendship and mutual respect.

Two hours later, Tess pulled into the already-packed parking lot adjacent to the Aspen County Sheriff's Office. Satellite trucks jammed into spaces designed for Volkswagens, and disjointed clots of TV reporters positioned themselves here and there surrounding the podium, already rehearsing their intros. The more relaxed newspaper writers and stringers simply stood around, some with cigarettes dangling from their lips, some with take-out cups of coffee, gossiping and catching up with colleagues they hadn't seen since the last Big Story. Sunglasses camouflaging at least part of her identity, Tess hung back to avoid getting waylaid by a colleague curious about why she was there. As an investigator with a magazine like *Panorama*, she was no longer part of the standard media crowd, and her attendance at something like a press conference could raise questions she'd rather not answer about the reason for being there.

Several minutes later, a small contingent of uniformed officers, men in plainclothes, and a woman Tess recognized as Susannah Applegate, stepped through the doors of the building and made their way to the front of the crowd. In the old days, you would have heard the pop of flashbulbs, but in this age of technology the only noise was the soft *snick-click* of dozens of digital cameras.

A short, bald, bowling-ball of a man in a green khaki uniform stepped up to the bank of microphones. "Good morning. I'm Aspen County Sheriff Win McCutcheon." Small beads of nervous sweat congregated on his upper lip and forehead, and he had to clear his voice before continuing. This kind of press event was clearly something he was unaccustomed to, and did not enjoy.

"I'm here to announce that a homicide investigation has been opened into the death of Rendell Matlock, the daughter of state Senator Simon Matlock. Ms. Matlock was found dead in a local guest lodge on January eighth of this year, an apparent suicide; however, since that time new details have emerged as a result of the exhumation and autopsy of her body, and her death has been ruled a homicide.

"Lieutenant William Schiffler"—he gestured to the uniform-clad officer to his right—"will be leading the inquiry into Ms. Matlock's murder, assisted by officials from the California Bureau of Investigation. We have no suspects at this time, but the investigation will be thorough and comprehensive, ultimately leading to the arrest of the individual or individuals responsible for the crime. Questions?"

A babble of voices shouted out a barrage of questions, causing the rotund sheriff to perspire even more profusely. "What made you decide it was murder?" "Why did you exhume Rennie's body?" "Do you have a suspect?" "What did the autopsy show?" "Who conducted the autopsy?" "Where is the body now?" "What will the CBI be doing to assist you?" "Do you have any theories as to why she was murdered?" "What does Senator Matlock have to say?" Many of their queries were drowned out by louder voices, some firing out the same question to score points and undercut the other. The event soon turned into a jousting match between media rivals.

Eventually, Deputy Coroner Applegate took to the podium, providing a thumbnail sketch of the autopsy results that led to the determination of homicide. More questions flew, which she handled with a great deal more aplomb than the sheriff. When it was clear that every question had been asked and answered at least twice, Sheriff McCutcheon stepped back to the microphone and announced that the press conference was over, and that his office would provide more details "as they become available."

By now, Tess had half-circled around the edge of the media crowd, and removing her sunglasses, caught the eye of Lieutenant Schiffler. He nodded, tilting his head toward the side door of the building. Tess waited until the sea of reporters began ebbing, then strode confidently toward the door as if she belonged there. Schiffler opened it for her.

"I was pretty sure you'd be here, Ms. Alexander," he said, his voice as arid as a desert landscape. The lieutenant had obviously resigned himself to the inevitability of having Tess Alexander in his life.

They stood in a long, cheerless, gray-walled corridor lit by ancient fluorescent tubes that painted both their faces a faintly sallow hue, while a series of unembellished, slab-like doors lined both sides of the hallway. The thought of working in a place like this made Tess want to run screaming for the exit.

"I'm glad the case has been reclassified," she said. "That's at least a first step toward justice for Rennie, and arresting her killer. How did Matlock react when you told him?"

"He wasn't happy, that much I can say. We off the record?"

Tess silently weighed her options, then nodded. "Sure."

"At first, the senator seemed shocked, then began suggesting a series of scenarios that implicated residents at Two Pines, homeless vagrants, or drugged-out lunatics. He was all over the boards, trying to show it was some psychotic stranger who didn't even know Rennie, that she was just in the wrong place at the wrong time. Then he shifted into threatening to make our lives miserable if we didn't wrap this up before the primaries in June. 'I can't have something like this hanging over my head when I'm running for re-election,' he said. I was kinda surprised he turned it to focus on himself, when no one breathed a word about anyone in the family being under suspicion."

"I'm not surprised at all," Tess said, her eyes narrowing. "Simon Matlock is the ultimate narcissist: everything is always all about him. Besides, he may be feeling a bit nervous now that Rennie's death is being investigated as a murder."

Schiffler glanced up and down the empty hall as his brows scrunched together like two caterpillars in a head-to-head confrontation. "I'm not sure why you think the senator has anything to be 'nervous' about, Ms. Alexander. The notion of him having anything to be concerned about…as if he were in any way involved in this…well, it's more than a little bizarre."

Tess's voice took on a hardened edge. "Do you recall what I told you the last time I was here? About the ring? The antique straight razor? Rennie's accusation that Matlock molested her? Perhaps it's time someone looked into those things. The senator isn't as lily-white as he'd have you believe."

"None of us is." Tess heard it in his voice, which cracked almost imperceptibly: he wasn't quite as unwaveringly benevolent toward Matlock as he was before. A tiny sliver of doubt was peeking out, which Tess had every intention of exploiting. If not today, then in the coming days and weeks.

"True enough, Lieutenant. But I have two other pieces of evidence that you can add to what I've already told you: First, I spoke to Butch Fogerty after I saw you last time, and he told me that Simon Matlock stopped into the Two Pines office the night Rennie was killed."

Schiffler's rocket-propelled eyebrows zoomed upward on his forehead. "What? Are you sure?"

"I'm absolutely positive: I showed him a photo of Matlock, and he identified him as the man he saw that night. Matlock gave him five hundred dollars to tell him what apartment Rennie was in."

Schiffler pulled out a small notepad and scribbled down the information. "We'll definitely check this out. I wish you'd told me before."

"Would you have believed me?"

Schiffler didn't respond.

"The second thing we've discovered is that Matlock bought a GPS tracker, which he undoubtedly attached to Rennie's car to track her comings and goings. Whether or not he had a suspicion that she was leaving San Francisco for a new life in Sacramento, I don't know. But what I *do* know is that's how he figured out she was in Hammond Mills."

Schiffler folded his arms across his ample belly, then shook his head. "Just because he bought a GPS tracker doesn't prove he attached it to Rennie's car, *or* that he used it to follow her to Hammond Mills."

"No, it doesn't *prove* it, but what other explanation makes sense? All of Matlock's cars have built-in GPS. He simply had no need for a tracker. Plus he wiped—or thought he wiped—his Internet browsing history for the day he bought it. Not the day before, not the day after. Just that day. Why would he do that? What was in that history that was so damned incriminating that he needed to delete it?"

"If it was deleted, how do you know about it? Come to think of it, how do you know anything about what was or wasn't on his computer?" The officer took a small step toward Tess, a vein on his left temple throbbing slightly.

Tess stood her ground. "Lieutenant, if you're trying to intimidate me, you need to know it won't work." Tension-filled silence hung between them, but then Schiffler took a deep breath and stepped back. Tess continued, "I can't give you the specifics, but I can assure you that the information was gathered not by me, but by someone with access to that computer. It may not have been strictly legal under the privacy statutes, which means it wouldn't hold up in court, but if someone were to one day obtain a search warrant...."

The comment hovered in the air like unexploded ordnance.

Schiffler broke the silence. "There's this matter called probable cause..."

"With any luck, your investigative efforts will soon provide you with that."

A slight tinge of red appeared on his neck and his eyes focused intensely on Tess's face, searching for any trace of derision.

Inwardly, Tess had limited faith in the tiny department's abilities to dig to the bottom of the muck and reveal anything significant about Rennie's death or at whose hand she died, even buoyed by the state's investigators. They'd been forced into admitting they made a mistake in their original ruling of suicide, and in Tess's experience, that kind of comedown seldom engendered enthusiastic motivation. Nevertheless, she mustered a sincere smile and touched the lieutenant lightly on the arm, knowing she couldn't risk insulting the man if he was going to be any good to her as a resource.

Schiffler's face softened and relaxed, and he returned Tess's smile. "We're all going to do our very best," he said, his voice carrying a hint of pride. "I'm confident we can solve this thing."

"I'm sure you will. And I hope I can come to you with any information I happen to unearth in the course of my own work on the…story." She was about to say "case," but caught herself just in time. No sense making the man think she saw herself as being on a par with law enforcement.

"Of course." He reached into his shirt pocket and pulled out a pen and a card, then wrote something on the back. "Here's my direct line, Ms. Alexander. If I'm not there, you can leave a message and I'll be notified. I'll get back to you as soon as I can."

"I appreciate that. Thank you for your courtesy." She offered her own card to the officer. "This is my contact information as well, in case you need to reach me." She held out her hand and they shook.

After letting Cooper out to stretch his legs and relieve himself, she pulled out of the now-empty parking lot for the drive back to Deer Valley. For a moment she thought about returning to Two Pines and re-questioning Butch Fogerty, then realized she had already squeezed everything she could from the man. Besides, his lecherous leer made her want to knee him in the groin, but what good would that do? None, she admitted to herself, but it sure would be gratifying.

17

BUTCH FOGERTY HAS DISAPPEARED." Lieutenant Schiffler's voice carried a note of frustration and concern. His call caught Tess just as she was emerging from her morning shower after a run.

"Disappeared? When?"

"We're not exactly sure. One of my deputies went up to Two Pines to talk with him yesterday afternoon, and he wasn't there. The folks there said he'd been gone for at least two days, even though his car was still there. Stone cold. TV was still on, and there was a stale, half-eaten sub sandwich on the front counter."

The image of a slug-like glop of some unidentifiable meat coated with mustardy mayonnaise slithering down the front of Fogerty's shirt galloped across Tess's memory. Of more consequence, however, was where Fogerty was. If he really vanished two days ago….

Tess heard Schiffler say something, but it sounded as if he were in a very far-away tunnel. Then there was no sound at all, just the image of a rocky slope dotted with drab, scrubby bushes and silver prostrate remnants of fallen trees, then a shallow, boulder-strewn river pushing its way through the barren landscape. In the blurry distance, a strange metal seven-sided behemoth spanned the water. Like film from a hovering drone, the image moved closer, exposing a parallel set of metal rods on the undercarriage, while next to it, on a pencil-thin bridge perched atop two weather-beaten rust and gray concrete pedestals, ran another pair of dark steel bars. Gradually, the vision faded, replaced by the alabaster floor and walls of Tess's bathroom.

Dropping the phone and falling onto one knee, she barely missed cracking her head on the tile countertop. A faint muttering elbowed into her consciousness. It was Schiffler, shouting out her name over and over on the phone's speaker.

She picked up the device and rose unsteadily. "I'm here, Lieutenant. Sorry about that: I just got a little dizzy and dropped the phone."

"That must've been one hell of a dizzy spell: you were gone for a good thirty seconds. Maybe longer."

"That happens sometimes. Low blood pressure." She wasn't about to tell Schiffler about the vision. She just needed to figure out the meaning for herself, and how it related to Fogerty. Which she knew it did.

"Do you have any idea of where to start searching for him?" she asked.

"Not yet. Doesn't look like he skipped town, since all his clothes, his car, and even his wallet were still in his apartment. No sign of foul play, but then...." He let the comment die of its own accord.

"Yeah, it's like what Rennie said when she called: the place *is* pretty sketchy."

"Well, just thought I'd let you know. Are you sure you're okay, Ms. Alexander?"

"I'm perfectly fine, Lieutenant. Please let me know if you find out anything about Fogerty's disappearance."

"Will do."

By now, the warm morning air had dried her body, so Tess set about getting dressed and preparing for a spontaneous drive up into the mountains: it was crucial that she locate the site of her vision, which she sensed somehow was near Hammond Mills. How near, of course, was another matter. Just in case, she packed toiletries and a change of clothes, then hollered for Cooper. The big dog came galumphing down the stairs and danced in circles around Tess as she gathered his leash, food, and bowls.

Oh, boy! A ride!

Detouring onto Interstate 80 past Truckee, she headed toward the exit that would take her north on old Highway 89 to Hammond Mills. Then something tickled her brain about the Truckee Chamber of Commerce: they were associated with the California Welcome Center, which meant they had not just stores of written materials on the northern Sierra, but the staff was likely well-versed in the features of the region, and might recognize the place in her vision as long as she could provide a detailed enough description.

She found the next exit, accelerated onto the overpass, and headed back west on the freeway. The right-hand lane looped off the freeway into downtown Truckee and onto Donner Pass Road, the town's main street. Parking a few blocks away, she and Cooper ambled toward the town's historic train depot, home to the Welcome Center. *Wait: train. That's what those steel lines could be: railroad tracks.*

The historic building, painted in Southern Pacific Railroad's trademark mustard-yellow with green trim, had served as the town's passenger railroad depot for over a hundred years, and was a point of pride for the community. Once she walked inside, Tess saw why. Time-worn oak benches from the 1900s spread throughout the lobby, alongside a bulky steel scale once used to weigh passengers' bags for their journeys east across Nevada and to Salt Lake City and Chicago, or west to San Francisco. Everywhere were historic photos—daguerreotype, albumen prints, autochrome and Kodachrome—and fascinating relics from the area's rich railroad heritage. Another area held modern-day maps, brochures, leaflets, and postcards, free for the taking. Always fascinated by history, Tess wandered through the building for nearly thirty minutes before reluctantly resuming her primary task and approaching one of the center's staff.

"I wonder if you might be able to help me?" she asked. "Years ago, a friend told me about a place where two bridges cross a river; one spans the river on a base that rests on big concrete pillars, while the other sits on some kind of steel base and is covered by a huge metal open framework with seven sections. I'd love to be able to see this for myself—do you have any idea of what and where it is? She said it was up in this part of the Sierra."

As Tess talked, the staff member's brows knitted together in concentration and puzzlement. "I can't say it sounds familiar to me, but let me get Robert, who's a second-generation Truckee native and also an avid hiker and explorer. If anybody knows where your spot is, Robert will."

A few minutes later, the woman came back, walking alongside a tall, rail-thin man that Tess guessed to be in his late sixties. He sported a massive, gray handlebar moustache and matching silver ponytail that dangled almost to his waist. Bending down to scratch Cooper's ears, he said, "I hear you have a mystery you're trying to solve. He smiled, revealing platinum-white teeth. "Can you explain it to me?"

Tess repeated the description from her vision, and about halfway through, noticed Robert's lips—what she could see of them—were curving into a smile. By the time she finished, he was nodding enthusiastically. "The one with the metal super-structure is the old Truckee River Railroad Bridge in Verdi," he announced. "Actually, it's called the West Verdi Bridge, but everyone around here calls it the Truckee River Bridge. It was built in 1906 or '07 I think, and trains still use it. It's called a truss bridge, on account of it's a truss. About two hundred feet long, as I recall, across the Truckee River. You can see it from I-80, no problem: it's about a mile or so past the Nevada State line on your right heading east. The other bridge is for the tracks going in the opposite direction."

"So, if I wanted to see it closer up, how would I get there?"

"Hmmm...best way would be to take the Verdi-Boomtown exit up a ways, then double around and go back heading west on the freeway. Then take the South Verdi Road exit and turn left under the freeway. The road kinda hoop-de-doos and makes a ninety-degree right, and you wanna take the second left onto Quilici Ranch Road. I'd be guessin' it's about two miles down to get close to the bridge, but the last part you'll have to walk. 'Course, I haven't been down there for years, so the road coulda washed out last winter or the one before.

"If that doesn't work out, you could take Forest Road 100, on the south side of the highway at Boomtown, and then head south. Just be careful that when Road 100 turns to the left, you stay straight ahead or you'll end up wandering in the wilderness darn near all the way to Mount Rose. That route's longer, maybe three miles, and I can't say the road'd be any better, but you could try. Either way, hope you got good suspension on your car."

Tess's mind was spinning with all the minutiae, but she could likely make it work by getting off the freeway at Boomtown and asking for directions if she needed them. Her Lexus wasn't ideal for off-roading, that's for sure, but at least it was four-wheel drive. If worse came to worst, she could go back to Truckee, rent a higher-clearance four-wheel drive Subaru or Jeep, and try again.

Now that Robert confirmed it, she was all but convinced this was the bridge from her vision, and that it related somehow to the missing Butch Fogerty. Who knows, she thought to herself: maybe the guy got a wild hair up his butt one day and decided to go camping with a buddy, and she'd find them both spread-eagled and sunburned beside the river, knocked out on dope or blitzed on beer, clueless that anyone was looking for them. Mystery solved.

Somehow, though, Tess didn't think so.

"Where can I get a Forest Service map?" Tess didn't want to take any chances on getting lost in the Nevada hinterlands.

"We've got 'em right here."

She took the map and thanked Robert and the woman who'd located him—Melanie, according to her nametag—and walked back to her car, Cooper in happy tow.

18

MAP IN HAND, TESS DROVE EAST on Interstate 80. Between Truckee and Verdi, the landscape becomes flatter, drier, scrubbier, and less mountainous. As the highway follows the Truckee River snaking through ancient, khaki-colored canyons burned even browner by the summer sun, mostly gone are the towering Douglas firs and less lofty Jeffrey pines that characterize the mountain landscape west of Truckee.

Verdi was just up ahead, and the just-across-the-state-line gambling mecca of Boomtown. Not quite two hundred years ago, the first wagon trains from the east thundered through that same land on their way to the fabled gold fields of the Mother Lode, following the ancient route traveled by native peoples as far back as the Stone Age. Tess felt the tug of history as she turned onto the road that would lead her to the terminus of her vision.

Google Maps was even more helpful than the Forest Service map in getting from the bedlam that was Boomtown to Quilici Ranch Road. Once on the gravel road, it was slow going, but the way was passable and marginally well-maintained. Sandwiched between the Truckee River on the west and the railroad tracks on the east, the road sometimes ran so close to the tracks that Tess could almost feel the rails humming their age-old hymns. A little over a mile and a half along, she passed a large residential compound on the right, nestled near the bank of the river at its widest. Tess surmised this was the Quicili Ranch, the road's namesake.

Now the passage became rougher, demanding her attention to the steadily increasing number of ruts and potholes, but still nowhere near SUV territory. Further ahead, the road dead-ended. To the right, a large graveled amoeba-shaped area stood empty, although dozens of tire tracks attested to other drivers who'd parked or turned around there. She shut down the Lexus, grabbed her phone and water bottle, and let Cooper jump out of the car. Crushed granite was underfoot at first, but soon, the pathway narrowed and then disappeared altogether, leaving Tess no option but to walk directly alongside the railroad tracks. Just to be safe, she hooked the dog to his leash.

She had wandered along railroad tracks like this before, in childhood on her grandparent's rural farm which was bisected by the railroad tracks, then later in college while exploring the Sierra foothill countryside where trains whistled through the night. Often, the only way from Point A to B was directly along-side or even on the tracks, through the layers of sharp, semi-crushed stones called track ballast, which was also packed between, under, and around the huge oak railroad ties. The ballast was notoriously difficult to walk on because of its size and irregularity. The creosote coating the ties was pungent and acrid, but to Tess, not altogether unpleasant.

As she rounded the gentle curve in the tracks, there it was, looming just ahead: the bridge she saw in her vision, the one Robert identified as the Truckee River Railroad Bridge. The loud, steady *whoosh* of traffic on the interstate, less than four hundred feet away, told her that whatever she was looking for was hidden from passing motorists, so she zipped her phone into a pocket on her cargo pants, let Cooper free from the leash, and began clambering down the loose rocks to the river itself. The dog followed eagerly, much more sure-footed than his mistress. Every few feet Tess looked up to see if the highway was still visible. It was.

They walked toward the looming bridge along the river's edge for nearly a quarter mile, completely out in the open and visible to any motorist who happened to be looking their way. And then there was the monstrous structure itself, a conspicuous landmark in the rough Nevada landscape. Gazing at the impressive structure, she realized she'd seen it herself dozens of times while driving over the Sierra.

After she scrambled back up the slope, she glanced ahead, then back to where she and Cooper came, just waiting for…what? Inspiration? Insight? A bolt from the blue? Unsure, she knew what she needed would likely reveal itself. Either that, or she'd get eaten by a bear.

Her eyes settled on a large copse of bushy pines maybe seventy or eighty feet from, and slightly above, the northwest side of the tracks. They were dense enough and situated so they would undoubtedly shield anything from freeway travelers, even if someone were directly focused on the spot.

Because she didn't know what she'd find ahead, she clicked on Cooper's leash again and started walking, slowly and carefully, looking and sensing for anything out of the ordinary. Traffic noise obscured at least some of the softer sounds she might have heard in this semi-desert landscape—the skittering of ground squirrels, small birds rustling in the scattered sagebrush, the *pip-pip-pip* of a startled chipmunk—leaving mostly her eyesight and sense of smell to guide her as she neared the cluster of trees.

Then came a sudden, loud crashing from the thick bitterbrush behind her, and Tess whirled around just in time to see a tawny, big-eared mule deer sprinting away, nose high in the air and white tail tucked against its hindquarters. Cooper's leash gave a Christmas-cracker snap as he lunged to chase the creature, but the leather held and foiled his escape, much to the big dog's dismay. Heartbeat galloping like a racehorse's, Tess couldn't help but laugh out loud at her moment of panic over this docile creature more terrified than she. *Get a grip, Tess—it's not like you're going to encounter the Loch Ness Monster.*

A shadow passed overhead, and Tess looked up to see a huge vulture on the wing. A second one followed, and a third and fourth, circling slowly on the warm air currents. Then came the scream of ravens, and Tess knew what she would find, hidden away under the piñon pines.

After making the grisly discovery, she drove back to Truckee, picked up a cheap prepaid phone at the local Walgreen's, then went back to her car and called 911.

She knew that eventually, the call would be routed to the Washoe County Sheriff, and from there Aspen County would be notified, because they had doubtless put out a missing persons alert to nearby law enforcement agencies. It might take a day or two, but eventually the authorities would have the answer as to the whereabouts of the missing Butch Fogerty.

"Hey, uhh, I want to report a body. At least, I think it's a body." She adopted a higher, much younger, nasal tone of voice, an uneducated vocabulary, and slight Texas accent. She didn't know who might end up listening to the call tape, but wanted to make certain no one recognized her voice.

"Did you say 'a body'?"

"Yessm', sure did. A body. Pretty sure it's a dude."

"Who am I speaking to?"

Tess ignored the question. "Me and a pal was…uhh…foolin' around on that big-ass iron railroad bridge that goes over the river by Verdi, and we seen these humongous vultures flyin' in and out of some trees that was up from the bridge. We went to go see what we could see, and when we got to the trees we could…well, we could smell somethin' bad. There was this mound of dirt with a few rocks off to the side and it looked like buzzards or coyotes or bears or whatever had been there and half-dug in the dirt to get to it…and we could see part of a body layin' there."

"What's your name, miss?" The 911 operator was persistent, but Tess once again skirted the question.

"It's on the left, off this road called Quill Ranch, or somethin' like that, runnin' alongside the railroad tracks, just up from that iron railroad bridge. It's after the road dead-ends, and under a bunch of ratty pine trees. That's all I know." She hit the red button to disconnect the call, stepped out of the car, and went around to the trunk and grabbed the tire jack. After removing the phone's memory card, she set it on the asphalt alongside the phone, and smashed them both.

In no hurry, she took old Highway 40 west from Truckee, past the impossibly blue Donner Lake that sparkled in the late summer sun as if it were sprinkled with a million diamonds, and ascended the summit past steep, granite rockfalls tumbling a thousand feet down the near-vertical slope.

As she drove, the land and the mountains whispered to her of enduring hope and bitter loss and the unbroken passage of time.

19

THE PHONE CALL FROM LIEUTENANT SCHIFFLER came at the end of that week. They received an anonymous tip, he said, about a body just below Verdi. Turned out to be Butch Fogerty. He was shot in the back of the head and buried in a shallow grave, but because of the hard and rocky ground, the grave was a lot shallower than it should have been to deter predators, and a few of them had already begun to unearth his remains. But no doubt: it was Fogerty.

"Any idea who might have killed him, or why?" Tess was pretty sure of the answer, but kept it to herself.

"Nope. No forensics to speak of, not even a shell casing. But the wound appears to have been made by a .22 pistol, according to the M.E., and fired at near point-blank range."

"An execution, then."

"Looks like it. But why someone would execute the manager of a seedy dump like Two Pines is beyond me. Yeah, Rennie Matlock was murdered there, but there's nothing to connect Fogerty to her, other than the fact that he ran the place."

Tess took a deep breath and hesitated, knowing her observation could antagonize the cop and destroy all the good will she'd tried so hard to cultivate. "That's not entirely true, Lieutenant. What about Simon Matlock? It was your deputy who went up to Two Pines to talk with Fogerty about Matlock's visit the night Rennie was killed, which means that at least a part of you believed what I told you about Fogerty identifying

Matlock's photo. Doesn't it make sense that Matlock wouldn't want that to come out?"

Schiffler struggled to answer. "I…I'm sorry, Ms. Alexander, but I still have trouble believing that Senator Matlock would…that he could…be involved in any of this. It's all circumstantial, what you've told me, and quite honestly, all I have is your word that Fogerty identified Matlock. It's not that I think you're lying, don't get me wrong. But Fogerty could have said it was the senator just to get rid of you. Or mess with you. Or he could have misidentified the photograph, accidentally or on purpose. Or a hundred other what-if scenarios. In the end, all we have is the word of a man known to use practically every variety of substance in existence, who very well could have been impaired when he spoke with you, and now that man is dead and can't confirm anything. In all honesty, we're no closer to the truth than we were on the night Rennie's body was discovered."

"Except for two things: we now know both Rennie and Butch Fogerty were murdered. And it's my belief that one way or another, either directly or indirectly, Simon Matlock was involved."

"I guess we'll have to agree to disagree on that, Ms. Alexander—at least until we uncover more solid evidence. I'm sorry."

"No, I understand, Lieutenant," Tess said, aware of her reddening cheeks and swatting back rising frustration. *If it's evidence you want, Lieutenant, it's evidence I'll find.*

Tess was struck with an idea, and she began turning it over and over in her mind to view it from every angle. Was it courage or lunacy? Confronting Simon Matlock about Rennie, telling him what she learned about the murder weapon, about what she unearthed in Hammond Mills thanks to Butch Fogerty.

What were the risks? Was there a downside to this kind of encounter? Sure, he might just erupt in fury and throw her out of his house—*No,* her inner voice cautioned, *don't meet at his house. A public place.* Okay, what else might he do, other than what he already did by concealing evidence and getting rid of the weapon and sabotaging her efforts to learn more about his larcenous activities?

Oh, yeah: chances are he also arranged for Fogerty's execution, so there was that.

As much as Tess wanted to put Matlock on the spot and make him sweat, she didn't want to put herself in danger with this man who may have escalated from a crooked businessman and corrupt politician to one capable of homicide. Unless, she thought to herself, he was *always* homicidal, and simply managed to control it all these years. Or hide it. The notion made the hairs on her arms stand up as if electrified.

She debated what to say to the man, and more importantly, what *not* to say: that she noticed Rennie's missing ring, or anything about Sofia's attempts to break into his computer. The former would risk him disposing of the ring, and the latter would risk him disposing of Sofia.

They agreed to meet at 8 a.m. on the north side of the small lake in Sacramento's William Land Park, a 166-acre oasis in the eastern portion of the city that was originally part of John Sutter's New Helvetia land grant. Even though it was early, several cars already squatted nose-to-tail along several of the nearby streets, their owners taking advantage of the coolness of the morning for a walk or run around the park.

She parked along the northern boundary of 13th Avenue, then walked the quarter mile to the lake. The park was just as lush and wide-open as she remembered from her childhood, with century-old planetrees, ash, sweetgum, and Chinese elms shading many of the pathways.

The lake was so small as to barely merit the description—in fact, Tess soon spotted a sign that designated it as the Anne Rudin Peace Pond. She only hoped that moniker would set the tone for the coming encounter, but it was doubtful. Surely Matlock would be on high alert as a result of her enigmatic phone call requesting the meet, and since their last get-together when she discarded her Tess-as-wide-eyed-innocent persona, he was likely primed for battle. *Fine. That way I don't have to dance around the facts.*

Now and then, someone walked or jogged or rolled a baby stroller along the path where Tess waited. It was just public enough to safeguard her, but not so populated that she and Matlock couldn't have a private conversation. Still debating whether to mention Butch Fogerty's unfortunate demise, she saw Matlock striding toward her, his face a mask of dark clouds.

Rather than sitting, he came to a stop and stood, legs spread wide, directly in front of her. Tess swiveled to the side and also stood, deftly forcing him to take a step backward; although he was a full head taller than she, at least she'd evened the playing field somewhat by not allowing him to trap her in a vulnerable seated position.

"So, what do you want?" he growled in irritation.

Good: she was already under his skin. "What I *want* is some answers, not that I expect to get any. At least, not honest ones." The muscles under one of his eyes twitched almost imperceptibly. "For starters, I understand that you're quite an antique collector." His head tilted slightly to the side as if he were unsure where she was headed. "Specifically, of antique straight razors. I also understand that one of your most prized artifacts—a particularly striking example with an elegant, fleur-de-lis engraved Sheffield silver handle—is missing from your collection. Oh, wait: it isn't exactly 'missing,' is it? It's in the evidence files of the Aspen County Sheriff. Any idea how it got there, Simon?"

Matlock hesitated for an instant, then declared, "Well, obviously Rennie stole it to use on herself."

Gotcha. "But Simon," she said, using the familiarity of his first name as an intentional irritant and her voice oozing with sweet sarcasm, "Rennie's death has been ruled a homicide, not suicide. You *did* get that message, didn't you?"

"Of course I know it, you little bi...." He stopped, not wanting to expose his irritation. The authorities connecting the straight razor to him was something that hadn't come to his attention, and it clearly concerned him. Then he smiled thinly.

"The only way I can think how the razor ended up with Rennie is that whoever killed her stole it from me and used it to frame me. Of course, it's not going to work, because I have an airtight alibi for that night. I was on a conference call with my chief operations officer, going over plans for a new office park in the East Bay."

Tess didn't want Matlock to see her frustration. Of course he would have an alibi, she reasoned, simply to ensure all his bases were covered. Nevertheless, she continued to press. "That doesn't make sense, Simon: how could someone have stolen the razor from your collection? Who? When? And what would be their motive for killing Rennie?"

"How the hell should I know?" he snarled. "It could have been anybody who was in my house, even one of my staff...." His voice trailed off, and his jaws set. "It could even have been Phillip. He never really forgave Rennie for Cliona's death. Oh, he put on a great act about wanting to exhume Rennie's body to prove she'd been murdered, blah, blah, blah—but that's all it was. An act. I know my son, and know he despised Rennie for killing his mother. I hate to say it, but ever since I learned it was murder, I've had my suspicions about Phillip."

Tess was disgusted, though not surprised, that he'd implicated his own son so effortlessly. Unfortunately, Phillip made a perfect patsy, especially in light of his youthful indiscretions. And that would be true for anyone investigating him. Which the authorities might already be doing.

Sidestepping his accusation against Phillip, Tess pressed on. "Are you *sure* that's the way he felt about Rennie, Simon? How would you know? After all, he was just a child when his mother was killed. Besides which, Phillip has never been terribly forthcoming with you about his innermost feelings." Tess hadn't a clue if this was true, but her instincts told her that the son wasn't close enough to his father to have confided in him.

Matlock's eye twitched again. *That's his tell.* "You know nothing about my relationship with my son," he spat. "We've always been close, more so after his mother died and he only had me to rely on. But he was always troubled. Sadistic, even. Did you know that he almost killed another kid once? Stomped him half to death." A tiny, victorious smile curved a corner of his mouth. "The only reason he didn't do prison time is because I saved him. Talked the DA and judge into giving him another chance. But now it looks like I was wrong: he turned out to be a killer after all." Matlock was clearly gearing up for a full-on assault on his son's character, testing the waters with Tess.

She just stared at him, flinty-eyed. "I doubt that, Simon. I don't think Phillip has it in him to be a killer, especially not of his sister. You, on the other hand...." The sentence drifted unfinished in the cool morning air.

"I don't have to stand here and listen to your ludicrous, baseless accusations. If that's why you brought me all the way out here, it was a waste of gas and time." He started to step away from her.

"Oh, it's not just the antique straight razor, Simon. There's a lot more that implicates you." *Like Butch Fogerty*, she almost said, then decided to back away from that particular precipice. "Like the tracking device you put on Rennie's car so you could follow her to Hammond Mills. Or like your abuse of Rennie since she was a little girl. Beatings, rapes, even when Cliona was alive."

Matlock exploded, furious spittle forming on his lips. "You fucking, lying cunt! What tracking...you can't prove...you have no right...I would never...how dare you accuse me of killing my own...you can't get away with...you're nothing but a lying *whore*!" By then he was shouting, completely out of control.

From the corner of her eye, Tess saw two refrigerator-sized men in dark suits running at full-tilt across the grass toward them, both with their hands at their hips.

Bodyguards—armed, she realized with a jolt, and raised both hands high above her head to show she was weaponless. She whipped her head to both sides, looking for witnesses, just in case the worst happened. Only an old man, seated on a bench on the far shore of the pond, asleep. *Where are all the soccer moms when you need them?*

"Hey fellas," she said, forcing a smile onto her face. "We were just having a conversation, and the senator got a little overwrought. Nothing to worry about." She kept her hands in plain sight, slightly above her shoulders.

The two human shields walled in Matlock. "Senator, are you all right?" one of them asked, while the second man never took his eyes off Tess, his hand still at his hip.

The master of disguise bobbed his head slightly as his face softened and his shoulders relaxed. His lips formed into a steely smile and he took a deep breath. "It's fine, guys. I'm fine. Just got a little hot under the collar and lost my cool, that's all. This *reporter*"—he spit out the word like it was a curse—"was just trying to shake me down. Get a *story*." He looked at Tess with a smirk. "But there's no story to tell. Never was, never will be." With that, he broke away from his protectors and strode away, calling over his shoulder, "Come on, guys. I have places to go, things to do."

With one last glance at Tess, both men dashed to catch up to Matlock, then hustled him into a large silver Chrysler sedan.

Tess eased herself down onto the bench and sat staring out at the inaptly named Peace Pond. *Well, you wanted to get a rise out of him, girl, and you sure as hell did. Damn near got yourself whacked by a couple of goons in the process. And for what? You're no closer to an answer than you were before, and now the man's even more supremely pissed.*

Then she thought of something else, and a tiny smile teased at her lips. Matlock was *so* pissed that he could easily make a mistake. Do or say something foolish, perhaps even incriminating. Angry people were often careless people. Angry, *guilty* people were sometimes even more rash. She only hoped it wouldn't come at a cost for her

20

PHILLIP, YOU NEED TO BE ESPECIALLY CAREFUL. Your father's foaming at the mouth, and you could get caught in his jaws."

"Why? What happened?"

"I confronted him with some things, and he went off on a tear about how *you* could be Rennie's killer."

"*Me?* Kill Rennie? That makes no sense." Across the phone lines, his voice sounded almost indifferent.

"He said it was because you despised her for killing your mother."

"Shit," he said dully, "that's old news. *Really* old news. Yeah, I was mad at first, couldn't understand why she did it. But then when I was older, we had a chance to talk for the first time, and I understood. I still thought it was fucked up, but I understood. She'd been through…a lot."

"So, you know about your dad? What he did to her?" Tess wanted to be careful in her wording, in case he didn't know the extent of Simon's abuse.

"You mean the molest? The whippings? Yeah, I knew. But only after she told me, and that was like years later. When she was in jail. I felt really bad that I didn't know before. Maybe I could've done something to stop it." Pain cracked his voice.

"Phillip, you were just a little boy. What, five years old? There's absolutely *nothing* you could have done. And probably no one would have believed you. They sure didn't believe Rennie."

"Yeah, she told me Mom hit her, said she was a whore."

"Anyway," Tess warned, "it's really important that you keep your head down and not cross your dad in any way. Just keep living your life in San Jose and be careful. Things are pretty quiet right now, but they could run off the rails anytime."

"Yeah, okay." Once again, his voice was flat and dispassionate.

In fact, things *were* quiet. Two weeks had passed since her volatile encounter in the park with Matlock, and she'd heard nothing. Nothing from Matlock, nothing from Schiffler about Fogerty's death or the investigation into Rennie's killing, and strangely, nothing from Sofia. But maybe there was just nothing to report.

As for Phillip…well, he was still a bit of an enigma. The stories about his youthful violence provoked an image in her mind of an old crone rattling chicken bones to foretell the future. You simply couldn't discount the fact that he had been an extremely disturbed kid. Whether he was just as disturbed now was a matter for the shrinks of the world. Sofia had dropped a few hints about what she saw as the young man's mounting instability, but in her own conversations with the Phillip, Tess didn't pick up on anything especially troubling except that his affect was a little lifeless. But then, Sofia had a lot more contact with him, and she could be right that the kid's seams were fraying. It wouldn't come as a surprise, probably to anyone.

Coffee cup in hand in the calmness of a still-dark early morning, Tess knew it wasn't doing her any good to keep ruminating on something she couldn't do anything about. She gulped the last of her coffee, headed upstairs, and with Cooper watching excitedly, dressed in her Shamrock green running shorts and short-sleeved T-shirt, and laced up her shoes. Cooper at her heels, she grabbed a bottle of water, some trail mix and the dog's leash, and jumped into her car as Cooper bounded into the back seat.

"Waddya say we take a drive over to Nevada City and hit the Pioneer Trail? Then we can grab a bite at one of restaurants that'll let you onto the patio." Cooper grinned enthusiastically, panting a quiet *heh-heh-heh.* Nevada City, a small town in the Gold Rush region of northern California, was about thirty minutes away from Deer Valley, and the part of the Pioneer Trail she wanted to run was another twelve miles or so north on Highway 20. Further away than she usually went for just a run, but it was a beautiful day, perfect for a drive into the mountains, and she needed to go somewhere new. She'd open the moonroof and roll down the windows, never mind what it did to her hair.

Nevada City was one of Tess's favorite towns: if she hadn't settled in Deer Valley, this place was her next choice. Nestled on the spring-green hillsides of the Sierra's western slope midway between Sacramento and Lake Tahoe, Nevada City is a perfectly preserved Gold Rush city, its downtown registered as a National Historic Landmark. The town itself shoulders up against the huge Tahoe National Forest with its multitude of glittering high Sierra lakes, wild rivers, and quiet forest trails perfect for hiking and running.

Once Tess made the turn onto Highway 49, in less than ten minutes the outlines of the small town of Grass Valley and then its sister, Nevada City, came into view. After slicing through Grass Valley and meandering up into the hills of Nevada City, the road split, with Highway 20 leading up into the high Sierra town of Truckee and then Lake Tahoe.

Along the way up Highway 20, she made an unplanned stop at the small pullout overlooking the breathtaking Washington Ridge, where she stood behind an aged rock barrier and simply reveled in the view. Cooper whined anxiously through the open window, eager to embark on the promised run, so Tess gave up and returned to the car. From there, the road began to coil and loop its way further up the mountain, through forests crowded with hundred-foot-tall, centuries old incense cedars and scattered maple, madrone and dogwood.

Once she saw the sign for the Skillman Horse Camp, she said to the dog in the back seat, "We're almost there, kiddo!" whereupon Cooper began whimpering excitedly while bouncing from one side of the car to the other. Past the camp, now on a dirt Forest Service road, Tess found a wide spot and pulled off. She grabbed her gear and opened the door for Cooper, who leaped out and immediately began sniffing every bush in sight. The Pioneer Trail was only a few hundred yards away.

Calling for the dog, Tess set off at a brisk walk toward the trail sign. While it follows the arc of the highway, this part of the Pioneer is far enough removed so that in the still of this early morning when the highway was empty, amidst the gathered trees standing silent sentinel, Tess could almost hear the drudging clomp of oxen hooves and squeal of rusty wagon wheels as the tired, early settlers wound their way down the mountains toward Nevada City.

But Tess and Cooper were going in the other direction, following the trail as it dove deep into the forest, looping and twisting and burrowing into the dusky mountain woodlands on its journey to Bear Valley and the towering cliffs of Emigrant Gap beyond. Despite the deadly attack on her in the coastal woods some years before, Tess carried no fear of the of the forest or its four-footed residents. *The two-footed ones are another story.*

While the highway remained still at this early hour, now and then she thought she heard the buzz of a dirt bike, but her run was mostly quiet and empty of anything but a slight breeze and the occasional rapid-fire barking of a grey squirrel alerting its brethren to a two-legged intruder.

By now, Tess was loping along easily, Cooper darting back and forth along the trail as he investigated all the wonderful new smells. Maybe a half-mile later, she heard the bike again, then remembered seeing on the map a handful of off-road motorcycle trails spidering out as they wound alongside the highway. Because motorized vehicles weren't allowed on the Pioneer, Tess blocked out the distant drone and shifted her attention to the imposing cedars and Douglas firs that mutely guarded the trail and its occupants, and the deep woods beyond.

Five minutes later, from somewhere in a nearby tree came the rattle of a woodpecker and again, the whine of a motorcycle, this time much closer. Nearing the trail's intersection with Chalk Bluff Road, Tess sensed that the bike was very close, so she slowed to a walk and called for Cooper. Chalk Bluff was nothing more than a dirt-and-gravel road just wide enough for a single car, probably a perfect place for a biker to practice tight turns and quick accelerations without worrying about oncoming cars. She began to step across the road, and then caught the bright blue of the biker's shirt as he hurtled toward her. At the last moment, he swerved and sped away down the road in a cloud of dust.

"What the fuck was that?" Tess screamed after the biker. Cooper stood nearby with a look of panic in his eyes and his tail tucked under his belly. Heart racing and mouth dry as the desert, she called for the dog, bolted across the narrow road, and ran several yards down the trail, even though her legs felt rubberized. Easing herself down onto the ledge of a huge granite boulder, she sat with her head in her hands and tried to get her breathing and heartrate under control. Cooper eased his nose under Tess's arm and licked her face.

"It's okay, fella. Just some stupid asshole who thought it would be a hoot to terrorize a woman and her dog. Some fun, eh?" Cooper lapped her cheek again, and Tess couldn't help but smile. "Let's have a drink of water, okay?" She pulled out a water bottle, took a deep swig then poured some into the dog's collapsible bowl. After a few minutes they were both ready to continue their excursion. "You've probably already forgotten what just happened," she muttered to the dog.

Further along, the trail spanned Lowell Hill Road, another one-lane track of dirt and gravel. This time Tess stopped and listened intently. Silence greeted her, so she skittered across. The trail hugged the highway for a while, then curved and began a slow descent through the woods until it reached the summer-dry Steephollow Creek. By now they'd moved far enough from the road noise that the only sounds were those of the forest: the songlike three-noted *fee-bee-bee* of a mountain chickadee, the insistent tapping of another woodpecker, and the ghostly footsteps of those dusty emigrants.

Finally, the pair reached the topmost spot where a small bench crouched, inviting sojourners to take in the sweeping view of the lush, emerald Bear Valley below. Tess had read and heard about the view, but nothing prepared her for its striking beauty. She sat, nibbling an energy bar and marveling at the scenic landscape stretching out before her as Cooper rested in a shady spot with his head on his paws, eyelids at half-mast.

Twenty minutes later, Tess roused the snoring dog and announced they were heading back. Retracing their route down the mountainside and across the dried-up streambed, once again they followed the route of those hopeful nineteenth-century pioneers through the slumbering woodlands.

Ahead, a hundred yards or so from where the trail crossed Lowell Hill Road, came the solid rumble of a pickup truck. It came into view, the silver-on-blue logo showing it was a Ford—maybe an F-150, but definitely dark blue—then slowly trundled down the road. In a few seconds, it disappeared into the dusty haze thrown up by its wheels, and the engine noise drifted away.

By this time Tess switched to walking, the words of Dr. Bones echoing in her mind: *If you don't quit running, one day you'll have the best-looking legs in the wheelchair division.* Yeah, yeah, Tess thought at the time. One of these days. Now as she approached Lowell Hill, she pondered whether "one of these days" should be now. Well, maybe tomorrow.

Not hearing an oncoming car, she stepped off the trail to cross the road. Two steps later the roar of a truck engine coming to life echoed through the trees, followed by a sudden clash of tires gnawing and spinning out of control on gravel.

Blinded by the curve from seeing down the road, she hesitated, questioning whether to go back or sprint the rest of the way across. She couldn't quite figure out the noise. Could someone have gotten distracted—maybe even hit a deer—and slammed on the brakes suddenly? Maybe the car fishtailed out of control into the trees and underbrush. Then no, she realized, the sound wasn't followed by anything like a car crashing through vegetation. All of this tore through her consciousness during the split second she was momentarily frozen near the middle of the road—then, just as quickly, she knew the safest thing would be to return to the trail where Cooper stood, immobile in uncertainty.

A flash of dark blue exploded over her right shoulder, punctuated by the snarl of an engine. *Close, way too close.* Too far from the shoulder to throw herself out of the way, she instinctively started moving in the same direction as the vehicle in the hopes of moderating the impact. *Impact. Someone is intentionally trying to hit me.* In the instant she felt the heat of the engine on the back of her bare legs, she frog-leaped to her left. The last thing she saw before being thrown in the air were the craggy hills in the distance, outlined against an impossibly azure sky.

21

THE MURMUR OF VOICES. A hand on her arm. Soft, mechanical clicking somewhere off to the right. Then a familiar voice among the others, closer, whispering in her ear. "Tess. *Tess.*"

Struggling against a monumental weight, she couldn't figure out where it was. It seemed like it was in her head, *on* her head, on her chest, like some impossible, immovable beast perching there. The woman standing alongside saw her thrashing weakly and called for help.

More voices. Now a deep one, once again speaking a name, but this time louder. "Tess. It's okay, Tess. *You're* okay."

Against what felt like insurmountable odds, she finally peeled open her eyes. Then the pain came crashing in. Screaming, thundering pain. An axe was embedded in her head. She moaned loudly and tried to lift her hand, but her arm wouldn't move. It was encased in cement. Her whole body felt that way, in fact. The behemoth still sat on her.

"Look at me, Tess. Focus." The man's voice again, insistent. *Who's Tess?*

But she looked up at him as best she could through the searing pain, peering through half-closed eyes.

"Good. Now stay with me. I know it hurts, but we've given you something that should help. Just keep your eyes open, okay?"

She nodded imperceptibly, moaning once more against the pain. Then slowly, the throbbing became a swan rising into the air on silver-white wings, and disappeared. She opened her eyes more fully, and saw scarlet macaws perched on the man's white-coated shoulders. The woman who'd spoken inched closer, carrying a huge golden retriever that was smiling broadly and carrying a purple balloon in its right paw.

"Pretty birds," she croaked. "Pretty dog. Balloon."

"Birds? Dog? Balloons?" The woman's voice carried notes of both confusion and fear.

"I suspect it's the morphine," the man said. "It causes hallucinations in some people. Obviously, one of those people is your sister."

"Can she…does she…know where she is? Or *who* she is?"

"I doubt it. Not yet. The concussion was a bad one, and scrambled things up pretty well inside her brain. Give it a day or so, maybe as long as a week, and hopefully she'll come back to something close to normal."

"Hopefully?? *Close* to normal??" Her voice went up an octave.

"Karen, the outcome of concussions is hard to predict. Some people pop out of them right away and have virtually no ill effects afterward. Some people take longer to heal. We just don't know. The science of brain injury has come a long way, but in many ways it's still a mystery.

"And you need to be prepared for memory loss. Often, concussed people lose what happened just before and just after the incident. But again, it's hard to predict. We'll know more once she comes around fully. Tomorrow I'll switch from the morphine drip to Fentanyl, which is much less likely to cause visual or auditory hallucinations."

He turned to the nurse standing on the other side of the bed. "Let's start with fifty in the morning and see how she responds. If she's still in pain, we can gradually titrate the dose up to 75 over a couple of days. Don't want to go much higher than that, given her size. Then in a couple of days we can try transdermal."

"That means you expect her to be in the hospital for several more days, right?" Worry still fissured Karen's voice.

"At least. Maybe even weeks. It all depends on her healing rate. She's fairly young, in excellent shape, so that should help. The fact that she pulled out of the coma so soon is a good sign."

Both of them gazed at the figure lying still in the bed, her swollen face a mass of purple, interrupted by two horribly black eyes. Her skull swathed in bandages, one arm was cocked at a forty-five-degree angle inside a pristine white cast and her left leg was immobilized by some sort of metal brace. Under the sheet, her entire body was a ghastly conglomeration of black and wine-colored bruises and great blue-purple welts and gashes, wide furrows of missing skin (not so laughingly referred to as road rash), and internally, three broken ribs and a ruptured spleen. They said she was lucky.

Tess didn't know any of this at that moment, since she'd drifted to sleep. She wouldn't know any of it for a while.

Three days later, she was alert and trying desperately to remember what happened. *Shit, this is getting old. Never been in a hospital before, and now twice in just a couple of years. Feels like damn Groundhog Day.* Her mind was a spider's web, and hours of memories seem to have slipped through the webbing to the dark nothingness that lay beneath. She picked at the corners of the web, sometimes plucking out a random thought or recollection, but the main chunks of memory eluded her grasp.

All she knew was that a passing motorist found her, lying on the shoulder of Lowell Hill Road near Nevada City—*how did I get there?*—barely breathing. Life-flighted to UC Davis Medical Center in Sacramento, the closest Level I Trauma Center, she went through surgery for a ruptured spleen and to repair the open fracture of her arm.

Tess remembered getting up that morning well before dawn, calling for Cooper—*Cooper. Where is Cooper?*—and driving somewhere. Beyond that, everything was blank until she woke up with her sister gazing down at her with an agonized expression on her face and tears in her eyes. And a beautiful, balloon-carrying golden retriever in her arms.

Both the dog and the balloons, not to mention the furious whole-body itching, disappeared by the next day, thanks to the replacement of morphine for a Fentanyl intravenous drip. *I've been down this road before,* she thought ruefully, after getting almost killed in Monterey by that creepy emissary from the sex trafficking ring. *Morphine and I just don't get along at all.*

While the Fentanyl kept the worst of the pain at bay, she hated having her arm in a cast. In all her years, she'd never broken so much as a finger, and the bulky piece of plaster on her arm was increasingly exasperating. They couldn't use fiberglass, they told her, because they had to reposition the bone. The leg splint was just as annoying: apparently she suffered a minor tibial shaft fracture, and the splint was there to reduce swelling. But she hungered to be up and walking: lying in the hospital bed all day was not just boring, it was creating painful havoc with her back.

Plus, ever since word leaked that Pulitzer prize-winning journalist Tess Alexander was almost killed in a mysterious hit-and-run accident in the northern California mountains, a swarm of reporters were begging for interviews, just like the ones who'd congregated after her last near-death event. Much as she loved her work, she hated being associated with the packs of media hyenas that passed for reporters these days, and pitied anyone who had the misfortune of straying into their Klieg lights. Now that she was the unwelcome focus of their attention, she empathized even more.

What made it worse was her inability to remember anything about what brought her to this point. And she couldn't find anyone who would tell her about Cooper.

"Sweetie, I've told you three times that Coop is fine," Karen said. "The man who found you looked at his ID tag then contacted the microchip company, who got in touch with your vet, who reached the neighbors you'd listed as a local emergency contact. Kip and Carla are taking good care of your boy, don't worry."

"I'm sorry to be so addle-brained, Karen. I'm sure you *did* tell me before, but I just don't remember." She shifted uncomfortably in the bed, trying to find a position that didn't hurt. "You know, you really need to go home and be with your family." Her sister lived in the oceanside village of Carmel with her husband of many years, Dan. Their daughter Elia was in London with British Airways.

"I'll be fine," Tess continued. "Really, I will. The headache is nearly gone, they're going to get me up and walking tomorrow, and they're weaning me off the IV pain meds. So you see: almost good as new!"

Karen let out a snort. "Good as new, my ass. It's been over a week, and you still look like you've been inside a cement mixer, you have a wrecked spleen, a cast on your arm, and a bum leg. Not to mention the holes in your memory."

"And what, exactly, can you do to affect any of that?"

Her sister was silent in the face of Tess's logic, then breathed a defeated sigh. "But what if something happens, and you…well, you need help. I'd be almost two hundred miles away."

"Yes, you would. And you *need* to be two hundred miles away. I'm not trying to get rid of you, hon—I appreciate you being here more than I can say. It's meant everything to have you here when I was feeling so lost and confused. But those days are over, and now all I need is time. In the interim, I have tons of people around who'll be there if I need help. You can tell that by the fact that this room looks like a damn flower shop."

She was right: just like it was after she was shot in the Del Monte Forest, bouquets and plants and mammoth floral arrangements were arriving in clusters, such that by now they filled every ledge, windowsill, table, and spare inch of floor space in the large and airy room. Tess even asked the nursing staff to take some of them to other patients, because there simply wasn't room for them all.

Karen looked around the room and laughed. "I can't decide if it looks like a florist or a funeral." Then she turned serious. "Who'll take care your yard if I leave?" Karen had been staying at Tess's house since the accident.

"Karen, you know as well as I do that it's not like my property needs the fine touch of a professional gardener. My yard pretty much takes care of itself. Plus, everything that needs water is on an automatic system, so that's not a concern. And Carla said she'd keep an eye out for any renegade gophers or nosy caterpillars."

"Are you *sure*, Tess? Absolutely, positively sure? That you don't need me to stay?"

"Yes, I'm absolutely, positively sure. Your husband needs you much more than I do. *Carmel* needs you. The *world* needs you. Now, go!" She reached up with her one good arm to hug her sister, glad Karen couldn't see the grimace as a lightning-bolt of pain shot through her middle. It would be weeks before she could move normally.

By late that afternoon, following a meet-and-greet torture session with the hospital physical therapist, Tess was miserable and ready for a nap. As she lay there, she started scratching once again at the cobwebs in her mind. Nothing. A vast, empty waste-land.

Until she saw the image of a vehicle. More accurately, a truck. Very dark blue, almost black. Maybe a big GMC or Dodge. Why did she think it was a full-sized pickup? Because it *looked* like a full-sized pickup. It looked like a…suddenly the image sprang up, fully formed. A Ford. A midnight blue Ford F-150.

The problem was, she didn't know what it meant.

Over the next several days, between fearsome skirmishes with her physical therapist and journeys down fifty feet of hall-way with a clumsy, halting gait reminiscent of Frankenstein's monster, Tess continued plucking and pulling at the brain-webbing. It was like trying to pick off a price sticker that refused to come loose.

Yet sometimes as she was in that twilight zone between wakefulness and sleep, shadowy, phantom images drifted through her mind, hovering just out of reach. One a bird in flight, another a sinuous, twisting path leading into the darkness. Then a vast, rolling landscape of trees and rocky peaks spread out before her, blocked by a stone wall. A dun-colored road, bordered by thickets of evergreens. And none of it connected to anything or got her any closer to remembering what happened. The neurologist kept reassuring her that she *could* get the memories back, but Tess recoiled at her use of the word "could." Did that mean they might *never* come back? She simply looked at Tess over the top of her glasses and smiled ambiguously.

Sometimes without warning, the headaches would come screaming back, and while not with their original ferocity, they were enough to make her stomach churn and even the faintest light feel like a bank of blazing LED bulbs. Once again, the bespeckled neurologist clucked reassuringly and pledged that the headaches *should* wane in intensity over time. Tess wasn't crazy about the woman's habit of hedging her bets when it came to the operation of her brain. She wanted certainty.

"You've been paroled!" The hospitalist made the announcement as if he were calling the Kentucky Derby.

"Paroled? Does that mean if I screw up, you'll haul my ass back in here and chain me to the bed?"

Dr. Birney chuckled, then shrugged. "Depends on how *badly* you screw up." Then he turned earnest, his face somber.

"Seriously, you really do need to take it easy for these first few weeks." He saw her start to object and held up his hand. "Tess, listen to me: how quickly and completely you heal is completely dependent on you and how well you follow the medical guidelines laid out by me, the neurologist, and your physical therapy team. The leg fracture is healing nicely, but you still need to use crutches for a while." Looking at her casted arm, he corrected himself. "Okay, crutch. Singular. You also need to do as little bending as possible, and no lifting at all. Remember, you had major abdominal surgery, which is going to hamper you for a while. As for your head, a concussion like yours is no small thing. You were in a coma for three days, and your brain needs time and tenderness—and patience—to recover. The onus is on you to exercise that patience, and not overdo it on *any* level. Your body suffered a major, major trauma, and you can't expect it to bounce back like a ping-pong ball."

Tess sighed loudly, her mouth downturned. "Yeah, I get it. Just veg out for a while. Something I'm not especially good at." That was a huge understatement. People who knew her thought of Tess as the Energizer Bunny, except her batteries never wore down. She was usually up for almost anything, willing to venture down literal or figurative dark alleys that few other journalists other than combat reporters would consider. Some people accused her of taking risks, but she knew how to analyze people and situations, and never—okay, seldom—embarked on anything that would be truly life-threatening.

It wasn't that she was an adrenaline junkie: she refused to set foot on roller coasters, and the idea of doing something like jumping out of a perfectly good airplane or off the edge of a canyon in a hang-glider made her break into a cold sweat of terror. But she was relentless when it came to flushing out the truth, reluctant to let anything stand in her way. It made sense that she would chafe at the notion of just sitting around waiting for the grass to grow. But those omniscient gods of medicine said she had no choice.

We'll see.

22

COOPER WAS AN AMBER TORNADO, racing from one end of the house to the other, dancing circles around Tess, then galloping away to undertake another mad kitchen-to-office sprint. Like a relay racer, he slowed only briefly to snatch a treat out of Tess's outstretched hand, then was off again. Even though he'd been perfectly happy staying with her neighbors for the last month, the dog was clearly ecstatic to see his own human again.

Even though her steadfast dog- and house-sitter Priscilla came by a few times and dusted during those weeks, leaving Tess a beautiful bouquet of roses on the coffee table and a refrigerator filled with fruit and wine and casseroles, the place still felt stuffy and airless. The first thing Tess did when she tottered in the door was throw open every window and the glass doors that opened onto the huge deck off the living room. Cooper leaned against her leg, and she bent over as best she could to pet him.

"Alexa, are you awake?"

The Amazon Echo's digital voice-controlled virtual assistant came to life almost instantly. "Hello, Tess. Yes, I am awake."

"Alexa, play Adele."

After a few seconds, the opening guitar riffs of "Rolling in the Deep" sounded through the house's speaker system. *Damn, that woman has some incredible pipes.* With her casted arm in a sling and only one good leg—the other was still splinted and her foot was in a soft boot—Tess's feeble attempts to take a few dance steps resulted in erratic stops-and-starts that resembled someone in the middle of an electroshock treatment. She couldn't help laughing at her inelegance. *Best leave that for another day.*

As she unpacked the toiletries and clothes her sister brought to the hospital, Tess mulled over the case she was bird-dogging when the accident happened. As far as she knew, there were no new developments: Aspen County was still investigating the murders of both Rennie Matlock and Butch Fogerty, with little luck according to her sources. Phillip called her once when she was in the hospital and seemed authentically concerned about her injuries. He told her things were quiet on his end, swearing he hadn't been doing any snooping or prodding that could put him in danger.

What was odd was the radio silence from Sofia. The last time they spoke was just after she discovered the unidentified folder-within-a-folder buried in the bowels of Matlock's hard drive. Over the last four weeks Tess continuously checked her voice and text messages, but found nothing from Sofia. Phillip said they talked about Tess's mishap, so it seemed a little odd that Sofia hadn't been in touch to see how she was doing. She wasn't exactly worried, more like a little troubled. If she didn't hear something soon, she'd take a chance and call Sofia, hoping it wouldn't blow the woman's cover.

"Tess, I apologize for not being in touch."

"God, Sofia, I was really beginning to worry." Her apprehension began to dissipate once she heard Sofia's lilting voice on the phone.

"My silence was…it was not intentional. My mother in *Venezia*—Venice—became gravely ill, and I flew back there at once to be with her. I know I should have contacted you, but there never seemed to be time."

"No need to apologize, Sofia—your mother should be your priority. How is she?"

"What? Oh. She died." Her words were so abrupt and her voice so wooden that Tess was momentarily stunned, but then realized that grief showed its face differently on different people.

"I'm so, so sorry, Sofia. I can't imagine what you must have been going through."

"Thank you. Phillip told me you were in a very serious accident, and that you could have been killed. Are you all right?"

"Nothing that a few weeks won't take care of. At least, that's what I'm hoping."

"Do you know how it happened?"

"Unfortunately, I don't. Hell, I don't even know how I got on that road. It's just one huge blank page. I've never experienced anything like this in my life."

"Do you, or do the police, know who hit you?"

"Well, *I* sure don't know. As for the police, I don't think they have any leads."

"Do you remember anything?"

"Nope. Nothing."

"What do the doctors say? About whether you will eventually remember?"

Sofia's questions felt a little like a cross-examination. "They use all kinds of words like 'might' and 'could,' which doesn't give me a whole lot of hope. But I'll keep working on it."

"Well, good luck. I really must go now, as Simon is due home. I just wanted to let you know I am back."

Puttering around the house, Tess replayed the conversation in her mind. She couldn't put her finger on what was bothering her about it, but something felt off. *Disconnected* is the word she kept coming back to.

Then came a loud crash, followed by Cooper sprinting through the room at supersonic speed. Hobbling into the kitchen, she found the dishwasher's silverware caddy—which she'd just started unloading when Sofia called—upended, and the floor littered with assorted cutlery.

"Cooper!" she called out in mock anger, then set to the awkward task of cleaning up the mess the playful canine left.

PART FOUR

Truth crept in on languid cat's feet,
in no rush to reveal itself.

~ Joan Merriam

23

 LARGE ENVELOPE FROM SOFIA arrived by overnight courier, along with a note explaining its contents and a flash drive.

Dear Tess,

I thought it would be safer if we both have copies of what I found on Simon's computer. Most of it is a duplicate of what is on the flash drive I have included. I have not been able to figure out what some of the files mean, but others will be self-explanatory. I regret the disturbing character of the photos, but wanted you to see at least some of them with your own eyes. There are more. I have included some of the source URLs that I found in his history, although I suspect I did not find them all. Hopefully this will be enough.

First was the Excel spreadsheet Sofia told her about, containing columns of IP addresses, names, and numbers linked with each one. Several pages long, it was obviously a scanned copy, as Sofia scratched notes and names beside a few of the addresses. "Toby Wrightsman." "William Berkhauser." "S. Enid Christopher." "M. Alphonse McThune."

Logging onto her computer, Tess searched a handful of the names and learned that the "S." designation stood for "Senator," and the "M" for "Mayor." Drilling down, she found that many of the IP addresses without names were masked by either proxy servers or VPNs, meaning she'd have to engage the services of her friendly neighborhood hacker to find out who they were and how they might be connected to Matlock.

Sofia was right: the most common entry was 10000, although a few were other five-figure numbers like 15000 and 50000. They *could* represent dollars, but they could also represent the number of times the guy blew his nose in the last month. There was just no way to know without a meticulous look into their identities, and even that might not reveal anything.

With a sigh of frustration, Tess set the spreadsheets aside. Next was a single piece of paper and a nine-by-twelve-inch white envelope held together by a small binder clip. Stuck on it was a Post-It note that simply said "P file." The top sheet was the list of URLs that Sofia mentioned, all of them darknet links, obvious by the .onion domain suffix the majority of them sported. Some references contained the actual designations of dark web community forums and chat rooms, which Sofia probably discovered by accessing the darknet herself, and it was those names that made Tess inhale sharply, and then made her skin crawl. *ChildChat. PedoForum. YoungLolita. SexyDolls.* The URLs were probably worthless, because administrators of sites like these shuffled and changed them frequently to avoid detection, but anyone with a site's name could probably track it down with little trouble.

Tess wondered if this was what Rennie discovered that she said would ruin Matlock. But if so, how did she find it? It had taken Sofia weeks of hacking to find the files, and from what Tess knew, Rennie had nowhere near that level of computer expertise.

Regardless, it was enormously incriminating stuff, although proving it was Matlock's could be problematic. As before, there was that little matter of probable cause that the authorities would need in order to seize his computer. A list of illicit kiddie-porn URLs was hardly evidence.

She set the paper aside and picked up the large white envelope. Tess pulled out the contents, and instantly dropped them as if they were radioactive, sucking in her breath with a strangled gasp. Here were five or six detailed photos of children and pre-teens engaged in the most perverse sexual acts, some with one another, some with adults. The images were slightly blurry, as if Sofia neither needed nor wanted to print them in high resolution, but there was no doubt about what they were.

Tess sat, her heart jackhammering and her stomach turning cartwheels. If she'd had two good legs she might have run just to escape the vile images, but the best she could do was hobble out of the office and into the living room, where she stopped, shocked and immovable, before dropping onto the couch. Cooper, sun-lazing near the office glass door, followed her into the room, jumped up beside her and lay his head on her lap.

Running her fingers through the dog's silken fur was calming, reassuring her that she didn't need to allow the ugliness she just saw change the way she looked at the world. At people. At goodness and decency.

After a few minutes, she took stock of everything Sofia sent her. There was certainly enough to destroy Simon Matlock, *if* it could be proven. That was a huge, possibly insurmountable "if" unless police had probable cause. As Matlock's live-in partner, Sofia could allow them to search the house without a warrant, but there's a very bright legal line in the sand when it comes to one resident's ability to give law enforcement the right to search another resident's private property *within* their home. Ergo,

Sofia couldn't give permission for them to access Matlock's private computer.

Simon Matlock was even sicker than Tess believed before. Despite the cruelty visited on Rennie, despite the incest, despite the allegations of larceny and illegal bribes and payoffs, his appetite for child pornography stunned her. She wasn't sure she'd have believed it without seeing it with her own eyes, and unfortunately, the images were now laser-burned into her memory. Then she heard Rennie's voice in her head: *What I've found will kill him politically, annihilate his reputation, and put him behind bars for the rest of his fucking life.*

Yeah, kiddie porn would sure do it.

"OK, DJ: do your magic." Tess sat beside her hacker accomplice in his tiny, cluttered loft on the outskirts of Sacramento. She wasn't often allowed into his lair, but for the sake of security she needed to hand-deliver the material for him to decipher. She included the flash drive that Sofia sent, as well as another containing the darknet URLs and pictures.

DJ inserted Sofia's flash drive and took a few minutes to scan through everything. Then he began typing, fingers flying across the keyboard at a mesmerizing speed. Indecipherable digital characters raced across and down the screen, one page spinning after another, a player piano roll on steroids.

Five minutes, then ten, then twenty. Tess moved to the postage-stamp-sized window that looked out on a sooty redbrick wall across the back alley. Not exactly an awe-inspiring view—but then, she didn't suppose DJ spent much time taking in the neighborhood sights.

"OK, here's what's what." His eyes stayed glued the computer screen.

Tess shuffled over beside him and sat down again. He hadn't said so much as a word about her splinted leg or casted arm.

"Most of the IP addresses were masked, like you said," he said in his deadpan voice. "But I unmasked most of them, enough so I have a pretty good idea of what's going on here. These guys are all, like, really heavy hitters, politically. Legislators, big company CEOs, appointed mucky-mucks like the head of planning commissions, JPAs, Transportation Commission, even, like, the PUC. Digging into their emails, it's pretty clear that these figures are dollar amounts. Like, bribes, kickbacks, donations, whatever. That's your territory. Of course, none of this would stand up in court because *technically*," he gave a little snort when he said the word, "you'd need, like, a search warrant to access the records. But this might be enough to put the DA on the trail, unless he's being paid off too. Didn't find anything pointing to that, but, like, you never know."

"Oh-kay," Tess said slowly, "I assume you'll transfer everything you found onto my flash drive."

"Yeah, obviously. *You* sure couldn't find it again by yourself." This came off as condescending, but Tess knew it was just because DJ was so confident in his expertise.

A few minutes later, he removed the first flash drive, handed it back to Tess, and inserted the second one. His reaction was swift.

"What the fuck! Shit, what *is* this?"

"It was hidden in Matlock's Folder Lock."

"How…who…who hacked into it?"

"Better you don't know." Bad enough that DJ knew about the kickbacks or whatever they were. Child porn was another matter entirely, and she regretted having to show him the files.

"Crap. I'm gonna have to sterilize my computer after this." He was only half-kidding.

"I'm really sorry, DJ."

"Yeah. Me, too." He shut down the window that displayed the photos, and began working with the data files.

After ten or fifteen minutes, he came up for air. "This is weird. I could, like, access the chat rooms and stuff, and found some chat logs, but the IP addresses didn't point back to Matlock's computer. Either he used a completely *different* machine and a *different* VPN and a *different* onion browser, or…well, I don't know 'or' what. Maybe, like, it wasn't actually him."

"Wait: what do you mean, 'maybe it wasn't actually him'? The stuff was on *his* computer."

"I know, but black hats have been known to hack into other people's computers and plant shit. It could happen."

"How easily? How easily could it happen? Would someone have to be a real computer nerd like you?"

"Hey, watch who you're callin' a nerd." Tess saw the barest hint of a smile cross his face, then it disappeared.

"Okay: a computer expert."

DJ twisted his lips sideways, and in the ultimate display of a mixed message, nodded and then shook his head. "Nah. Not as good as me, but pretty kickass."

"All right: How hard would it be for someone to use different VPNs?"

"Well, he could chain VPNs, but that's pretty tricky. Or he could set up multiple protocols to connect multiple devices to the same VPN server, but, like, that wouldn't really help disguise his identity…." DJ seemed to be mumbling to himself, but then actually turned toward Tess. "Yeah, like, you can set up separate VPN services on the same computer, each with their own client. Really convoluted, though, and I'm not sure why someone would want to do it. Not really any point to it, for security. Or, like, for hiding your identity."

"Shit, DJ: I thought you were going to be able to give me *answers*, not more questions." She was only half-teasing.

"Well, seeing as how I aim to please, here's a little tidbit for you. Whether this was Matlock or somebody else, he, like, always used the same nickname. Prodigal66. Usually, people choose handles that mean something to them—not likeABC123—so, like, 'prodigal' must have a meaning. Waddya suppose it means to Matlock? And what the fuck does it have to do with this kinda shit?"

Tess was at a loss: something about the handle just didn't fit. "I haven't the vaguest idea. Maybe it means something, maybe it doesn't." But her inner voice told her it *did* mean something. Something important.

DJ didn't respond, just pressed a few dozen more keys, then pulled out the flash drive and tossed it to Tess. "Here ya' go. Good luck figuring this one out. Glad I'm not you."

Tess smiled and passed the young man five one-hundred-dollar bills. "Don't spend it all in one place, okay?"

DJ's eyes momentarily lit up when he saw the cash, then returned to their normal implacable state. "Yeah, like, thanks."

"Like, you're welcome." Tess didn't expect him to get the sarcasm. The word "like" was now so ubiquitous that it felt to Tess like fingernails on a chalkboard. Except that nobody even knew what a chalkboard was any more.

24

TESS HAD HIT A BRICK WALL. She'd amassed some powerful information about Simon Matlock's illegal dealings—again, as DJ said, maybe kickbacks, payoffs, illegal campaign donations, or any combination thereof—but unless she could convince someone like the district attorney to take it to the next level, it was practically worthless. Nothing but idle innuendo and numbers on a page.

The same went for the evidence of dealing in child pornography. Right now, all she had were some nasty chat room logs, along with a stash of incriminating photos that could easily get her arrested if they were found in her possession.

It was like having a boxing match with fog.

She decided to call Javier Coelho and offer to fly down to Los Angeles to meet with him. Maybe he could point a way through the murk.

The next day, she sat across from the former detective enjoying a decadent pastrami sandwich at Langer's Delicatessen on the corner at Seventh and Alvarado streets where it had been since the 1940s. Tucked into this west Los Angeles Latino neighborhood, Langer's boasts what some regulars say is the best hot pastrami in the world.

"Hey, kid: you got mustard on your chin." Coelho grinned and offered Tess his napkin.

Tess laughed and wiped away the offending spot, then took another bite of the overflowing sandwich. "God, it's almost enough to make me want to convert," she joked. "Why is it that no one else can make a pastrami sandwich like this place?"

"I dunno, but even in New York they can't come close to topping this."

After they finished and were settled over a cup of coffee, Tess brought Coelho up to date on the case, and what DJ discovered.

"Well," Coelho said thoughtfully, "seems to me you have a real hornet's nest here." He paused, then said quietly, "I really hate to suggest this, because it scares the hell out of me, but the first thing that pops into my head is that this 'accident' of yours was awfully coincidental. Do the local cops or the CHP have any leads at all?"

"None. There was absolutely nothing left at the scene pointing to the truck that hit me, like paint or a broken headlight or anything."

"Wait: you said 'truck.' How do you know it was a truck?"

Tess frowned, eyes fixed on a spot high on an adjacent wall. She cocked her head slightly to one side as the frown deepened and the silence intensified. Finally, she pulled her gaze back to her companion, but it was more like she was looking *through* him than at him. Her voice was monotone and trance-like. "I'm running along a forest trail with Cooper…trees on both sides…quiet. I'm watching for a road. Dirt, gravel. I see it in the distance. Then a loud clacking—no, crunching—sound. Tires crunching on gravel. Then a roar. An engine. I see it in my peripheral vision, just over my shoulder. A blue—dark blue, almost black—Ford truck. It's just a few feet away, coming fast. I know it's going to hit me; it's actually *aiming* at me. I feel the heat of the engine on the backs of my legs, and then everything goes dark." Her complexion had transformed to ghostly white as she relayed the story. At the end, her eyes lighted on Coelho as if seeing him for the first time, blinking repeatedly to bring him into focus. Her whispered, "Oh," fluttered on the air.

Coehlo stood and moved to her side on the bench seat, then turned toward her and took her hand. "Tess, are you okay?"

"I, uhh…yeah. I'm fine, Javier. Just give me a sec." She shook her head to clear it, then smiled weakly. "Whoa, wasn't expecting that. The docs said memories might come back without warning, or not come back at all, but that was one hell of a jolt."

"You looked like you were watching a movie. A horror movie."

"That's a little like how it felt."

"So, you have two pieces of information you didn't have before: one, why you were on that trail, and two, that you were hit by a dark blue truck. A Ford. Anything else?"

"150. It was an F-150. How the hell I know that is anybody's guess."

"Okay: remember anything else about that day? Beforehand?"

"Mmm…it's really fuzzy. Wait: I'd decided to take Coop on a run that morning. It was still dark, but I wanted to drive up to…to…Nevada City. Above Nevada City. For some reason I see a motorcycle…a dirt bike…speed past me. But beyond that, and the truck coming at me from behind, nothing's there."

"Don't suppose you can remember the driver."

"Nope. Just an outline in the driver's seat."

"Well, at least you remembered something," Coelho said, returning to the other side of the table. "That's a help."

Tess took a sip of her coffee, now barely room temperature. Scanning the room for their waitress, she caught the woman's eye and with a slightly trembling hand, pointed to her coffee cup. Within a minute, the old cup was replaced with a fresh, steaming one, plus a fresh mug for the detective.

"So," said Tess, regaining her composure, "let's go back to where I was when I so rudely interrupted myself. Beyond my uncertainly about how to prove any of what I found about Simon Matlock, I also have the totally unfounded feeling that Fogerty's murder may hold the key to at least some of this."

"Agreed. Somebody who saw Matlock at Rennie's murder scene doesn't just fall off the face of the earth and end up buried near some railroad bridge in the middle of nowhere. It's not like gypsies came in the middle of the night and spirited him away. Nah, the whole thing stinks, and somehow Matlock is part of it. What part, I don't know, but definitely a part."

"Wait: are you saying that Matlock might not be the killer? Who else would it be?"

"Don't know the answer to that one, little lady," Coelho said with a smile, fingers smoothing his moustache. "But I believe in keeping my options open, my cards hidden, and my eyes on the horizon."

"Jeeze," Tess laughed. "Talk about mixed metaphors." Then she turned serious. "Thanks to Dr. Dambudzo, Rennie's autopsy gave them enough to reopen the case—but do you think the local and state investigators will find enough to implicate Matlock in her killing? Or are they on a fool's errand?"

"Can't say on that one either," said Coelho. "The problem is the lack of forensic evidence like prints, fiber, hair, DNA. You know the drill. Ruling it a homicide is a step in the right direction, but just finding Matlock's antique razor at the scene doesn't prove he was responsible. All it proves is that the razor was the murder weapon. They need to put it in his hands, in the murder room, and right now there doesn't seem to be a way to do that."

"Hold on: you said DNA. They didn't do any testing for DNA evidence because they believed it was a suicide. Now that it's officially a murder, do you suppose…I mean, with a killing that violent, and with something like a razor, is there a chance Matlock could have gotten cut and left his DNA on it?"

Coelho paused, then nodded. "Sure. Lots of times when a killing involves a knife or something sharp, especially if there's any kind of a struggle, someone other than the victim gets cut. I'm sure the state guys will investigate that if they have any sense at all."

"What about the GPS?"

"All that proves is that he *bought* a GPS locator. Doesn't mean he attached it to Rennie's car, or that he followed her to Hammond Mills, or that he killed her."

Tess bobbed her head. "Yeah, yeah, I know all that. Intellectually. Just that sometimes wishful thinking gets in my way."

"Don't tell me the great Tess Alexander is actually fallible?"

"Very funny. Yes, indubitably fallible. If you'd seen me lying in the hospital several weeks ago, you'd have no doubt of that."

"I'm just glad you're okay. Well, more or less okay. Gotta say, that cast doesn't add a lot to your *je ne sais quoi*."

The two joked and chatted their way through one more cup of coffee, and then Tess glanced at her phone. "I'd better get moving, Javier, or I'll miss my return flight. Thanks again for meeting me on such short notice—and I really hope that somewhere in the dark recesses of your mind, you'll figure out a way for me to make the case against Matlock."

Two hours later, the plane was cruising at thirty-five thousand feet over the brown, summer-parched landscape of the great Central Valley, as flat as if it were ironed. Stretching some 450 miles over eighteen counties, the valley is one of the world's richest agricultural regions. While appreciating its culinary bounty, it was nevertheless one of Tess's least favorite places in the state. She hated its oppressive summer heat and impenetrable winter fog, and most of all the tedium of the land itself. She looked out the tiny window to the east, where the great Sierra rose in the distance. *Just give me my mountains.* As she stared, a face appeared in her field of vision, barely visible, but there. She put her palm against the window, trying to grasp it, but the apparition moved away, then slowly faded, leaving only the cloudless sky and yet another enigma to solve.

25

IT STARTED WITH ANOTHER PHONE CALL.

"Ummm…is this Tess Alexander?"

"Yes—who am I speaking to?"

"My name is Stella, and uhh, you stopped by our place at Two Pines a couple months ago. You gave my husband your card, said if we remembered anything about the night that woman was murdered, to call you. My husband don't know I'm calling…didn't want me to call…." her voice trailed off.

"That's okay, Stella. No need for me to tell him."

First a throaty sigh of relief, then she continued. "Okay, great. Well, uhh, I *did* see something. Someone. Heard it first, then looked out the window and saw somebody stuck in the slush, and Butch was tryin' to get them out. The car didn't look like a four-wheel drive, and she for sure didn't know how to drive in the snow. Was makin' a real mess out of it."

"Excuse me: you said 'she.' Was the driver a woman?"

"Oh, yeah, thought I said that. Dark hair, pretty, from what I could tell, but didn't get a great look at her. Anyways, thought you'd want to know."

"Could you tell what kind of car it was?"

"Not like the beaters around here. Expensive. Big. Don't know one car from another."

"Color?"

"Dark. Hard to tell, 'cause there's no lights in front."

"Any idea of what time it was?"

"Mmmm, I'm not sure… it was late. Oh, wait: the news just ended. Ralph was already asleep, but I like to stay up and watch them late-night shows. So, it was just after *The Tonight Show* started, maybe around 11:45 when I heard the ruckus outside. Butch was really pissed that he had to go out in that shitty weather."

The meaning of Stella's revelations eluded Tess. A strange woman in a big luxury car shows up at a seedy no-tell motel in the middle of a blizzard, then leaves just before midnight after doing…what? Meeting her drug dealer? Not in that kind of weather. Why the hell was she there? And *who* was she? She certainly couldn't be connected in any way to Rennie's murder, but her presence was bewildering nevertheless. Just one more damn thread to follow.

"Is there anything else you can tell me?"

"Nah, that's it." The line went dead.

Tess sat down, thought it all over, and wrote out a mini-timeline.

8-8:30   Matlock arrives.
11:15   Rennie calls me.
11:45   Mystery Woman gets stuck in the snow.
?? Sometime between 11:45 and 12:30, Matlock and the woman leave.
12:30   I arrive & discover Rennie.

That meant the murder occurred sometime after 11:15 and before Tess's arrival around 12:30. She grabbed the sheriff's Incident Report to refresh her memory. The Deputy Coroner showed up a little after 2:00 and concluded that Rennie had been dead between two and four hours.

But that didn't square with Matlock arriving so much earlier. Unless, of course, the man took his time with Rennie. Time to make everything perfect. She winced at the idea. She really *did* need to find out the identity of the mystery woman. If she saw something, it could help break the case wide open.

Exactly how she was going to find her was another matter.

"We caught a break on the Fogerty case." The perpetually taciturn Lieutenant Schiffler sounded positively jaunty.

"What kind of break?" Tess's pulse began to sprint.

"We got a hit on the gun that killed him: turns out it was linked to a couple of murders-for-hire in Reno and Tucson last year."

Tess was taken aback by this news. "Jesus. A hit man?"

"Would seem that way."

"So, the question of the day is, why would a hired gun want to off somebody like Butch Fogerty?"

"That's something we haven't figured out yet." The buoyancy disappeared.

"Okay, so not just any Joe or Jill on the street knows how to hire an assassin, right? Plus, I don't imagine they come cheap…"

"$30,000 to $50,000 seems like the going rate. Unless you can find some nut-case on the dark web who'll do it for a hundred bucks."

"Right. That means whoever hired this guy has money. And probably power. And knows enough about the underbelly of society to find the hit man in the first place. Remind you of anyone?" Tess knew she was playing with fire, but figured it was worth a shot.

A long-suffering sigh made its way across the phone lines. "Are we back to that again? Really, Ms. Alexander, there's just no evidence to tie Senator Matlock to Butch Fogerty's—or for that matter, Rennie Matlock's—death."

"But the two *killings* are tied together, don't you agree? It's beyond coincidental that a woman is murdered in a squalid backwoods motel, and just a couple of months later, the manager of that motel is also murdered."

"Yes, I've come to suspect that the two are somehow connected, but that connection is tenuous at best."

"Unless you believe that Fogerty actually *did* see Simon Matlock that night."

"Yes, unless you believe that. Unfortunately, we have no evidence to support that contention, and we can't fashion a case to fit a suspect. It just doesn't work that way."

Tess knew he was right, and knew she had to find something beyond Butch Fogerty's assertion that he saw Matlock.

Two days later, Schiffler called again with more news: state investigators ordered a DNA analysis of the blood on the murder weapon.

"How long will the analysis take?"

"Probably a while. The Bureau of Forensic Services has a pretty substantial backlog. It could take anywhere between thirty days and six months."

"Oh, great. Meantime, the case is dead in the water."

" 'Dead in the water' is a bit of a loaded phrase. We're continuing to work it as best we can, but there just isn't a lot to go on."

Tess debated about whether to tell him what she learned from Stella about the anonymous woman at Two Pines, but figured he'd be just as flummoxed by its significance as she was and would likely brush it aside.

Might be one of those clues that wasn't really a clue at all, one that leads nowhere except straight into a blank wall.

☍

At La Note restaurant on Berkeley's Shattuck Avenue with her oldest friend Barbara, Tess was in the middle of a delicious sandwich of French ham and melted Emmental cheese on a lightly buttered half sweet baguette.

"I guess I'm lucky that it wasn't a worse break," she said, referring to her leg, "but I really hate having to wear this……" Suddenly she stopped with the sandwich halfway to her mouth, and her eyes lost focus. Another memory missile.

"Tess, are you okay?" Barbara leaned forward with concern.

Silence. A sliver of ham escaped and landed on Tess's plate.

Then finally, eyes still unfocused, she spoke in a dry, wooden chant." It's… I'm…I…remember…"

After about thirty seconds, her head shuddered and she looked across the table at her friend with a feeble smile. "Wow. Just got smacked with another memory of my accident. It seems to happen that way: no alert beforehand. At the risk of delivering a terrible pun, it's like getting hit by a truck."

Barbara laughed in spite of herself. "So, tell me: what was the memory?"

"Well, I'm driving up into the hills on Highway 20, a really beautiful road that someone once told me is actually a State Scenic Route. I'm just poking along, pretty much all alone on the road that early in the morning. Then I pull over to look at this really incredible view of the canyon and mountains. Funny, one of my earlier bits-and-pieces memory was of this short, long rock wall with lichen on it. I couldn't figure it out then, but now I realize it was that overlook at…at…oh: Washington Ridge, I think.

"Then I see myself starting to walk across a gravel road, and a dirt bike comes racing by and almost hits me. I can't see his face, but his hair, kind of blondish brown, is sticking out at the back of his helmet. Then I'm standing with Cooper on the hiking trail, on the *other* side of that same gravel road, going in the opposite direction. Finally a repeat memory of the crash, except this time as I look back over my shoulder, I see the driver in my peripheral vision, but his face is blank, like one of those cardboard cutout head-on-a-stick things."

"That's it?"

"Yep, that's it. Not much help, but at least now I know I *can* bring more memories back from the dead. If I could only see his face…"

"You will, Tess. It'll come back, I know it. Then maybe you'll have at least part of the answer to what happened."

26

TIME TO DO SOME SERIOUS DIGGING into the Excel file Sofia found on Matlock's computer. Tess hadn't a clue if she could find anything useful, but thanks to DJ she had some leads and a road map. Who knew where it might lead.

The green spreadsheet with its list of names, numbers, and hyperlinks popped up on her computer screen. She went back to the flash drive's menu, clicked on the file containing DJ's data, then split the screen so she could view both documents.

DJ found names for almost all the IP addresses, even though they were hidden behind proxy walls or VPNs. There had to be at least a hundred of them. Not alphabetized, so apparently in random order. She went through Sofia's original list and found two with the "S" designation and three "M"s. Two senators, three mayors. But according to DJ, that was just the tip of the iceberg: these names represented not just legislators and mayors, but public officials at every level.

Now came the biggest challenge: figuring out the meaning of the five-digit numbers beside each name. She decided to start with the senators, since much of their lives were in the public domain. Senator Enid Christopher was the first to appear. *Okay, Senator Christopher: let's see what dance steps you've been doing with Simon Matlock.*

The FPPC, the state Fair Political Practices Commission that's the repository for all the financial disclosure forms that every public official has to file, was her first stop. A notice at the top of the FPPC website read: *This search only includes state-level elected officials, elected judges, city councilmembers, and certain other officials. Local planning commissioners, special district board members, school board members, and many other local officials do not file Form 700s directly with the FPPC. You must contact the local filing officer to determine how to obtain Form 700s for these other officials.*

Tess groaned, knowing that according to what DJ said, at least some of the names belonged to local officials. It was going to be a long, long day.

There were six different categories of FPPC forms, from Candidate Statement of Economic Interests to Amendment to Statement of Economic Interests to Recipient Committee Campaign Statement. Tess clicked on "all," then "View Forms," and started reading. She skimmed over Schedule A, listing stock and bond ownership, and moved on to Schedule A-2, showing business entity investments, income, and assets. Nothing remarkable there.

Schedule B itemized income from real estate, including some from rental properties, but nothing earth-shaking. Schedule C showed income, loans, and business positions. Again, nothing of interest. Schedule D and E recorded income from gifts, travel payments, and advances, all of them paltry amounts.

The problem was, the FPPC records went all the way back to the late 1970s, and Tess had to look at the forms for every year Senator Christopher had been in office or was a candidate for office. Ditto for every other state-level bigwig on DJ's list.

This wasn't just going to be a long day, it was going to be a long week.

As the days ticked by, Tess recorded the FPPC information about the financial disclosures of each state official on Matlock's list, but none of it was even vaguely suspect. Of course, what officeholder would intentionally reveal that he got a free Maserati in exchange for a political favor?

She closed down the FPPC site and moved on to the Secretary of State and its campaign finance disclosure system called CAL-ACCESS. Now that DJ uncovered the names behind the hidden IP addresses, Tess could use the site's Power Search and input each name in the Matlock database to see if they made any campaign contribution in any of his Senate runs.

That's where she struck gold.

Every name in the Excel file turned out to be a campaign donor to either Matlock's first or second senatorial campaign. Tess was under no illusion that the dollar amounts recorded in the database would align with the numbers in the Excel file: CAL-ACCESS showed only *legal* campaign contributions, limited to $4,200 per Senate candidate, whereas the numbers beside the names on Matlock's list clearly represented each donor's actual bequest. Welcome to the era of kleptocracy.

But once again, none of this was proof. It was only numbers on a page that could have come from anywhere, maybe from someone with a grudge against Matlock. Every time Tess unearthed a worm of suspicion, it tunneled back underground before it could be dissected.

The next afternoon, Lieutenant Schiffler's name popped up on her caller ID.

"Hi, Lieutenant. Please tell you have some good news. I'm drowning here."

"As a matter of fact, I do. Butch Fogerty's killer's been caught."

"Whoa—really? How? Where?" Tess reached for a pen and paper.

"An off-duty Sac City officer was parking on the 6th floor of a downtown garage when he witnessed a shooting and saw a man running toward a parked car. He called it in, then had them call the attendant to shut down the garage. The suspect got to the blocked exit, the officer boxed him in, and arrested him."

"The guy that got shot…"

"Hurt bad, but he lived."

"So, how did you find out the shooter was the hit man?"

"He was carrying a Ruger SR22 Rimfire, and a few days later ballistics proved it's the gun that killed Fogerty and two other victims in Nevada and Arizona, and also shot the victim in the garage. The shooter wasn't exactly talkative before we informed him of that, but afterward was more than willing to give up the 'clients' who hired him. Said they found him on the darknet."

Inexplicably, goosebumps sprouted on Tess's arms. *Why'd that happen? Something about the darknet reminded me of some-thing…*

"…was a woman."

"Sorry, Lieutenant, I missed that."

"I said, the person who hired him to kill Fogerty was a woman."

Tess was stunned. *How could that be: a* woman? *Who?* Her mind was racing, trying to search out an explanation. "Did he identify her?"

"I'm not at liberty to give you anything more, but the simple answer is no. Said they only met once, and she was disguised. I figure he'll cough up more once the DA and his lawyer finish negotiating a deal."

"So, who is this guy?"

"His name's Benny Barbosa. Benjamin. Has a long rap sheet, including robbery, assault and battery, attempted arson, witness tampering, fraud, and one homicide that he skated on. The feds have never been able to nail him for doing a contract kill, even though they've known about him for years. He's left victims behind in every state in the west, and probably further."

"So, I presume the FBI will be taking him into custody?"

"Yep. Dear old Butch Fogerty could never have imagined that he would be the lynchpin in a nationwide federal case against a hired killer."

Tess chuckled at the thought of Fogerty becoming a celebrity, even in death. God sure had a wicked sense of humor.

"Well, this thing about a woman is sure a new wrinkle," Tess said, then steeled herself for Schiffler's onslaught once she finished talking. "I need to tell you something that may or may not be related, Lieutenant: I got a phone call a couple of weeks ago from someone at Two Pines who said they saw a woman on the night of Rennie's murder, somewhere around 11:45. Apparently her car got stuck in a slush-pile, and Butch had to help her get clear. Was pretty pissed, I gather, that he had to leave his nice warm bed and go out in the storm. Anyway, the person couldn't describe or identify the woman except that she was attractive, and drove a big, expensive car."

The silence at the other end of the phone spoke volumes. When he finally spoke, his voice was gruff and irritated. "Is there some reason you waited until now to tell me this?"

"I apologize, Lieutenant. Honestly, I just didn't think it meant anything. And frankly, I also didn't think you'd take it seriously. But now that a woman is apparently involved in Fogerty's death…well, I'm sorry. I didn't intend to withhold anything."

"What's this person's name? The one who called you."

"Now it's me who's not at liberty to say." She interrupted Schiffler's expletive. "But I *can* tell you that the person still lives at Two Pines. I can also say that this individual is part of a couple, and the other partner didn't want this person to get involved, so you'll need to tread carefully."

Again, silence from the lieutenant. "Okay, at least that's something to go on," he grumbled.

Tess could only hope she wouldn't stay on his shit-list for too long.

27

E D WILLOUGHBY'S VOICE GROWLED across the ethereal cell phone network. "Got something for you."

"Don't suppose it's a raise?"

Her editor gave a guttural laugh. "Yeah, in your dreams. Nah, it might be something even better: a tip."

"About what? And by the way, good morning."

"Hadn't noticed." Peevish, as usual. "About your little mishap up in the hills. Caller—sounds like a younger guy on the recording, really nervous—said a dark blue pickup truck came into a body shop with the front end a mess, cracked-up bumper, smashed headlight, huge dent in the hood. Driver said he'd hit a deer.

"While this body-shop guy was getting the truck ready for repairs, he saw some bright green nylon fabric stuck in the front grille, covered with blood. Figured that most deer don't wear pants, so he mentioned it to one of the other guys in the shop, who blew it off and threw the material in the trash. Fellow couldn't stop thinking about it, so he fished it out and wrapped it in a plastic bag.

"That night he saw a news story that the cops were looking for information about a hit-and-run on Highway 20 above Nevada City, that the woman who got hit was you, and you were wearing bright green nylon shorts and a light green T-shirt. He Googled you, saw you worked for *Panorama*. At first, he didn't want to get involved, didn't want to get in trouble for not reporting it right away, but it just kept eating at him, so he called us."

"Well, it *was* a dark blue pickup that hit me, Ed. Don't suppose the guy said it was a Ford F-150?"

"One and the same."

Breath caught in Tess's throat. Other than the sporadic surfacing of her memories, this was the only real lead they had about what obviously *wasn't* an accident. She hadn't spoken about her suspicions to anyone, but Javier Coelho reasoned it out right away. His words--*The first thing that pops into my head is that this 'accident' of yours was awfully coincidental*—rang in her ears. What he *didn't* say out loud, because he didn't have to, was that the crash was somehow related to Matlock. She couldn't prove it, but knew it nevertheless. The problem was, just like every other aspect of the story that got uncovered, it just didn't fit with anything else.

The whole case was like the frayed end of a rope, with individual strands raveling out in a dozen different directions, each one disconnected from the other. She would start off following one thread, then another appeared, and another, and another. Cliona's murder…Rennie's killing…Phillip's past…Sofia's discoveries…the hit-and-run…Simon's corruption…Fogerty's homicide…a hired killer and a mystery woman…and all the little filaments that scattered out from each one.

Willoughby said the kid only left a cell phone number, and so far hadn't returned their calls. "Maybe you'd have more luck," he added.

Knowing she was once again attempting a potentially wrath-inducing end-run around the police, Tess took down the number and made the call. Voicemail.

"Hi, this is Tess Alexander. I'm the woman who was hit by the pickup truck in the Sierra, near Highway 20. I'd really like to talk with you about what you found at the shop, so please give me a call back." All she could do now was hope.

That night around nine, her phone rang. Caller ID unknown. "This is Tess."

Static on the line, but she could hear breathing. She waited.

"Uhhh…this is the guy you called. Earlier. From the body shop outside Grass Valley." His voice quavered, and he took deep, uneven breaths before almost every word.

"Hi. I'm really glad you called back."

"You're, umm, not recording this or nothin', are you?"

"Nope. Couldn't do that without telling you first."

"Oh. That's good."

"So, what's your name?"

"Is that important?"

"Only so I can call you something other than 'Dude.' "

The barest hint of a chuckle. "Yeah, okay. How about…uhh…John."

Right. As in, John Doe. "Okay, John: why don't you tell me what went down?"

The young man repeated his story for Tess, almost exactly as Willoughby told her, but with slightly more detail. The strip of material was actually wedged in the space between the grille and the front of the hood, scrunched up and not visible unless you were really looking. It wasn't *covered* in blood, but had a lot of blood splatters on it. There was also something that looked like blood on the hood where it was dented. And some hair caught in the windshield wiper. Deer blood and hair, the driver said, but the kid didn't believe him, especially not after he found the material. And especially not after seeing the news report.

"Did they take pictures of the truck? Like, for insurance?" Crap: she was slipping into like-speak.

"Huh-uh. The guy was paying cash."

"I know you saved the fabric, but don't suppose you saved any of the hair?"

"Nah. Probably should have, huh?" He sounded almost forlorn.

Tess tried to hide her disappointment. "No, it's okay. At least you have the material. That's huge."

"What…what do we do now? Like, I can't afford to get fired. Or to get in trouble with the cops." The fear raised its head again.

Tess wasn't sure how to answer without terrifying him even more. "Okay, John—and I know 'John' isn't your real name, is it?"

"No, it's not," he said resignedly.

"Well, we can talk about that later. But let me ask you something: The other guy you talked to at the shop doesn't know you recovered the piece of my shorts from the trash, does he?"

"No. Nobody seen me pick it up."

"And you still have it?"

"Yeah. In one of them zip-top plastic bags."

"Good. Just hold onto it. Don't touch it any more than you already have. And don't say anything to anyone, okay? You haven't, have you?" She was genuinely concerned for his safety if word got back to the driver.

"No. I was too…scared to tell anybody."

"All right. First, know that you *won't* get into trouble with the cops. You didn't do anything wrong, except not reporting what you found right away, but that's not a problem because you didn't know it involved a crime until later. But here's the hard part: you have to turn it into the police *now*. It's evidence, and you can be prosecuted for hiding evidence, and that's just not worth it. Ideally, the police would have collected it themselves from the pickup, but since *you're* the one who found it, you need to be the one to take it to the police. I'm sorry, but you just don't have a choice."

Again, nothing but static. Tess was afraid she'd lost him.

"Are you still there?"

"Yeah." He barely squeaked out the word.

"I know this isn't the way you wanted things to turn out, John—but you've done the right thing by coming to me. Now you just have to keep on doing the right thing by going to the police." Then she had a thought. "Would it help if I went with you?"

"M…maybe. Yeah."

"Okay, we can work that out. But before we do, I need to ask you a couple more questions. First, did the driver tell you his name?" Tess figured it would be phony, but it was worth a try.

"Yeah: Peter Jones."

Phony for sure. Too simple. "Anyone at the shop write down the license plate?"

"Yeah, the boss did. Like, the guy didn't want him to, so my boss said he wouldn't, but then he did. Said the guy's story seemed a little fishy. He got the VIN, too."

Tess was elated. "Terrific. That, along with the fabric from my shorts, should be all the police need to arrest this guy."

A few more seconds of silence. "Do you…you don't think I'll, like, have to testify or nothin', do you?"

"I wouldn't think so: with this much evidence, the guy will probably just cave, and the case will never go to trial." *At least, that's what I hope. If there ever was someone who'd rabbit rather than sit in the witness box, this kid is probably him.*

"One more question, John: do you remember the license plate?"

"I only remember it had three eights in it. But there was those, like, little barcode stickers on the truck windows—front, side, back—and that means it's a rental. The guy musta thought it was cheaper to get it fixed himself and not turn it in to his insurance. And not tell the rental outfit."

No, it's probably not a good idea to tell Hertz that you carried out an intentional hit-and-run on someone with their vehicle.

"Okay, that's really good information. You've been great, and I really mean that. It'll be because of *you* that this guy is caught and punished for trying to kill me. You're a real hero." Tess was worried that the fellow could flake out at the last minute, maybe just disappear without going to the police, and one way to help ensure his cooperation was to stroke his ego. Make him understand just how valuable he was. "Are you willing to tell me your real name now?"

"Yeah, I guess so. It's Rodney Weatherstone. Rod is okay."

"Thanks, Rod. I appreciate you trusting me enough to tell me."

Tess suggested they meet the following day at Java John's in downtown Nevada City. From there, it was just a fifteen-minute walk to the Rood Center, Nevada County's administrative headquarters where the sheriff's offices were. Rod said he could find the café, and that he'd meet her at 10. I'll call in sick, he said, because that's what I'll be feeling after I talk to the cops.

"Don't forget to bring the evidence bag," Tess reminded him.

When they hung up, Tess added Rod Weatherstone's name to the incoming phone number, saving them both. Just in case the kid decided to bail.

Rod Weatherstone was a chunky, long-haired kid who couldn't be more than nineteen or twenty. He had carrot-red hair, freckles and a nasty case of rosacea, a serious overbite, and ears with huge, floppy lobes. Tess could only imagine the bullying he'd suffered over the years.

She bought him an iced mocha with a generous glob of whipped cream and chocolate sprinkles on top, then led the way up Broad Street, onto Orchard Street at the Y, then across Highway 49 and into the administrative complex. During their walk, the young man switched from being monosyllabic to a veritable chatterbox, telling Tess about his work at the body shop and the 1956 Chevy he was restoring. He seemed happy for the momentary distraction from the plastic bag in his pocket and the looming sit-down with the sheriff.

The encounter went much better than Tess envisioned. The sergeant in charge of the case barely reacted when Tess explained about the tip to *Panorama* and her decision to follow it up. In fact, he told Tess he would keep her informed as the investigation proceeded.

"We've got it from here," he said, looking directly at Tess with what almost looked like a twinkle in his eyes. "Nothing more for you to do. Except be careful." She realized he was telegraphing that he was well aware she would stay involved, and that he wouldn't try to stop her. "Oh, one other thing. Say hello to Javier the next time you talk. We go back a long way." *So that explains my amnesty. Let's just hope it holds.*

"Thank you, Sergeant Ross. I hope you'll keep me informed. And I'll certainly let you know if anything else comes up on my end."

He nodded, a vaguely bemused expression on his face. "Good deal."

They had reached an unspoken agreement.

28

THAT AFTERNOON, TESS CANVASSED the few regional car rental agencies that offered pickup trucks. Using the license plate information from Rod Weatherstone, it didn't take long before she had a hit. It was a small, one-office operation that specialized in renting commercial vehicles, and the manager was especially cooperative when she said she was investigating a hit-and-run that this pickup might have been involved in.

"So, Mr. Buskirk, what can you tell me about the truck?"

"Well, the guy brung it back, three days late, and said he'd hit a deer up in the hills somewhere. Said he went ahead and had the damage fixed so's he didn't have to file an insurance claim. Told him that wasn't what he agreed to in the contract, but by then it was too late. Not a damn thing I could do about it. Just hadda hope it was a decent repair job."

"I presume you got his driver's license information?"

"Yeah, o' course. Uhh, what department you say you were with?"

"I didn't say." Tess wasn't about to impersonate law enforcement, but the guy opened up when she used the word "investigate." Who was she to disabuse him of his opinions? People make assumptions all the time.

"Oh. Okay."

"Do you have that information, Mr. Buskirk?" she pressed.

"Yeah, just gimme a minute to find it." A file cabinet drawer clanged open, and papers rustled in the background as the man mumbled to himself. Another phone began ringing. "Uhh, lemme get that. Hold on." The line went silent and stayed that way for a good two minutes.

When Buskirk came back, he sounded confused. "That was the Nevada County sheriff's office. They was askin' the same questions as you, and I told 'em that I was already talkin' to a cop on the other line. They says no, that this was the first time they'd called. So, who *are* you?"

"I never told you I was a police officer, Mr. Buskirk. I merely said I was investigating the case."

"Shit! I dunno who you are or what you want, lady, but I'm not sayin' another word." He slammed down the phone.

Tess was disappointed, but not surprised. It was a gamble, and if the Nevada County SO hadn't called when they did, she would have succeeded. The good thing is that Buskirk would give the sheriff the information they needed to identify the driver, and that would provide resolution to at least one mystery.

That resolution upended Tess's world.

Sergeant Ross called her two days later with the news that they made an arrest. "Do you know a Phillip Matlock?"

A legion of spiders crawled across her skin, and for a few seconds, no sound came out of her mouth.

"Ms. Alexander, are you still there?"

"Y…yes. Could you repeat what you just said?"

"I said we arrested Phillip Matlock for the hit-and-run. Do you know him?"

Her mind raced over every interaction with Phillip, frantically searching for a key to unlock the puzzle of this bewildering information. Then a picture zoomed into her mind of a dark-haired young man in sunglasses, framed in the window of a pickup truck. It *was* Phillip. Her deep breath emerged as a labored wheeze, as if all the air had somehow been squeezed from the room. Finally, she found her voice. "Yes, I know him. Quite well, in fact."

"He said it was his father's idea. Do you know *him?*"

The spiders resumed their unnerving march. "I think perhaps I need to come in and talk with you."

"Absolutely, Ms. Alexander. Anything you can do to help us understand what's going on."

I'm not sure you'll be able to understand. I sure as hell don't.

An hour later she was sitting with Sergeant Ross and the crusty sheriff Aaron Dreyfus, who looked none too happy to have her there. It took nearly forty minutes for Tess to describe the major twists and turns of the story, from Rennie's killing up to her own hit-and-run, and explain the few connections between events she could decipher. She didn't mention Sofia or the files the woman purloined from Matlock's computer, though she made clear her own suspicions about the man's role in both Rennie's and Butch Fogerty's deaths.

Utter skepticism paraded across the sheriff's face. "Ms. Alexander, do you have any idea of who you're accusing? That's *Senator* Simon Matlock."

"I know very well who I'm accusing, Sheriff. Unfortunately, I don't have any rock-solid proof...."

Dreyfus interrupted. "And I can guarantee you won't find any. The whole idea that the senator could be implicated in not one, but *two* murders is preposterous."

"But how do you explain Phillip's contention that his father convinced him to murder me?"

Dreyfus glared at the sergeant accusingly, but Ross refused to return his gaze. Neither man responded.

Finally, the sheriff stood, signaling the end of the interview. "I'm sure we'll have further questions, Ms. Alexander. I suggest you not plan on leaving the country—or the state—any time soon."

Back home, she played and replayed every conversation she'd had with Phillip, everything she knew about the man. The ambiguity persisted, hanging like a veil of dark, impenetrable smog.

The next day came word from Sergeant Ross that they'd seized Phillip's computer. A few hours later he called back. "I'm not officially authorized to reveal this, but because Javier thinks so highly of you, and since you're so closely involved in the case…." He allowed the comment to drift unfinished. "I trust this isn't going to show up in the press?"

"Nothing about this case is going to show up in the press, Sergeant, until it's over and done."

"Fine. We discovered a cache of child pornography on Phillip Matlock's computer."

The news hit Tess like a grenade. Once again, she found it difficult to regain her voice. "What kind of…never mind. Sergeant, I need to see Phillip Matlock. But first, I need to meet with you."

"Uhh, all right," he said carefully, "but can I ask why?"

"I'll explain when I see you. How about in two hours?"

☙

Tess fanned out the six photos from Matlock's computer across the conference room table. "I need you to know these are *not* mine. I understand that even possession of child pornography is a crime, but when I tell you where these came from, I think you'll understand."

The sergeant's eyes narrowed as he scanned the photos.

"You recognize them, don't you?"

One by one Ross turned them face-down. "What makes you say that?"

"Because they're the exact same images you found on Phillip Matlock's computer." It was a shot in the dark, but Tess was fairly sure she'd hit the mark. The moment Ross looked up, she knew she had.

"Maybe you'd better tell me where these came from, and where you got them." His affable disposition was gone, replaced by a tight-lipped, just-the-facts-ma'am law enforcement demeanor.

Tess explained as best she could without implicating Sofia, handing Ross the printout of darknet URLs and chatroom names. He studied the information for several minutes, absently biting the inside of his cheek. "So who's Prodigal66?"

"That's the strange part, Sergeant: without a doubt, these came from Matlock's computer, but now that I know about Phillip, I'm suspecting *he's* Prodigal66. The prodigal son?" A nod from the officer. "But what I don't get is how the hell the pictures got from Phillip's laptop to his father's computer. It's pretty improbable that they would share this same…interest. So that's why I need to speak to Phillip. I think he'll talk to me."

Thirty minutes later, Tess was sitting in the Wayne Brown Correctional Facility's visiting area across from a pale, defeated Phillip Matlock. His dehydrated lips stuck together every time he tried to open his mouth, nd he laced and unlaced his long fingers as he stared at the floor.

"Phillip, look at me." No response. "*Phillip.*" He jumped at the force of the commandment and glanced sideways at her.

"Phillip," she said softly, "I know what you did—the hit-and-run—but I don't get why. You've told the police that your father convinced you to do it, but for what reason?"

"I dunno."

"You don't *know?*" The authoritarian voice again, full of skepticism.

"I…I…he just made me. Forced me."

She took one last stab at it. "I have a hard time believing that your father could convince you to do something like attempted murder, for no reason."

He just shook his head, his eyes back on the floor.

She tried a different approach. "I have something to tell you: the same photographs that were on your computer, were on your father's. Can you explain that?"

Phillip's head snapped up, and his eyes widened so much that she could see the whites. "Wha…what? What do you mean?" His voice was barely above a whisper.

Tess proceeded to explain about the locked files and the record of URLs and chatroom logs on Matlock's computer, without telling him who found them.

"You're facing some fairly serious prison time, but the DA might be willing to go easier if you could help us figure out how the same porn ended up on two different computers. Especially since yours was in San Jose, fifty miles away from your father's."

Phillip stared at her blankly.

"It looks like you were trying to frame your father for possession of child pornography. If it *was* you, you may as well tell me now, because your electronic fingerprints will be all over that file." This was a bluff, but she needed to put the fear of God into him.

"Fuck no, it wasn't me! No way. You're not gonna find my 'electronic fingerprints,' whatever that is, because I didn't do it. Shit, I wouldn't even know how. I'm a complete techno-idiot. Ask my roommate, he'll back me up. He's always having to show me how to do stuff like get my printer to work with my laptop or update my programs. I just don't get it most of the time." She recalled DJ's comment that some malicious hackers are savvy enough to break into another person's computers and plant something nefarious, but it sounded like Phillip was no computer whiz. Something in his denial struck a chord of truth—but at the same time, she knew he was hiding something. Maybe not about the porn, but something.

"All right. But one more thing: you need to keep this matter about the duplicate photos just between us for right now. I'll tell the police eventually, but I need to talk with someone first. Deal?"

"Yeah, deal." His voice was dry as parchment, and just as lifeless. If the man looked defeated when he came into the room, he was now shriveled even further into himself. As she left, Tess suggested to the guard that they put Phillip on suicide watch

PART FIVE

*Revenge: the sweetest morsel to the mouth
that was ever cooked in hell.*

~ Sir Walter Scott

29

EVERY HEAD IN THE SMALL UNIVERSITY CAFÉ turned toward the beautiful woman as she drifted across the room to join Tess at a secluded corner table. Sofia was dressed in simple narrow black slacks and a vivid violet-blue satin blouse that shimmered as if it were luminous. Wearing an unpretentious gold chain bracelet and slender hoop earrings, she was the epitome of elegance. The earrings peeked out from her deep walnut-brown hair which hung in long, loose waves that perfectly framed her full face. She smiled warmly as she sat down.

"It is good to see you, Tess. You still have the arm cast, I see."

"Not much longer, they tell me." Tess raised her formerly splinted leg off the floor. "And look: I'm finally rid of that damn splint."

Passing over the comment, Sofia signaled for a waiter and asked for coffee and a scone. After it arrived, Tess broke the news about Phillip's arrest for the hit-and-run, and the child pornography found on his computer. At the last minute, she chose not to reveal that the lewd photos on Phillip's laptop were exactly the same as those on Matlock's PC.

Sofia's face was an impassive mask as she listened and picked at the scone with her left hand, which featured a stunning amethyst ring. The marquise-shaped stone was a shade of violet that perfectly matched her blouse, and was accented with two leafy curves of round diamonds inlaid into the wide gold band.

Tess was sure she'd never seen it before, and wondered if it was a gift from Matlock. As the stones winked and sparkled in the light, something scratched at a corner of her mind, a riddle that had no form or structure. Impatiently, Tess pushed it away.

Finally, Sofia spoke. "I frankly do not understand why Phillip would do such a thing as go after you with a car, and it is also difficult for me to believe that he has been…engaging…in this terrible filth on his computer. Perhaps he is much more troubled than I knew, but it is shocking."

But the woman didn't *seem* terribly shocked: the words were right, but something in her affect was off. If anything, she appeared dispassionate. At the same time, it was odd that she said nothing about the striking coincidence of finding child porn on both the father's and the son's computers.

With a promise to remain cautious, Sofia left the coffee shop for the drive back to San Francisco, leaving Tess to ponder the implications of their interaction. Or maybe there weren't any implications. Maybe, Tess scolded herself, I'm just fixated on looking for significance where none exists.

An insistent buzzing, like a hive of angry bees. Tess pulled a cushion over her head, trying to shut it out, but the irritating whirr continued. When she opened her eyes, she realized she'd fallen asleep on the couch, and the drone of irate bees was actually her phone. She reached for it, not even bothering to look at the caller ID.

"Yes? Hello? This is Tess." Her words came out thick and fuzzy.

"Oh—did I wake you? I'm sorry, this is William Schiffler."

Tess blinked to clear her head and sat up. "No problem, Lieutenant. Just an unintentional nap. What can I do for you?"

Well, he said, there's been a break in the Rennie Matlock case. "The state lab finished the DNA analysis of the blood on the razor. Turns out there *was* a second sample, and it belongs to a woman."

"Wait: a *woman*? That makes no…are they sure? Did they identify her?"

"Yes, they're sure. No doubt. Unfortunately, there's no match in CODIS." CODIS, an acronym for Combined DNA Index System, contains DNA profiles collected from convicted offenders, crime scene evidence, and missing persons all across the nation. No match in CODIS meant that the woman's DNA didn't match any of the profiles in the database.

"But there *is* some good news," he continued. "Once the profile came back, they did some other DNA tests—I don't really understand all this genotype-phenotype stuff—and they say she probably has brown hair and eyes, and what they call 'intermediate' skin color."

Tess was familiar with the technology that allowed for this type of classification, and it was a true game-changer in law enforcement's ability to identify both suspects and victims. The tool, called HIrisPlex-S, allows scientists to assemble physical features from genetic data by genotyping forty-one markers for eye, hair, and skin color, and then isolating three eye colors, four hair colors, and five skin color categories. Tess knew that researchers were also working on perfecting DNA phenotyping systems based on biometric and facial recognition, which would advance the field into the stratosphere. Grab an unknown subject's DNA, and you could reconstruct his face.

"Female DNA. I just…I'm flabbergasted."

Without warning, Tess's theory of Rennie's murder was annihilated. So apparently it *wasn't* Matlock. But if not him, who? Why would a woman want to kill Rennie? Her mind felt as if it were inside a washing machine on spin dry.

"Yeah, it came as a shock to us, too. Ideally, there'd have been a hit in the database, but guess that's just too much to hope for. We just need to keep working the case. At least we have more than we had before."

Tess had a thought. "Did you talk to the person at Two Pines I told you about? The one who saw the mystery woman who got stuck in the snow the night of Rennie's killing?"

"Yeah, I did. All she could remember was what she told you. Pretty, dark-haired woman in an expensive car. Not much to go on."

"No, but it could match the DNA phenotype the lab came up with."

"It could, but it could also match a hundred thousand other women in this state, probably a million in the country."

Tess had to admit he was right. She needed some time to sit and study and regroup, and simply digest this unsettling news. "Thanks for calling, Lieutenant. I'll let you know if lightning strikes and I come up with an answer to solve the case."

Schiffler chucked softly. "Yes, Ms. Alexander, you do that."

The next day, Tess got a collect call from Phillip in jail, asking to see her.

Seated across from the young man once again, she almost felt sympathy for him. His eyelids drooped and his face was an unappealing cast of gray. His arms wrapped around his body as if protecting himself from some unseen fiend, and one leg bounced incessantly. Tess sat quietly, waiting for him to speak.

Several minutes went by, with the only sounds the soft murmur of other voices conversing in the room and Phillip's rapid breathing. *If he keeps this up, he's going to hyperventilate.*

"I…I have…" He stopped and swallowed, then gulped in a breath. "There's something I need to tell you. But you need to find a way to protect me. Knowing what I know.…" His voice trailed off. By now he'd brought his hands to his waist and was furiously clenching and unclenching his fists. The leg continued bobbing.

"Phillip," she said gently, resting her hands on the table between them, "just say what you need to say. We can figure out the rest."

He finally raised his head and glanced at her, but only for an instant. Looking off into space, he spoke just above a whisper. "It wasn't Simon."

"What wasn't Simon?"

"It wasn't Simon who got me to run you over. It was Sofia."

Tess froze, a fallow deer in someone's headlights. One quivering hand rose to cover her mouth. She tried to respond, but the words wedged in her throat.

"I…I'm sorry I lied to you."

"Tell me. Everything." She could barely whisper the words.

Slowly, painfully, Phillip recounted how Sofia confronted him with photos of child pornography and records of chat room logs she found on a SIM card he accidentally left in the San Francisco house when he moved to San Jose. At first she threatened to go to the police, but then said she had a better idea: transfer everything to Matlock's computer and use it to ruin him.

"She knew how much I hated Simon for killing Rennie, how much I wanted to see him punished for it, and she said this would destroy him when it came out that he was involved in child porn, so I agreed. I didn't know she'd blackmail me with it later.

"For a while she was cool, but then you got involved, and she said you were about to figure out about the porn, and to protect our secret you needed to be exterminated. That's how she said it: 'exterminated.' Like you were a bug. She said if I didn't do what she asked, she'd turn me in and my life would be over. I'd go to prison for years, and she'd make sure Simon disowned me, so I'd be left with nothing. Then she said she'd cover for me by pinning the hit-and-run on Simon, and say it was because he thought you were getting too close to proving that he killed Rennie, and he wanted to shut you up. In the end, he'd go to jail for life. Murder, plus child porn. I'd be in the clear and Simon would be finished."

"But it didn't quite happen that way, did it?" Tess was regaining her composure, even though her heart still hammered against her chest, and she'd developed an excruciating headache. Worse, she'd been totally hoodwinked by Sofia, and the fury swirled in her gut like sulfuric acid.

Phillip's eyes returned to the floor. No, it didn't, he agreed. First, of course, Tess wasn't killed in the hit-and-run. Then, when push came to shove, Sofia didn't protect him at all. She made sure Phillip was the only one linked to the accident, and he was left twisting in the wind. That, and the child porn. His life *was* over.

"If she…if Sofia finds out I told you any of this, she'll kill me, I know she will. And she'll find a way to implicate Simon.

For some reason, she hates him even more than I do, and she'll do anything to wipe him out and protect herself at the same time."

If you only knew.

Tess looked at the clock and wondered if she had enough time to catch Sergeant Ross before he left. Barely. At least the jail and the SO were in adjacent buildings. She told Phillip not to worry and that she'd talk with him soon, and called the department's duty officer. Yes, he said, Sergeant Ross was still in. Yes, he'd tell the sergeant she was on her way over.

Her world was still gyrating, but Tess knew she couldn't present herself as some hysteric if she wanted Ross to take her seriously. She found a quiet spot and took a few minutes to calm and center herself, then made her way to the sergeant's small cubicle. It would be hard to make her case without anything except Phillip's word, but she hoped the argument was convincing enough that Ross would agree to contact the state Bureau of Investigation and Schiffler up in Aspen County.

All the frayed strands of the case were finally coming together.

30

JAVIER COELHO MUST HAVE DONE a superior job of championing her, because Sergeant Ross listened intently to everything she said, only interrupting to ask a question or get clarification. When she finished an hour later, he leaned back in his chair and looked upward for several seconds, his eyes narrowing, before he returned to gazing steadily at her.

"If what you say—if what Phillip Matlock says—is true, it's blown the cover off all these cases at once. Let me talk with Lieutenant Schiffler first thing in the morning and find out who the CBI investigator is. We don't have enough to get an arrest warrant for Ms. Frantonio, but I think that we can issue a BOLO for her as a person of interest, just in case she decides to leave the country. Don't suppose you happen to know if she carries an Italian passport, or has dual citizenship?"

"No, sure don't. In fact, I didn't even think of it until you mentioned it just now. Great investigative journalist I am."

"Don't beat yourself up, Tess. Sounds like she's incredibly devious, and you got completely blind-sided. I don't blame you at all for trusting her."

"Thanks, Sergeant, but it's going to be a long time before I get over the sting of this. I'm not accustomed to being the rube, and between you and me and the lamppost, it really pisses me off."

"If it makes you feel any better, it pisses me off too."

❦

Tess had an idea, and hoped it would work. She texted Sofia that she had some important information about the case. It would only take a few minutes, she said, so maybe they could meet at the Starbuck's at 12th and L, across from the state capitol, so Sofia wouldn't have to drive all the way to east Sacramento. They set the meet for the next afternoon at four-thirty.

Tess waited outside for several minutes after she saw Sofia enter the coffee shop, then dashed in as if she were late.

"So sorry to make you wait, Sophia," she puffed. "It's turned out to be one of those days when nothing comes together on time. I desperately need some coffee—how about you?"

"Yes, that would be good."

Tess got their drinks and the two women settled at a table. The place was fairly quiet, but give it another half-hour and it would be a madhouse with all the state employees getting off work.

For several minutes, Tess spun a tale about how she was finally going to be able to retire, how she'd already been looking at second homes in Carmel, and how she envisioned herself getting another dog. Maybe a horse. She wanted time for Sofia's coffee to cool.

Then she looked at her phone and feigned surprise that it was nearly five o'clock. People began dribbling into the café.

"Didn't mean to go on and on about that," Tess apologized. "Better get to what I came here to tell you. It's about Phillip. Or, rather, about Matlock. The Nevada County sheriff has put a lot of pressure on him to talk, and he finally broke. Confessed that his father convinced him to run me down."

At first, all Sofia did was raise her eyebrows, but then she gave a tiny gasp. "His father?" she whispered loudly. "But why?" She sounded genuinely appalled.

"Apparently—and I only have this information from a source inside the jail, so no telling how accurate it is—it had something to do with the pornography they found on Phillip's computer, and how his father threatened to expose him if he didn't do what he wanted."

"But why would Simon want *you* killed?" She sipped at the coffee.

"According to my source, because I was getting too close to unearthing damaging information about Matlock that would ruin his career. He convinced Phillip it was damning enough that I needed to be taken out. The word I believe he used was 'exterminated.' " She waited for a reaction from Sofia to the word she herself apparently used, but the woman remained unruffled.

"That's truly amazing," she said, taking another drink. "I can hardly believe that Simon would go so far as to have you murdered. What will they do now?"

"I haven't heard, but as soon as I know something, I'll let you know. It feels like everything's beginning to come together." She reached across the table to touch Sofia's arm, and when she pulled it back, her hand clipped the rim of Sofia's coffee cup. Still partly full, it tumbled over, splashing the brown liquid on Sofia's blouse and creating a coffee lake on the tabletop.

"Oh, crap—I'm so sorry! Shit: there's coffee all over your blouse!" She grabbed Sofia's arm and propelled her to the counter. "Can someone get a towel? And a damp rag for me?" she commanded, then turned back to their table, rag in hand.

Too intent on blotting the coffee on her shirt, Sofia didn't notice Tess surreptitiously slip her paper coffee cup into a plastic zip-top bag and into her purse.

"It is all right," she said as Tess returned. "The shirt is washable, and I shall take care of it the minute I get home. I am sure it will be fine."

"Oh, I can't apologize enough, Sofia. This just puts a perfect ending to what was already a lousy day."

"No worry. Just relax and be careful driving home. And let me know if you find anything else."

Tess promised she would, and they both walked out of the shop into the valley's summer blast furnace.

That night, she called Schiffler, told him about purloining Sofia's cup so they could compare the DNA to what the crime lab found on the razor, and said she overnighted the cup to him. What followed was yet another minor dressing-down for taking matters into her own hands.

"Sorry, Lieutenant , but you know what they say: you can't make an omelet without breaking a few eggs."

"What worries me," he grumbled, "is that *you're* going to end up as the broken egg."

"The lab is running the DNA from the cup." It was three days later when Schiffler called. "In the meantime, I talked with your pal Sergeant Ross, and he told me quite a tale. You've been busy, Ms. Alexander."

"Lieutenant Schiffler, after all this time and all we've been through, I think you can call me Tess. And yes, I've been busy as hell, even though sometimes it's felt like I was barely treading water. But these last few days made up for a lot of that."

"I'm sure. Based on what you learned from Phillip, seems that your suspicions about Senator Matlock may not have been terribly well-founded."

"At least with regard to the hit-and-run, yes," Tess said a little defensively. "But there's more, a lot more, that I have on the man. Strangely, thanks to Sofia Frantonio, who's obviously deeply involved in this whole thing."

"Perhaps you'd finally like to enlighten me with what you know."

Tess spent the next half-hour going over everything: her encounters with Sofia, the Excel file and her discovery that the figures represented illegal campaign contributions, the pornography and how Sofia planted it on Matlock's computer to frame him, and about the woman's role in the hit-and-run accident.

"And here's the *coup de grâce*: I'm convinced it was Sofia who murdered Rennie." She heard Schiffler inhale abruptly and start to say something. "Once you get the DNA results back, " Tess interjected, "and once I talk with her, you'll have all the proof you need."

"Once *you* talk with her?" he rumbled. "Ms. Alex—Tess—that's not your job. You're not a law enforcement officer."

"I know, Lieutenant, but *I'm* the one she trusts. *I'm* the one she thinks she conned. She has no clue what I know, what I found out, and that makes me the perfect person. I'll tell her I have more news about the case, that I finally have proof that Matlock killed Rennie, and that will draw her in. We can meet in the little café where we met several times before, so she won't be suspicious."

"Again, that's *our* job, not yours."

"There's no way she'll give anything up to you, or to any other cop. She thinks she's smarter than all of us, and in a way she is: she damn near pulled this off. But if anyone's going to be able to get the truth out of her, it's me. You know that."

His only response was indecipherable muttering.

"Look, you can fit me with a wire, and if you're worried, even post someone in the café as a customer. She's not going to pull out an AR-15 and start mowing people down. That's not her style. If you want evidence that she killed Rennie, that she's responsible for Butch Fogerty's death, that she's the mastermind behind my so-called 'accident,' you need to let me do this."

The line was silent for at least fifteen seconds. She could almost see the man's tight-lipped expression.

He drew in an audible, long breath, then let it out in a loud *errrr*. "All right: I'll talk with the Sacramento County sheriff, see if he can set you up with a covert listening device, then position a team to monitor your conversation. And of course I'll make sure he has someone in the coffee shop in case things go south. I don't like this...."

"I know you don't. You're not used to civilians mucking about in police business, especially if they're part of the dreaded media. But this is the only way you're going to get anything on Sofia Frantonio beyond what we got from Phillip. She's clever, she's deadly, and she's covered her tracks extremely well."

"Speaking of leaving tracks," the lieutenant said, "I have another piece of information for you: Remember our friendly neighborhood hit man, Benny Barbosa? Just before we turned him over to the FBI, he told us something very interesting: he still can't ID the client who hired him to take out Butch Fogerty, but he said she had an accent. Maybe Spanish, maybe Italian."

After a moment, Tess's mouth set into a hard line. "Yeah, Lieutenant, very interesting indeed. How much do you want to bet that Benny's client, our Two Pines mystery woman, and Sofia Frantonio are one and the same?"

31

TESS WAS THE FIRST TO ARRIVE AT THE CAFÉ. It was late afternoon, and the owners had agreed to stay open later than usual. Of course they'd be closed to any customers except for Tess and Sofia and the young couple seated at a table in the opposite corner, who were actually undercover officers. For the sake of authenticity, they hung a sign on the door reflecting the "new" later closing hours.

An outside pocket of her purse held an inconspicuous pen that was actually an extremely sensitive GSM listening device and transmitter. An earlier test run showed it could pick up two voices in conversation, even when one of them was speaking just above a whisper. Lieutenant Schiffler and the police officers in the San Francisco Baking Company van in the parking lot could hear perfectly.

Everything was ready. Four o'clock came and went. Four-ten. Four-fifteen. Schiffler was getting nervous, but Tess assured him that Sofia would show. At four-twenty, the sun flashed off the window of a blue-black Mercedes as it pulled into the lot, and less than a minute later, Sofia walked in. This time she was dressed casually, in russet brown leggings and a silky, cream-colored sleeveless tunic with a soft cowl collar. She smiled apologetically as she joined Tess, saying she was held up by construction on Howe Avenue. No problem, said Tess, signaling the waitress—also an undercover officer—to bring them coffee.

"So," said Sofia, "you said you had proof that Simon was involved in Rennie's killing. What has happened?"

"Turns out, a great deal." As Sofia lifted the cup in her left hand, Tess suddenly grasped the reason for that nagging itch of discomfort she'd felt when looking at the woman's amethyst ring the last time they met.

Sofia was left-handed.

The mortal wound on Rennie's neck was from right to left, exactly how it would be if a left-handed person stood behind her and slashed her throat. Tess flinched unconsciously.

"But first, about Butch Fogerty." She kept her voice steady and amiable.

Sofia cocked her head questioningly, and her brows scrunched together just a bit. *This woman is really good. Playing like she can't remember who he is.*

"You know: the manager at Two Pines."

"Oh, yes, of course."

"His killer was actually a paid assassin. Thanks to a little luck, they caught the guy and arrested him. Benjamin Barbosa." She waited for a reaction from Sofia, but her face was perfectly blank. "Benny said he couldn't identify the person who hired him because they were in disguise, but he knew one thing: it was a woman." Still, not a muscle twitched on Sofia's face. "And the woman had an accent." Nothing. Just a languid blink of her eyes.

"But let me go back to the night of Rennie's murder. I discovered Matlock *did* show up. In fact, he gave Fogerty five hundred bucks to tell him what room Rennie was in. That's a big part of what convinced me that he'd killed Rennie.

"But later, one of the guests at Two Pines told me about something she saw and heard through her window just before midnight: It was Fogerty, out in the middle of the parking lot in the blizzard, grumbling and swearing while he tried to help an attractive, dark-haired woman get her big black Mercedes out of a snowbank.

"I just couldn't figure it out: Matlock got there a little after eight, but it wasn't until 11:15 that Rennie called me, slurring her words because she'd been drugged. About thirty minutes later, the mystery woman got stuck in the snow, and forty-five minutes after that I arrived and found Rennie's body.

"Here's the strange part: the coroner put the time of death between ten o'clock and midnight, but I was talking with Rennie at 11:15, so we know she was alive then. That just doesn't square with Matlock arriving just after eight. You see my problem?"

Sofia simply gazed at her, expressionless.

"If we believe Matlock killed Rennie, that means he spent over *three hours* with her before he killed her. Why would he do that? There's no rational explanation."

"Perhaps he was trying to convince her not to move out." Calm, composed.

"But how could he have known she was leaving? You yourself said she was afraid to tell him. That got me thinking about the commotion in the Two Pines parking lot just fifteen minutes after Rennie called me. It all came together when I learned that the murder weapon contained *two* sets of DNA: Rennie's, and an unknown woman's."

Sofia's eyes widened ever so slightly at this new information. "A woman's?" She sounded genuinely perplexed. "How could that be?"

"I wondered the same thing at first. I mean, all of us—you, me, Phillip—were certain Matlock killed Rennie. Everything pointed to it. And then I met with Phillip a few days ago, and he had some very interesting things to tell me that shed a whole new light on everything.

"I'm afraid I wasn't entirely truthful with you the last time we spoke," Tess continued, placing her palms flat on the tabletop and leaning slightly forward. "Phillip didn't say that Simon blackmailed him into running me down." She paused to give her next words more impact. "He said you did."

One eyebrow arched up, and an infinitesimal smile raced across Sofia's face. "Really?" she said. "Me? That's preposterous." She looked almost amused.

"No, not preposterous at all." Tess went on to divulge what Phillip said about Sofia discovering his child porn collection on the SIM card, and essentially blackmailing him into carrying out the hit-and-run, saying she would set up Matlock for it as punishment for him having killed Rennie. Sofia sat motionless and serene throughout Tess's story, indifferent to it all. Her breathing was slow and even.

"This is all quite interesting," she said coolly, "but I cannot see what it has to do with me. Phillip is obviously very disturbed, as I mentioned to you after you told me about the sordid images on his computer, and he is clearly attempting to escape blame for your accident by pushing it onto me. But why would I want to hurt you, Tess? I care about you, deeply. I was feeling that we were becoming friends as we worked together on solving Rennie's killing." She reached across the table to touch Tess's hand when she said the word "care," but her deep brown eyes were glacial.

Listening to Sofia's practiced rationalizations and the supple ease with which she produced them, the wings of a thought fluttered against the edges of Tess's mind, but for the moment it was just out of reach.

Still touching Tess's hand, Sofia continued speaking, smoothly and dispassionately, reminding her companion of how much she had done to help her, the wealth of evidence against Matlock she brought to light in the past months. Phillip is trying to trick you, she insisted. He is the one who is responsible. He and his father.

With a jolt, Tess realized this wasn't the first time she'd noticed Sofia's lack of affect. She always seemed to say the right words, but it was more like she was reciting them from a script, as if she said the words *not* because she felt them, but because she knew the effect they would have on her listener.

The moth glided out into the sunlight on delicate wings. It was a lecture she'd attended a year or two before given by Robert Hare, one of the foremost experts in criminal psychology and creator of the Hare Psychopathy Checklist. Known colloquially as The Hare, the checklist is used worldwide by researchers, clinicians, and forensic psychologists to identify psychopathic characteristics.

Tess recalled the researcher's explanation that what makes psychopaths different is their natural talent for deceit and manipulation, the remarkable ease with which they lie, and the cold-heartedness with which they do it. Once caught in deception or deviant behavior, they often candidly admit their actions, calmly denying any sense of guilt, and are utterly unconcerned about the pain and devastation they've left in their wake. And although these individuals lack the capacity for conscience or empathy, they can put on an extraordinarily convincing show of caring.

Tess conceded that the woman sitting across from her fit this description in every way.

She pulled her hand back and made direct eye contact. "I know that's not the truth, Sofia, and so do you."

"Why don't you tell me what the truth is, then?" Sofia's voice was almost mocking.

"The truth is, *you* forced Phillip to run me over, *you* had Butch Fogerty killed, and *you* murdered Rennie."

A tiny smile played at the corners of her mouth. "I am interested to know how you believe I did all these things."

"Okay, let's start at the beginning. At some point, Matlock told you that he put a GPS device on Rennie's car because he wanted to keep track of where she was going and what she was doing. When Rennie told you she was going up to Hammond Mills to think about her future, it presented the perfect opportunity: You could tell Simon that Rennie was driving into the mountains to plan her escape, and you knew he'd track her there. Which of course he did, probably hoping to convince her to stay—which you knew wasn't about to happen. Rennie was absolutely determined to get away from him. He would leave the motel, then you could show up and kill Rennie using Matlock's antique straight razor, which you figured would throw the spotlight of suspicion on him once the cops figured out it wasn't a suicide after all.

"But you didn't count on two things happening that night: you getting stuck in the snow, and someone at the motel seeing you as Butch Fogerty was trying to get you out. Poor Butch couldn't have imagined that little act of chivalry would cost him his life.

"Next, you very effectively roped me in as your after-the-fact accomplice to frame Matlock. You strung me along with the story of how you hacked into his Folder Lock and 'found' the incriminating child pornography, which of course you planted after you lifted copies from the SIM card Phillip accidentally left in the mansion when he moved out. That gave you an opportunity to put another nail in Matlock's coffin: Not only was he involved in illegal campaign contributions, but he was into child porn as well. That, and the suspicion that he killed Rennie, wouldn't just ruin him, but would be all the authorities needed to put him away.

"But that wasn't good enough: you also wanted to destroy Phillip for some reason. So you told him I was about to uncover his pedophilia, and the only way to keep that from happening was to get rid of me." She thought for a second. "I believe the word you used was 'exterminate.' How am I doing so far?"

Sofia only gazed at her dispassionately.

"I'll take that as a 'good.' In the midst of all this, you decided Butch Fogerty needed to be eliminated, because he saw you that night at Two Pines, and sooner or later he'd put two and two together. With your computer expertise, it was no problem at all for you to access the darknet and find yourself a hired gun in the person of Benny Barbosa. I can only guess how you lured Butch out into the wilderness where I found his body."

Sofia's forehead puckered, and her mouth formed a small "O" of genuine surprise.

"Ahh, I see you didn't realize it was me who found Butch. Of course, the critters had gotten to him first, so he wasn't looking so great, but there was enough left to ID him. Shot in the back of the head.

"It's funny: Life has a way of upending the very best of the best-laid plans, and in your case, it was that I survived the hit-and-run. And eventually got enough of my memory back to make a start on figuring out what happened. The frosting on the cake was a fellow at the body shop where Phillip took the pickup who had a conscience, and contacted me with what he knew. That was pretty much it for poor Phillip, particularly when you didn't honor your promise to protect him. But then, honor isn't really one of your strong suits, is it, Sofia?"

Her face bore the blasé half-smile she wore before.

"I'm guessing you figured that Phillip would stick to his story about his father being the one who blackmailed him into going after me, but after we talked, he realized there was just no percentage in protecting you."

Silence hung in the small café like a thunderhead. Sofia turned her head and looked out into the near-empty parking lot, her face unreadable. Then she turned back to Tess and met her eyes once again, and her face broke into what appeared to be a genuine smile.

"You are much smarter than I anticipated," she said. "That was my error, underestimating you. If it hadn't been for that…. Oh, well. In the end, Simon will be ruined, even though they will not be able to charge him with murder or child pornography. But adding to the information you gathered on the illegal campaign contributions, I have a large, well-documented file of his many payoffs and kickbacks over the years. Between the two, he will go to jail. Perhaps for not as long as I had hoped, but at least I will have avenged Francesca."

So in the end, that's why Rennie's died: to satisfy Sofia's need to exact retribution against Simon for her sister's rape and suicide. Tess shook her head sadly. All this death and destruction, all the lives shattered, all in the name of vengeance.

At that moment, the café doors swung open and a small cadre of uniformed officers streamed in. Sofia looked at Tess, then tilted her head back slightly and gave a little chuckle. Just before they walked the handcuffed woman out the door, Tess put out her arm to stop them.

"One thing still puzzles me, Sofia: what happened to Rennie's ring?"

Sofia's smile widened. "Oh, I have it. Once the police came to arrest Simon for her murder, I would have planted it in his leather jewelry valet." She paused. "I thought of everything."

Epilogue

TESS SAT, HYPNOTIZED BY A FLOCK of crimson and purple clouds hovering above the horizon. Something smooth and wet against her hand interrupted her reverie, and she turned to the golden dog perched beside her, his soft tongue lapping gently at her fingers. She ruffled his head and threw one arm around his broad back.

"Ahh, Cooper, you're my good boy, aren't you?"

The big dog huffed and grinned in appreciation, leaning contentedly against his human as they watched the sun rise over the indigo mountains.

Eight months before, Sofia Frantonio was convicted of the murder of Rennie Matlock and solicitation of murder in the death of Butch Fogerty, whose real name was Percy. *No wonder he went by Butch.* Apparently, Sofia paid Fogerty to stay quiet about seeing her, but he got greedy and tried to extort more from her. That was his death sentence.

Expelled from his Senate seat by unanimous vote, state police arrested Simon Matlock for violation of campaign finance regulations, fraud, bribery, and a host of other felonies including accepting kickbacks and bribes from a crooked lobbyist. All of it netted him fifteen years in state prison. Tess desperately wanted to see him indicted for child sexual abuse, but other than herself, Phillip was the only person still alive whom Rennie told, and he too was sitting in a prison cell for attempted murder and child pornography. Not the most credible witness. Plus, since neither he nor Tess had personal knowledge of the crime beyond what

Rennie told them, it would certainly have been ruled inadmissible in court as hearsay.

Along the way, Tess learned what Rennie hoped could destroy Matlock, and it turned out to be one more twisted road that led back to Sofia. She'd told Rennie she found a stash of child porn in Matlock's closet safe—in actuality, prints of the photos she lifted from Phillip's SIM card—and evidence of Matlock's many years of providing payoffs to city and county officials for favorable treatment of his construction projects. Like so many people caught in Sofia's noxious web of deceit, Rennie was blind to the fact that the kindhearted, compassionate woman who pledged to help her was in fact a murderous psychopath.

Tess heaved a deep sigh of sadness and resignation, and Cooper looked up at her apprehensively. "It's okay, Boo," she said, tears choking her voice. "There's just been a whole lot of pain and sorrow, and a good woman died an awful death. I'm just sad for it all."

She picked up her coffee mug as curls of steam lapped at the cool morning air. Pulling the soft blanket around her shoulders for warmth, she tilted her head back and watched the last of the evening's stars surrender their light to the approaching day. The pungent scents of fir, cedar, and piney mountain misery perfumed the air as she offered up a silent invocation for Rennie, for Kathleen, for all the souls shattered by life, now finally at peace.

Here, among the deep green forests of the magnificent Sierra Nevada, her beloved dog at her side and the gilded rays from the rising sun breaking free from the darkness, a soft, shadowy image materialized in front of her. It was Roger, his gentle smile voicing a thousand unspoken words, words that would carry her forward into whatever lay ahead.

The road to this place had been long and torturous, filled with terrible loss and profound grief, but also illuminated by great love, abiding friendships, and incalculable kindness.

Above the lilac mountains, the sunrise called to her soul in the language of the ancients, whispering its comfort and deep approbation as it cast the earth in crimson gold.

She was home.

ABOUT THE AUTHOR

A Cruel Oblivion is Joan Merriam's second book in the Tess Alexander Mystery series. The first book, *A Just Reckoning*, was published in February of 2021.

Career-wise, Joan has led a peripatetic life, ranging from fine jewelry sales to real estate appraisal to running a nonprofit agency devoted to child abuse prevention to her current work as a college instructor and freelance writer.

Author of the nonfiction book, *Little Girl Lost: A True Story of Shattered Innocence and Murder,* she currently writes a syndicated newspaper column on life with dogs.

She lives in northern California, in the Sierra Nevada historic Mother Lode region.

Visit her website at www.joanmerriam.com, or on Facebook at www.facebook.com/JoanMerriamAuthor

READ

the first book in the Tess Alexander
Mystery series,
A Just Reckoning

Available in paperback at your local bookstore and as a paperback or e-book on Amazon, Barnes & Noble, Google Play, and other internet retailers

THANK YOU FOR BUYING THIS BOOK!

To receive special offers, bonus content,
and my monthly newsletter,
visit me at
www.joanmerriam.com